THE BRIGHT YEARS

A Novel

Sarah Damoff

SIMON & SCHUSTER

New York   Amsterdam/Antwerp   London
Toronto   Sydney/Melbourne   New Delhi

Simon & Schuster
1230 Avenue of the Americas
New York, NY 10020

First Simon & Schuster hardcover edition April 2025

Interior design by Wendy Blum

Manufactured in the United States of America

ISBN 978-1-6680-6144-2

For
daughters and sons
parents of all kinds
and
the discomforted

Sorrow eats time. Be patient. Time eats sorrow.

Louise Erdrich, *LaRose*

THE
BRIGHT
YEARS

1958

HE'S COLORING A NIGHT SKY ON THE UNDERBELLY OF the kitchen table. His parents are too busy fighting to notice. It always starts with his father's thirst. Next comes the television set. His mother turns up the volume so the antics of Wally and Beaver or Lucy and Ricky will drown out the yelling.

A pound cake sits on the oak table above him. The sugary smell teases the boy. He forced down his peas, but now he might not even get a slice.

Behind his parents' bedroom door, there's a thump. What sounds like a loud clap. A crash. His mother, her voice muffled, says something about upsetting the landlord.

With a chunky white crayon, the boy adds a star to his sky. He bites his lip and narrows his eyes, neck craned upward to study his work. Now the challenge is how to make clouds show up. He decides to try purple over the black of night. Doesn't work. He adds a faint white outline along the wood grain, tracing the purple. Better. He smiles proudly.

His mother's navy pumps cross the yellow linoleum. He watches her apron swoosh and braces for his father to follow with his grass-stained socks and loudness. But the only sounds are his mother's steps, cabinets opening and closing, and June Cleaver asking Wally where he's going.

The boy watches his mother's busy calves. Then, suddenly, her red-streaked face appears. She grips the table above her head, squatting down into the shadow of the boy's world. He holds his breath. He knows good and well that he shouldn't be drawing on furniture, but the blank wood was pleading for color.

"Play a game with me, dear?"

He frowns.

She touches his face softly with her thumb and whispers, "You know how silly your father is. He's playing a little hide-and-seek game with the Oldsmobile key. Help me find it?"

"Hide-and-seek?"

"When we find it, we can take a drive."

His eyes widen. "With you driving?"

"Hey now." She manages a playful smile. "I can drive." With the offering of this smile—the corners of her lips raised, frown lines softened, a peek of teeth—the desire to protect awakens within the boy, the force of helpless love that children have for their mothers. So he emerges from his oak shelter. And even though he finds her game dull, he does not complain.

After they've looked unsuccessfully inside every cabinet and drawer, the boy eyes the cake. His mother exhales and leans over the tile counter, her palms pressing hard into it, chin tucked into her neck. The boy's eyes dart between mother and cake. Then she stands up straight, lifts her chin, smooths her apron, and says, "Okay."

He waits, mouth watering.

She says, "If we can't take a drive, how about a little walk?"

His nose scrunches as he looks away from the cake and out the window. "It's dark."

She squats again, placing her hands on her son's shoulders. Up close, she smells like Palmolive. Her skin under each eye is purple like his clouds. She's his Palmolive sky.

She hesitates, but only for a second. "Walking will do. Go find the new coat we got from that yard sale." She stands and moves something from a drawer into her handbag.

"But it isn't cold." The truth is that he doesn't like his "new" coat. It smells like dog and cigarettes.

Down their dark hallway, the flush of a toilet. His mother whispers, "Shoes. Now."

He glances at the hallway, the cake, his crayons on the linoleum, and, wiggling his shoes on, he follows his mother out the back door.

He needs help with his shoelaces, but she says to hurry and leads him through their neighbor's side yard. Her apron is still around her waist, dotted with hot sauce and oil. A bush rustles. The boy shivers and realizes his mother was right—it is cold.

As they trudge a trail through wet grass, he chastises her. "You said don't go in the Thompsons' yard without their permission."

"I have permission."

The boy doesn't think this is true.

Trying not to trip on his laces, he realizes his bladder is full. He reaches down to hold himself as they walk and walk. Even by moonlight, he can see a bruise on his mother's face. It looks like a green-yellow flame. She chooses a path away from the road.

Eventually, her voice flat, she says, "Your father just needed—"

"I hate him." This startles the child as much as it does his mother. He would never have dared to even think that at home, but there's something about the still air. Something about the effort it takes to move deeper into the night, like moving into a swamp. He feels smaller, angrier, and much more afraid. Reckless. A fresh wildness growls low inside him. He's young, but he's old enough to have watched his father hurt his mother again and again.

She stops walking and sinks into tall grass and bluebonnet buds. She tucks thick hair behind her ear and says, "I don't." She's looking past him, her eyes sweeping across their surroundings and back again.

"Huh?"

She sighs, her breath like milk and her eyes like water. "I love your father," she says, "very much." She takes a shaky breath. "But"—she reaches for her son's small hands as muscles gather and tighten around her bottom lip—"I love you most, Ryan."

As she begins to cry, he imagines that the dark clouds beneath her eyes are raining. His heart wobbles. He wets himself. He realizes they aren't going home, not even for dry pants. He wonders what will happen to the cake. To his night sky. And to them.

Part One

LILLIAN

1979

THE LIBRARY TABLE IS UNSTEADY ON ITS FEET, SHIFTING its weight from one cold metal leg to another. I should be preparing a work presentation, but I can't stop turning pages in *A Tree Grows in Brooklyn*. It was left on the table where I always sit.

Early 1900s Brooklyn is quite different from 1970s Fort Worth. Still, Francie is strikingly relatable, admiring her parents without seeing fault and saving pennies without seeing poverty. I'm too interested in the gradual opening of her eyes to pay much attention to my notecards that will hopefully move me from bank teller to public relations manager at my branch.

I glance around the sleepy Saturday library and plump my inky mess of hair. It's past time for a new perm. I look back down. One more chapter, then I'll work on my presentation.

Three chapters later, a whisper. "Lillian?"

I look up at a man I don't know; Johnny and Katie look up at me from chapter eleven.

"Yes?"

"Ryan." He touches fingertips to his chest. "I've come to your bank a couple of times." Ah. We have nameplates at work.

"Oh, um, hi."

"I thought that was you."

It's an odd thing to say to your bank teller.

Ryan has dark, shaggy hair, paint flecks on his fingers, and beard scruff down his neck. A gap between his two front teeth. His eyes are a sinking dark; I can hardly see the pupil for the iris, like a tree in a night wood. His clothes are plain, his build unthreatening but not weak. He's like an understated book cover, which is the type I'm inclined to open.

I give an internal kick to Morning Lillian, who thought it would be silly to wear makeup to the library on a Saturday. I don't even have a barrette for my hair. But at least Morning Lillian had the good sense to throw on this flattering green blouse at the last minute. I smooth the front of it.

Aside from confirming that I am indeed Lillian From The Bank, Ryan doesn't seem to have more to say. Though he doesn't take a step away, either.

"Need a spot?" I gesture to the three open chairs. In the distance, a child whines for *Madeleine* instead of *Frog and Toad*.

"Thanks." He scoots a chair back and settles in with paperwork. I put *Brooklyn* aside and focus on my presentation notes. I have a decent shot at this promotion if I prepare well. I pretend not to notice Ryan's glances.

He whispers again, "So what're you working on?"

Before I can answer, he shakes his head. "Sorry. We don't know each other. What I mean to say is that"—he clears his throat—"I would like to get to know you." Pinpricks of pink dot his cheeks like salt.

A few people are reading near us, their *shush* glares like spider eyes in starlight. A woman flashes a frown at us from behind her paperback because a whisper can sound like a foghorn when you're in the dazed silence of a story's pages. I study Ryan, decide to finish my presentation tomorrow, and nod toward the people trying to read. "Getting to know me is worth more than begrudged library whispers."

Ryan reddens, and I chase my nerve-racking display of confidence with more of it. I gather my work and stand up. Give him a half smile and a *Let's get out of here* head tilt. He meets my eyes as understanding fills his own. Not even trying to mask his widening smile, he follows suit and collects his own scatter of papers. Then he fumbles to trail me out of the Fort Worth Public Library and into the shock of sun.

The hole-in-the-wall Greek restaurant across the street is an obvious choice. My stomach is embarrassingly noisy from missing lunch. We order gyros, no more whispering.

Sauce drips onto Ryan's shirt, but he doesn't seem bothered. I learn why he's been frequenting my branch: he's trying to secure a loan to open an art gallery downtown. He claims he noticed me as soon as he walked into the bank. I laugh it off, but he's so sincere that my warming cheeks betray me.

Ryan waits tables at Matteo's Italian Café and moonlights as a starving artist. It's a dinner restaurant though, so he actually works there at night and sunlights as an artist. The walls at Matteo's are covered in Ryan's murals too. His ultimate dream, he says, is a gallery. I ask why.

"Why what?"

"Why a gallery?"

"Well, why a bank?"

"I didn't take out a loan and open the bank."

"Touché. I still want to know though."

I consider. "I like the bank. It's stable. I have good coworkers and make enough money for things like books and meat and gifts for friends." I've learned how big of a dream it is to have a small life. That the cost of ambition is high. "Now tell me about your gallery. And your art."

"A gallery is something I've dreamed of since I first went to one as a kid. I thought it was a museum until I saw someone take home this enormous painting of mountains. I just wanted to give people that. The ability to take home mountains."

11

"And you paint too?"

He nods. "The already realized dream."

"How so?"

"I already paint." He shrugs. "So, that's it. And take photographs."

I'm skeptical. "Isn't it every artist's dream to have big commissions and exhibits at fancy galleries?"

"Not this artist. Industry pressure changes the art. I'd rather paint what I want and open a gallery where other artists can do the same." He pauses. "I don't need recognition. I just want something stable where I can make enough money for things like books and meat and gifts for friends." He smiles; I laugh.

"So the café isn't cutting it?"

"Matteo is a friend. Working at a restaurant is unpredictable, though. One night your Alfredo-stained pockets overflow with tips, and the next they're empty and you get a meatball thrown at you."

I nearly spit out my food, covering my laugh with a napkin.

He studies me. "What about you?"

"What about me?"

He traces the rim of his glass. "Dreams?"

My hand moves instinctively toward my stomach like I have something to protect. "My dream is . . ." I pretend to consider. "More pita and hummus." I sit taller, looking around for a waiter.

Ryan raises bushy, unsatisfied eyebrows before dragging his eyes from me. He tracks down a waiter and makes my hummus dream come true.

When our red plastic food baskets are empty, we linger beneath the fluorescent lights. We talk about art and books, even grazing the outer edges of our childhoods. I can't remember the last time anybody listened to me like this. Nobody since Mama, I don't think.

We keep the table for hours.

Twilight and an increase in diners mark the shift from dead afternoon to the early dinner crowd. A tarnished bell announces each new patron. With the next chime, a lone man stands in the entrance beneath

12

the polyester Greek flag and a sign that reads KOUZINA! A gray beard crawls up his face like vines. He could be sixty or forty; I can't say. He walks toward the counter, one foot landing heavier than the other, the smell of gin like a kite tail as he passes.

Ryan and I resume a conversation about the pieces Van Gogh painted while hospitalized. The line lengthens behind the bearded man as he counts nickel after nickel after nickel onto the counter. Ryan starts fidgeting but keeps talking about how art can heal. He grows increasingly distracted until he finally says, "Sorry, excuse me a minute." He stands and leaves the table. I grin, endeared. Poor guy didn't know how to excuse himself to pee.

While he's in the restroom, I sneak a compact from my purse for a quick face and hair check. Still no makeup and still need a perm. Still Dad's thin lips and Mama's big eyes and my dark circles. I sigh and snap it shut. When Ryan returns, he's less antsy, but it's becoming clear that we should give up our table soon. Neither of us is ready for that.

As he asks if I'd like dessert, we're interrupted. The man with the nickels and uneven gait is standing over our table. He leans down close to Ryan like he's going to whisper, but then he nearly rams a finger into Ryan's nose and says, quite loudly, "Thanks again! You're a good man!"

The man is already walking away with that heavy-footed saunter by the time I understand. He has a bag full of food while his pocket still rattles with change. Ryan's cheeks turn as red as raw lamb. He didn't leave the table for the restroom.

I sit back in my chair. I underestimated this man who not four hours ago materialized from between library shelves. He tries to brush past the exchange by recounting a time he and his mom went to a local Greek festival and ate themselves sick. I bite my lip as my intrigue deepens, and I tell him yes. I'd love some dessert.

I try to tell myself how little I know of him. How this could go south. How he could have a long disease or a short fuse. Or children. Former lovers with stories that would make me run for the hills. There's endless possibility for pain inside these potent wanting feelings. But while everyone's engrossed in appearances and money and themselves, here is a man who attends so little to those things that he actually sees the people around him. The tired stranger on his hunt for food. The bare-faced bank teller who usually keeps to herself. The woman who, after everything, still falls in love fast and hard. Who, with every bite of baklava sliding down her throat, is trying to convince her heart not to go hog wild.

When we stand to leave, he asks with another blush if he can see me again. I scarcely refrain from asking, *How soon is too soon?*

I carry a torn napkin home with Ryan's phone number like a firefly in my pocket. On the other half of the napkin is my number, held somewhere against his body.

At home, I pin his seven digits under the terra-cotta lamp beside my bed, leaving it where I can see what it says: *ryan brighton (from library)*. No capitals.

When I fall asleep, my dreams dilate with Ryan. The patient intensity of his forest-dark eyes and the paint-dotted hand that pulled my chair out for me. I gave up long ago on the myth of a good man. Yet here I am, ready to let *ryan brighton (from library)* try to prove me wrong.

1980

AFTER THE LIBRARY AND BAKLAVA, RYAN AND I PASS SIX months together like a morning stretch, that carefree inhale before the day picks up with its work and worries.

The afternoon that he takes me to meet his mother, I'm one long denim dress full of nerves.

Ryan opens the passenger door of his Mazda for me, and I touch my fingertip to some new dots of paint on the seat. Dry. I drop into the car. The last thing I need is paint on my rear end to meet Ms. Brighton. Or does she still go by Mrs.?

Starting the car, Ryan turns down the sudden blast of music and shifts into drive, his bomber jacket across his lap. His neck is shaved. Razor-burned, if I look closely, which I do.

"You're the first company Mom's hosting at her new house. Fair warning, her excitement will probably come out in being particular."

"Particular?"

"Taking your purse and serving snacks in only certain dishes and, 'Now dear, are you sure you want the tea bag instead of loose leaf?' That sort of thing."

"That sounds wonderful."

He clicks his tongue. "That's one word for it."

It's like fingernails scraping my skull when people complain about parents doing perfectly fine parental things. "I'm just sorry I don't have parents for you to meet."

His face blanches. "Shoot, I'm sorry. I shouldn't be embarrassed about my mom. I know how lucky I am. Really." He looks over at me and then back at the road.

We've been slow to climb each other's family trees, and I'm reminded of what a daunting climb it can be. Branches might snap.

I drop my gaze to my hands folded in my lap beside the tea Ryan suggested when I asked about a housewarming gift. No wine, he advised.

I fidget with the tea packaging. "What should I call her?"

"My mom?"

"Your first schoolteacher." Ryan shoots me a look, and I smile. "Yes, of course your mom."

"Elise?"

I make a face.

"Also, Mom was my first schoolteacher."

"What?" I knew she was a teacher, but for some reason didn't consider this.

"One of her earliest classes. First grade." His mouth ticks up in a half smile. "She'd give me the sternest look if I called her 'Mom' at school." He reaches over to hold my hand. "Anyway, call her Elise."

A first name might be fine if I were meeting a dad, but Ryan doesn't understand that mothers care more about this stuff. Especially single mothers of only children. And especially mothers of sons. I sigh. I should have chosen something nicer than this denim dress. We have just enough time to turn around so I can change clothes. I'll do my teal cotton dress from Kmart, with the collar and cap sleeves, that I should have put on in the first place. And I will call her Mrs. Brighton.

Before I can say any of this, Ryan takes an unexpected hard turn with, "If we have kids, I guess they'll essentially have only one grandparent."

I cough. We have never talked about kids. Or much about the future

16

at all. We've kept both past and future at arm's length, a Frankenstein embrace of the present moment only. Ryan, though, does tend to say whatever pops into his head. So now I have a much bigger concern than whether Ms. or Mrs. Brighton will approve of my denim dress.

He frowns. "You okay?"

"Uh, yeah." I clear my throat. "So, you want kids?"

His expression lightens, his smile pure. "With you, yes."

I should be giddy. Ryan should be with a woman who's thrilled to hear those words from him. *With you, yes.* But dread coils inside me, leaving no space for the children he imagines.

I say nothing.

He frowns again. "Don't you?"

"I just want to make a good impression on your mom." I smooth my dress and casually ask, "Should I have worn something nicer?"

My pivot doesn't go unnoticed. His brows furrow into a deep V, but he responds with stabbing sincerity. "You're perfect."

When his gaze sears me at a long red light, I swallow and say, "So tell me more about your dad." I know what I'm doing.

Ryan grinds his teeth, and I immediately want to kiss the spot beneath his ear to release the tension I invited into the car. But instead, I flip over his Beatles cassette and wait.

Here's the little I already know: Barton drank too much and it made his hands loose. Elise and Ryan left when Ryan was young, but she got back in touch and Barton became an erratic presence. He'd show up occasionally at their duplex and beg Elise to take him back, while Ryan would tuck into a corner, drawing and making wishes on his mother's crucifix. Elise usually refused Barton, but not always. She sometimes let him stay for a while, whether from strength or weakness.

Ryan decided to stay teetotal. Even when college friends would chug drinks and do body shots, he'd get a Shirley Temple topped with a cherry. I don't know how long it's been since he and Barton have seen each other.

I don't know Barton's profession or if Ryan looks or laughs or chews like his father. I don't know if Barton's gotten sober or what happy memories they share. There must be *some*.

"Not much to tell. He's a drunk."

"I'm sure there's more to him than that."

"If there's more to him, then I don't know about it, Lillian!"

The angry pop of my name ricochets off the windshield and hits me between the eyes. This is the first time I've ever heard Ryan yell. I stare at him, feeling my pulse in my wrist.

He shakes his head as if waking up. "Sorry."

His edge is unfamiliar. I say, "I shouldn't have asked." I stop shy of saying, *Let's leave behind what we need to leave behind.* And I try not to think about my trip to Nashville.

He signals and pulls onto a side street. Puts the car in park and turns toward me, his eyes like dark fire. "I really am sorry. I am *not* a yeller." His frown creases so deeply that it goes all the way into the years before I knew him. An acorn plinks on the hood of the car as he continues in a heady voice, "I love that you care about my family. In fact—" He chews his lip and says for the first time, "I love you."

We're stacking emotion on emotion like a block tower nearing collapse. Still, I know Ryan means what he's saying, unlike some men. Dark tangles fall across his eyes, and my heart pirouettes like it's been doing since the day we met. My fingers on his forearm, I say it back. And I mean it, too. For us, it was love at first whisper, first put-down-my-novel-for-you, first cheesy Ryan line: "I think gyro beautiful." Yes, I've loved him for a while now.

I lean over and kiss him, my tongue finding the gap in his teeth, the seat belt tightening across my chest. *This*, I think, is us. Not our childhoods or parents or wounds.

I peel back and tilt my forehead into his. "Your mom's expecting us."

"We can be late." He starts to unbutton my dress. "I'll explain that we had to pull over and—"

I slap at his hand and re-button myself with a snort of a giggle. "You'll explain no such thing."

We're fine. Better than fine. We love each other! And I'm ready to meet his mother.

He grins, shifts the car into drive, checks the mirror, and eases back onto the road.

I play with the back of his hair as he drives, both of us lost in thought as acorns crunch beneath the tires.

Elise opens the door of her gray-bricked ranch-style home, pulls me toward her, and makes a kissing sound beside my cheek. "So good to finally meet you." She looks me in the eye with a shade of Ryan's exact sincerity, still holding on to my arms. "Can I take your purse, dear?"

Ryan raises his eyebrows at me, smirking.

I ignore him. "Thank you, Ms. Brighton!" In addition to sounding overeager, I've apparently landed on calling her Ms.

"Oh, please call me Elise." She takes my purse.

Ryan's *told you so* eyebrows lift so high that his forehead practically disappears. I elbow him after Elise walks ahead of us, and we repress snickers.

She's wearing jeans and a pink blouse with lips to match. Her shoulder-length, graying hair is freshly curled, but her feet are slippered, which leaves me reassured about my denim dress choice.

The house is immaculate, with only a few unpacked boxes remaining in a back room. Ryan was spot-on about her particularities during our visit. Tea in this cup, not that one. Turn on that light, not this one.

What I wasn't prepared for is how close she and Ryan are. It makes sense. She lost everything and then gave all her reserves to her son. He, in the way of a child, did the same for her. All of a sudden, my six months with him are a drop in the bucket. Now that we're here in his mother's house, I hardly know him at all. Women reflexively size up the mothers of their men, with some small smugness for knowing their sons in ways they never will. But mothers, I realize at this moment, have this. All the years. The man as a boy. My hand pulls toward my stomach.

Elise asks proudly, "Has my son told you he's a brilliant artist?"

Ryan rolls his eyes as I smile up at him. "Something like that." Elise and I both know he's too modest to make such a claim, despite its truth.

She points toward a canvas hanging on the living room wall between a crucifix and brass sconce. "That's a Ryan Brighton original right there."

I turn to see a painting of a mother and young son. I blow the steaming surface of my (loose leaf) tea and ask, "Is it—"

Elise nods. "That's us. From an old photo that's always been a favorite. Ryan painted it for my fiftieth birthday."

I brush Ryan's arm approvingly as I walk over to get a closer look. His talent and devotion are evident. In the painting, he's wearing red overalls, hugging his mom. I've seen him in action enough to know how he must've labored over the selection of colors, come back day after day, worked until each shadow was just so. How he must've thought about it even when he stepped away, problem-solving angles and details even as he scrubbed reds and blues and browns off his hands with turpentine. I look from the two of them in oil paint to the two of them in the flesh, and I'm struck again by the length of it, being someone's child.

Examining the boy in the portrait, I smile. "What a sweet little guy."

"Wasn't he?" Elise beams.

"Uh, ladies?" Ryan interjects. "As much as I love the attention"—he vigorously shakes his head to demonstrate that he does *not* love the attention—"should I start dinner?"

Elise laughs with her head tilted back. She's beautiful, the headwaters of the man I love. She gestures to the backyard. "Grill's ready when we are."

The screen door slamming behind us, we migrate to the patio. Ryan mumbles that he needs to fix that hinge. Then, as he grills, I hear all about his playing baseball, winning art awards, and going camping in weather so cold that Elise had "a serious spike in blood pressure" worrying about frostbite. I shiver.

Elise offers me a sweater and doesn't wait for my response. As Ryan goes inside to get a spatula, she puts a hand to his arm and instructs, "Hall closet. My thick cream sweater."

Ryan retrieves the sweater, and I shrug myself into it as the sunset coats us in an orange film of relaxed contentment. Two floodlights click on while night enters placidly as if to say, *No hurry.* Tiny bugs flock from nowhere and bump against the light.

Reclining at her wrought-iron table with burgers and grilled squash, I answer questions about my recent promotion and then hear about Elise's favorite and least favorite students over the years, her neighbor with the four cats, and the rhubarb pie recipe she's perfected, which Ryan and I confirm by practically licking our dessert plates clean.

When we hug goodbye, Elise makes the kissing noise by my cheek again and says, "Don't be strangers."

I sense the precarious dance behind her words, the loss that comes with a son falling in love, her decreasing necessity, the fear of his drift.

Halfway out the door, I turn, remembering. I slip out of her sweater, which has the distinct and comforting smell of a woman of a certain age. Like nutmeg, but gentler. I wonder if my mother's sweaters would have smelled this way. I thank Elise again and follow Ryan to the car.

What if I want to be strangers? What if I'm not ready for family or *only one grandparent* or—

"IloveyouIloveyouIloveyou." As Ryan opens the Mazda door for me, he whispers this in quick succession like beads falling from a necklace. Before I can respond, he closes the door behind me and all but skips around to the driver's side.

Sitting, he faces me. "Now that I've said it, I don't ever want to not be saying it." He looks me up and down. "It was torture looking at Little League pictures with my mom when all I want is to be alone with you."

The best parts of the day rise to the surface. Ryan has fanned into child and teen and man, past and present and future. Being ready becomes irrelevant, and I swell with affection. "Ryan"—my palm rises to his cheek—"I've never loved anyone as much as I love you." This is almost the truth.

He pushes the speed limit on the drive to my apartment, where I have his jeans at his ankles by the time we get to my bedroom's threshold. A craving comes over me for his pleasure. Something about how he did his mother's dishes, the paint lodged in the creases of his knuckles, the smell of his patchouli shampoo, what he looked like as a little boy, that he ever *was* a little boy and is now this whole man who lets my fingertips trace his ribs, my tongue his teeth.

Our passion heightens in an attempt to keep the highlights from stopping, the lowlights from breathing, the tower from falling. We tumble onto my bed, my old quilt, where *if we have kids* is like an unseen hair tickling my skin.

It would break us if he knew I already have one.

1981 to 1982

WHEN I OPEN MY FRONT DOOR, RYAN HAS A CHAMBRAY tie and a hairless chin. I straighten the tie and kiss the chin. We walk to his car, our dress shoes rhythmically tapping cement. It's the heart of summer, and launch night has arrived.

I distributed flyers all over the city while Ryan navigated contractors and the tedious process of getting the lighting how he wanted it. According to him, most of art is light. He has acquired a collection from local artists and is already dreaming of acquiring nationally. He's determined to showcase work of all price points and never to franchise.

He stoppers the gallery door with a rubber wedge. There are paintings, photographs, and even a few small sculptures—a lion, a top hat, and two embracing lovers.

Caterers arrive looking like well-groomed Oreo cookies with white shirts sandwiched between dark pants and dark hair. They prepare Merlot, fudge, and an assortment of pastries. The AC blasts. Jazz musicians set up and play, their instruments saying, *Don't let me interrupt*, and also, *No pressure to talk*.

Our first buyers are a couple in their seventies who saw a flyer at the senior center where they use treadmills twice a week. By the time they purchase an expensive piece, we've heard about all dozen of their grandchildren. And at least twice that many guests have come through the gallery door.

I shoot a giddy *Can you believe this?* glance at Ryan, but he's focused on a *Fort Worth Star-Telegram* journalist who wants to feature the gallery. When she learns that Ryan plans to give a percentage of the night's earnings to Catholic Charities, she mentions the potential of a cover story. I pinch myself and meander with a clipboard, asking who'd like to be on our mailing list or register for a class. The lists fill. A couple of hours ago, we wondered if anyone would show up besides Elise. And here we are.

As the evening winds down, Ryan and I stand in a side-by-side embrace, my head resting against his arm. We watch a young woman carry off a silhouette of downtown, the last piece to sell for the evening. Behind her, Elise congratulates Ryan with a sophisticated squeal. She hugs us goodnight. Trays and wineglasses exit after her. Next, a saxophone and drum kit.

After he pays the caterers and musicians, Ryan dead bolts the door in slow motion, like the click of the lock might make everything vanish.

There's an echoey quiet. He turns toward me, exhales a long-held breath, extends his arms, and says in disbelief, "We did it."

I run to him. "You did it."

"Nobody would have known to come if it weren't for you, Lil." His thumb on my cheek, he adds softly, "I love you so much."

I buzz with affection and success.

Ryan looks around, wipes his palms on his slacks, and kneels. He takes my hand and stares up at me with mischief and nerves. I laugh, assuming it's not what it looks like. This is impulsivity, the emotions of the moment getting to him, as often happens with Ryan.

But then he pulls out a velvet box.

Goose bumps parade up my spine, and I smooth my taffeta dress.

This is exactly what it looks like. He's been planning it.

The moment lingers like whiskey circling the glass before it hits the tongue, then circling the tongue before it hits the throat.

He creaks the box open and says, "Lillian."

Unlike when we first met, my name is not a question. It's a declaration, solid as the small stone gleaming up at me. My breath quickens as his calloused hand holds my trembling one, his thumb drawing soft lines across the back of it.

Yes bubbles up in me like I'm a flute of champagne, but I won't let it surface until he says the words. So instead I ask it, like that day in the library. "Yes?"

He lets the pause breathe, the moment expand, the memory grow roots.

His eyes are locked on mine. "I have loved you since the day I met you. I love you more with each passing hour, and I want to build a life together if you'll have me. Lillian Wright," he says, "will you marry me?"

The question barely escapes his mouth before I yank him up, laugh-cry out a definitive yes, throw my arms around his neck, and kiss him as hard as if a priest has already pronounced us.

Months later, in February of 1982, we take vows in that same spot of his fledgling gallery, dancing to Village People and celebrating late into the night. A fragile new tree of our own is planted. Beyond my wildest dreams—and against my better judgment—I have a family again.

Galveston is brown. The sand, water, even the sky. But we're honeymooners, so I couldn't care less if our surroundings are dull. We explode with enough color to fill the Gulf Coast.

A friend of Matteo's owns a two-bedroom bungalow with a blue porch ceiling. It's a seven-minute walk from the beach. Because it's February, we're apparently doing him a favor by staying at his place, and the cost of a winter's week at a friend of a friend's beach rental is to check a few plants, wrap a pipe, and look in on Mrs. Fischer next door. All of this is done within an hour of our arrival. After that, we have a week together, blank as a fresh canvas.

The first morning, we stay warm in bed for half an hour after waking, my hand across Ryan's chest as he fiddles with my ring. His voice still has the husk of sleep when he asks, "So how do you want it to start?"

I prop up on an elbow, moving the pillow corner out of his face. "The trip?"

A small shake of his head. "No." A turn of his neck and his molasses eyes meet mine and even now my heart reacts with a little flip. "Our story."

"Our story?"

"Yeah." He lifts my ring finger, kissing knuckle and metal. "We're here at the beginning. It can be anything we want. So how do you want it to start?"

I would never think of it that way. Our story started two days ago when we made vows. Weeks ago when we chose flowers and cake. The night the gallery launched and Ryan sunk to his knee and looked up, bursting with anticipation. It started the first time he took my photograph, the first time he called, the day of the Greek food and a wobbling library table and our entire histories panting inside of us during our first blushing hug. It started when our mothers cradled us decades earlier. But I don't say any of this. Instead, I smile at my husband's charming way of seeing things, and I answer his question. "Pancakes."

He grins.

I get dressed and go out for ingredients.

When I return, Ryan has a hammer in his hand. I smile-frown my curiosity as he explains, "Just earning our keep." In the time it took me to get flour and sugar and syrup, he has fixed the loose leg of a chair, a drawer handle, and a wonky light fixture.

I rise onto my toes and greet him with a slow kiss on the mouth. Something I learned early on is that Ryan Brighton doesn't miss his surroundings. If there's a need, he meets it. If there's beauty, he photographs it.

As he flips pancakes, he requests that I wear my swimsuit when we go to the beach.

"But it's cold."

His dark eyes slant playfully. "I don't mean *only* your swimsuit. Obviously."

"Under my clothes? What difference does that make?"

He gives me a shrugging *Come on* face, and my cheeks warm.

Then he drizzles syrup over my pancakes. "Say when."

I smile, shy and euphoric as I watch maple pool. "When."

While we walk the gravel stretch of road toward the beach, he toys with the red halter strap of my swimsuit peeking out from beneath my sweatshirt. I think of last night, his mess of hair against the pillow, his hands, tonight. I get a chill of memory and want, and I scoot closer toward my husband as we walk, wind coming at us off the sea.

He has brought his easel and high hopes, but as soon as he attempts to set it up, he mutters, "That was stupid." The wind knocks it over once, twice, three times like a tireless child. Ryan packs it up and says that we'll settle for photos, his camera emerging as the easel is banished.

He takes pictures of my veiny feet in the cold surf, jeans rolled to my knees, goose bumps prickling my calves, and foamy waves placing seaweed across my toes before taking it back again. He takes pictures of the clouds, the pier, a young family down the way, seagulls congregating near a trash can, a trio of teen boys laboring to get their truck out of the sand. Naturally, he then sets down his camera and jogs over to help them.

A good half hour later, Ryan has shed his top layer, and his forehead is glistening. He heaves his weight into pushing the truck, the boys doing the same. Little do they know that he's on his honeymoon. I watch their sincere efforts and scrawny frames next to Ryan's full-grown-ness, and I snap some amateur photos of their process and of my miniature sandcastle. Well, sand bungalow. Well, okay, sand lump with what you can almost tell are windows. I'm not the artist here. A crab skitters over it.

Another rev of the engine and I look up to see the truck's rear wheels finally find purchase as the four men cheer. I hear Ryan invite them to get ice cream with us (I guess we're getting ice cream), but they admit they're supposed to be at school. Something about a math test from one of them and an expletive of realization from another. Ryan shakes their car-greased hands goodbye, and I feel the familiar jealous attraction that I sometimes feel when the needs of the world monopolize Ryan. The truck drives off down the seawall with a blast of exhaust.

By way of apology, Ryan reaches both hands out to pull me up from the sand. I dust off the seat of my pants as he asks, "Ice cream?"

I laugh. Shiver. Ice cream sounds delicious.

We start walking down the beach toward the pier, imposing with the massive Flagship Hotel suspended above the water. Once upon a time, this was the Coney Island of the South. But then storms came.

Ryan is as excited about the prospect of ice cream as he is about the swimsuit under my clothes, which is to say, overly. Trudging through sand, he turns and walks backward, taking more photos, a too-close one of my face, wind whipping my hair across it. I blink up at the overcast sky. "You're going to have a bunch of brown pictures."

"I'm going to have pictures of where I was with my bride on our honeymoon, exactly how it is." He hop-steps to a different angle and clicks again, my profile, my wild hair. Pleased, he says, "The work of the artist is to freeze time."

I laugh though nothing's funny. It's simply a happiness big enough for laughter, big enough to want a moment frozen and kept. I'm overcome with untouchable joy as I regard my groom. His complete otherness, given to me. His beloved camera. His forehead damp from selflessness. His eyes their rich hue that convinces me brown is the best color in the world.

I hoist myself onto his sturdy back and he runs, wind drawing tears from our eyes. I could be anywhere with anyone, but here I am joined in marriage to not just any man, but a good one.

Eventually, we get to our ice cream. And later to the little bungalow with the blue porch ceiling and a ready hammer and leftover pancakes and the red swimsuit that my new husband is impatient to uncover.

We're here at the beginning. It can be anything we want.

Ryan Wells Brighton and Lillian Irene Wright. We want to do something unusual and combine our last names, but "Brighton-Wright" and "Wright-Brighton" remind us too much of "night-light" or the Lite-Brite toy. We consider this dilemma as we adjust to newlywed life.

One evening after work, Ryan cooks spaghetti and Bolognese as I distribute wedding gifts throughout our apartment. A toaster. A cordless phone. A new sage towel set for the bathroom. I nod approval at the towel color against the rust tile that covers the counter and walls.

I shelve a couple of books on our living room built-ins. Ryan and I decided our gifts to each other would be related to books and art. I got him a camera, and he got me a special edition of *A Tree Grows in Brooklyn*. As Ryan browns beef in the kitchen, I slide the torn paper napkin with his old number in between the book's pages, warming at the memory.

I place our new VCR beside the television and then focus a few degrees north, adjusting the southwestern wall art that Elise got us. It looks nice with our brown plaid sofa and recliner. I toss a blanket into the bedroom, carry Ryan's easel to the living room, and bring gift wrap trash to the kitchen, making a mental note to get another small trash can or two.

I squeeze behind Ryan, pleased with how our first home is coming together, the bliss of tinkering around our apartment as my husband makes dinner.

"I need to get out the address book and start thank-you cards. People were so generous. Matteo got us the towel set, right?"

Ryan is stirring the noodles.

"Ry?"

"Hmm?"

"Did Matteo give us the towels?"

"Oh, uh, not sure."

"I'll check my gift notes." I get Parmesan from the fridge. "That reminds me. I need to replenish my stationery."

He gives the softening noodles a tired smile.

I look up at him. "You okay?"

"Yeah, why?"

"I don't know. You're just quiet." I pull two plates from an upper cabinet. When we set up the kitchen, Ryan had this baffling idea that plates should go in a lower cabinet. I said I couldn't get used to that and he said he couldn't get used to my way, so we split the difference. Plates in both cabinets. In case we should want to grab them with our toes, I teased. He laughed but pointed out that we don't get other lower cabinet items with our toes. Then he gave me a peck on the forehead, and I leaned into him and into this work of grafting ourselves together.

"I'm just tired. Turns out, running a gallery is hard work." He gives me a wink and taps the spoon on the pan's edge to shed excess sauce.

We serve straight from the stove and shuffle over to our oak table, where I toss down place mats, needing to check my gift notes about those too. It's already dark outside, so I light two taper candles as Ryan grabs napkins.

We sit down and dig in. Spaghetti is an easy favorite of mine. I wipe sauce from the corner of my mouth and sprinkle grated Parmesan. Ryan twirls his fork and says with a thoughtful frown, "Where'd we get this table again?"

I scoot the Parmesan toward him and say, "My great-aunt. Queen of estate sales."

He mumbles, "Estate sales?" He scoots back, bending and twisting to look under the table.

"What in the world?"

"It reminds me so much of the table I had when I was little." He shakes his head. "I used to color on the underside of it."

I bend to look under the table, knowing what I'll find: naked wood. I sit back up and take another bite. "How crazy would that have been?"

He drops his fork onto his plate with a light clink and goes to refill his water glass.

I swallow and spin more noodles around the tines of my fork. "So cute that you colored underneath. Ever the artist."

"Not sure Mom found it cute."

"Uh-oh, were you scolded?" I smile, envisioning young Ryan sneaking under the table while Elise baked or hummed or counted for hide-and-seek.

When my eyes drift up from my food to my husband's face, I stop smiling. He's seated again, shadowy thoughts across his face. Whole years seem to have been added to him.

"What is it?"

"Nothing." He stabs his spaghetti and takes a bite. "Last time I colored that table was the night we left."

He chews and gulps and blinks, his fork stilling beneath a limp wrist. He never talks about that night. Ever. I set my fork down as silence surrounds us like an ambush.

A tear slides down my husband's face, over his stubble, like rain down a window. We both avoid our pasts, but on the occasion that we

31

face them, we do so in opposite attitudes. I go at mine with downplaying and busying myself. Ryan, on the other hand, can't do anything but feel the enormity.

Then, the sound of my arm lifting. The fabric of my blouse. My bent knuckle to his cheek. Skin, salt water, skin.

With a crackling edge, his voice cuts the quiet. "What a stupid thing to cry over. Especially in front of you." That edge is in his words—I've come to think of it as The Barton Edge, because it emerges when Barton comes up.

"Why especially in front of me? I'm your wife."

"I didn't even *lose* my dad. You lost so much when your parents died."

I ignore the perpetual sting of it, the flash of Mama's hair falling out in clumps, the chemo not working, then Dad's accident and two funerals in as many years.

Ryan labors to control his voice, but in an anguished crescendo he yells, "I'm crying because of a table!" He pounds the table with a fist. Plates rattle. I startle. The candle flames bow low.

Ryan swallows, squeezing his eyes shut.

I take a long breath, push my chair back, move to him, and sit on his lap, unable to get close enough to his hurt. "I didn't lose my parents until I was older. And death is different than . . ." I say what neither Ryan nor Elise ever says: "violence."

He clenches his jaw and opens his eyes. Part of me wishes he'd close them again. Looking into their dark, heavy need is like being at the bottom of an ocean. But the other part of me will stop at nothing to heave him up to the surface. I press his head to my chest and say, "You can cry." I tilt his chin up and add, "Especially in front of me."

With memories thick in his throat, he grips me and says into my neck, "You're like light, woman."

I disagree, but I keep this to myself. I have my own darknesses; I just don't wear mine like he does.

In a thick voice, he whispers, "Wait, that's it." He leans back. "Bright."

I blink. "What?"

His shoulders release, and the shadow across him dissipates. "Hear me out. You'll think it's cheesy. But give it a chance."

He sniffles, smiling small, and I try to keep up. I hand him a napkin, and he blows his nose. Then he grabs my shoulders and pauses, always one for a subtle brand of theatrics. In an announcer's voice, he says, "Ryan and Lillian Bright. It combines our last names!"

"Can we do that?"

He shrugs. "Why not?"

I exhale away the preceding moments and stand up, carrying our dishes to the sink. "Yes, it is cheesy. But . . ." I return his melodramatic pause and take a minute to consider. "It might work?" A smile sneaks over me. "It's certainly better than our other options."

I find Tupperware for the leftover spaghetti and nod, persuading myself. "I think I love it, Ryan . . . Bright." I smile wide. "And I love you." Of this I need no persuasion—Brighton or Bright or Big Bird, my love for him is sure. Which remains a marvel after Zack Melendez.

Ryan's voice has a gravelly glow. "I love you too, Lillian Bright."

"Your mom will have opinions."

"She usually does." He shrugs. "But she considered changing back to her maiden name, so she might appreciate this." He pulls me toward the living room. "Besides, it's not her name. It's ours."

Ours. Happiness blooms inside me.

We leave the dishes and use my darkest eyeliner to write our new name on each other's skin, testing it out. Sitting on the living room rug, he writes around the crook of my elbow. We sign in cursive and heart-dot the *i* like high schoolers decorating book covers. Ryan seems to shed the years the table added.

I pull his shirt over his head and write our names vertically between his shoulder blades, no capitals: *ryan and lillian bright*. He reaches beneath my skirt, leisurely rolling down my hose like a scroll. In the kitchen, sauce hardens in a neglected pan. He scrawls my name up my leg, my skirt bunching. He abandons the eyeliner and keeps a hand on me, inching upward.

I shake away the linger of pain. His. Mine. No need to think about Lillian Wright or Ryan Brighton. We are now proud canvases of a new name, a new life.

1982 to 1985

DOWNTOWN IS RIPE FOR BUSINESS, AND THE GALLERY establishes itself in the new Sundance Square. We call it the Sundance Gallery, later shortening it to the SG. I'm soon able to work full-time at the SG, managing books and publicity. Ryan's artistic ambition coupled with my execution makes us an excellent business pair. The gallery thrives.

Our early married years pass like the happy dream I didn't let myself have over that first hummus and pita. Summers take us to the seawall, and autumns find us eating corn dogs under the shadow of Big Tex. Whenever we leave work together, we buy ice cream cones and stroll by street performers or drink hot cocoa on our way to Burnett Park to see the giant Christmas tree in December. Walking through the Sundance bustle, we share hopes, plans, and line items to add to the SG's budget. In the evenings, we host gallery events, ravage rhubarb pie with Elise, or cook a simple dinner at home with an in-progress canvas on the easel, Ryan's work as vibrant and personal and captivating as ever. Currently, a teal-toned painting of an old chapel with a contemplative man on the front step, hat in hand, the slight lift of clothing and grass showing that it's a windy day.

One evening when we get home from work, Ryan disappears into the bedroom and returns with a goofy grin and something behind his back. I'm still shrugging off my jacket, setting down a stack of registrations and supply lists for a charcoal drawing class. "What's going on?"

He reveals a red cardboard box. *Standard of the West Since 1879* is emblazoned at the top, *Justin* at the bottom. I raise my eyebrows. "Boots?"

"Open it." He's still just smiling.

I open it. Boots. I look up for an explanation. All he says is, "Do you like them?"

I swivel them, slipping my current shoes off to try them on. They're light brown with fringe. At least they don't have rhinestones. I pull them on. Perfect fit, just need to be worn in. "They fit great." I haven't owned cowgirl boots since I was little. "Hope I have an occasion to wear them." I can't imagine any.

"Let's go to Billy Bob's."

I look around. "Now?"

He shrugs. "Sure."

I chuckle and shake my head a little. When the landmark honky-tonk opened, Ryan wanted us to check it out. I said I didn't have boots, so with an exaggerated drawl, he gasped and teased, "Then you ain't a real Texan." That was over a year ago, and I haven't thought about it since.

"I think the last time I did any country-western dancing was a do-si-do with my dad." I get a fleeting whiff of Dad's aftershave.

Ryan laughs. "Nobody cares if you know the steps."

So I change into jeans, a thick belt, and my new boots.

On the Billy Bob's dance floor, I discover that Ryan, for one, knows the steps. He's front and center for the Cowboy Boogie and the Electric Slide and something called the Tush Push. I'm not the only one who enlists his help. Over the twang of music and roar of people and flow of beer, Ryan demonstrates line dances slowly for anyone who needs a refresher. I didn't realize I was going out dancing with an expert, and it's all too much fun for me to care if I forget to tap my toe or push my tush.

Ryan turns to me as I yell over the music, "You're so good at this!"

He smiles and takes my hand to two-step.

I relax into the quick-quick-slow rhythm until the music picks up and I realize there are a lot more than two steps. With strong arm motions, Ryan leads me through twists and spins. As he moves me to the side, front, behind, side, he whispers cues. "To your right." "About to spin left." "Ready for a dip?"

Rising from the dip as a song ends, I laugh and say breathlessly, "Full of surprises."

Women line up to dance with him. As another song starts, I yell, "Go ahead! I'm getting water anyway."

He turns to a woman in rhinestone boots, shakes his head, and yells, "Sorry!" His hand slides from my waist to the small of my back as he guides me off the dance floor and says low, "You're wonderful out there." I feel the women's eyes on me as we walk away. *He* is wonderful out there. I'm beyond rusty. But beauty's in the eye of the beholder and whatnot.

As we drink our water against the bar, he asks me what's wrong.

"Why would something be wrong?"

"You're taking those deep breaths you take when something is wrong."

I can't hide from him, which is both unsettling and comforting. "Just a headache."

"Want to call it a night?"

"But it's so fun!" I roll knuckles across my temple.

He has already set his water down. "And so loud. Come on." His hand finds the lower curve of my back again. "Let's go home."

"You sure?"

"Yes." He looks at my feet. "You have boots now. We'll come back soon."

I smile.

In the car, he sings Eric Clapton's "Wonderful Tonight," the part about the aching head and the help to bed, and then he tenderly calls me *darling* in one of his unashamed cheesy moods. I laugh and say, "I just got dehydrated. That was more of a workout than the do-si-do I remember. Where did you get so—"

"One guess."

"Your mom?"

"Bingo. I was nervous about my first school dance. We took lessons. Swing, too. And—don't tell anyone—also ballroom."

I giggle as I imagine him waltzing.

"Hey now."

"Sorry." I bite my lip.

We hold hands atop the center console. At home, he does in fact help me to bed.

We return to Billy Bob's every so often. Matteo and his girlfriend join. My boots get worn in, and one wild weekend I even let Ryan flip me. We get good enough for circles to clear around us.

We're so happy that we pretend otherwise around less-happy friends. Our once-faltering tower is not only sturdy. It's luminous.

Then the day comes when we sell the Anand piece.

Arjun Anand is an exceptional photographer whose work Ryan acquired all the way from L.A. The piece is a four-foot-tall photograph of three women in vivid saris in the middle of a crowded Indian market. The people and rickshaws and fruit stands around them are blurred. Still, the noise and aromatic spices nearly jump from the frame. It's titled, simply, *Khan Market*. One of the women looks into the distance, the second woman looks at the first, and the third—younger than the other two—looks straight at the camera. And straight at Mrs. Patel as she enters the gallery, neither the baby on her hip nor her three-inch heels slowing her down. She came for this piece; she came with cash.

After she lays eyes on the piece and confirms that it's as magnificent as anticipated, the crew starts getting it ready to be moved, and Mrs.

Patel passes her baby boy to me as if handing me a cup of coffee. She follows Ryan to take care of payment, and I'm left standing alone on the gallery floor with the gurgles and warm weight of her doughy son.

The baby dons a two-toothed unadulterated smile like I'm some favored auntie. I look away fast—I don't deserve that smile. He must be something like six months fresh to this world. Barely here. And yet fully here. The wind is knocked out of me by a wave of something akin to morning sickness. I steady myself on a smooth white wall as crewmen across the room maneuver *Khan Market* with rumblings of "Cuidado, jefe, cuidado."

Suddenly the baby's hand is on my cheek, his laughter making its way through my chest, arteries, womb. I have to get him out of my arms. With my free hand, I wipe sweat from my neck as I speed walk toward Ryan just as he and Mrs. Patel round the corner. Mrs. Patel offers a crisp smile and takes her baby to go oversee her purchase. Her footsteps click away, quieter and quieter.

Ryan's expression shifts from sale-triumphant to something softer. I realize I might look sick. My skin feels clammy. But he pulls me to him with one arm, kisses the crown of my head, and says, "You look amazing." I search for the inspiration for this strangely timed compliment, which starts to make sense when he adds, featherlight, "We should have one of those."

"One of what?" It takes me a minute.

With a smile, he nods toward Mrs. Patel's baby. I cough and say something about the sale instead. Ryan looks like a wounded puppy, but I pretend not to notice.

I thought that when the time came, I could be ready. I love Ryan, after all. But when he broaches the subject over dinner a few days later, and again a few days after that, I tell him I'm not ready. I do not tell him why.

After a few months, my guilty conscience presents as his dream come true: I'm ready, or so I say. Too slow for Ryan and too fast for me. Much of marriage is some permutation of mismatched desires, like a three-legged race. And desires become indistinguishable. I can't tell if I want to have a baby or want to make Ryan happy. Or pay penance. But if perfect understanding of our own motives were a prerequisite for action, the world would be motionless. One way or the other, I move our condoms to the back of the drawer, next to out-of-ink pens and disposable razors.

When Ryan realizes what I'm doing, he looks at me the way he did while sliding a ring onto my finger—like pain can't touch us. Never mind that it has touched us all our lives, and our parents before us. He lives as though we've hit our limit; I live as though pain has no limit. Our pasts have molded us in opposite directions. *How does he do this?* I wonder, bitter and pitying and also clinging to his hope like a lung to oxygen.

Four months after moving the condoms, I'm five days late. The liquid unapologetically changes from red to white in its tiny tube. Positive. I take another home test to confirm. This one also turns white within an hour. To my great surprise, some rebel seed of joy sprouts within my garden bed of fear.

Three weeks after that—after just enough time to dream—I start spotting. My back aches. My stomach cramps. Faster than I can get in touch with a doctor, the spots mushroom into a surge, white underwear to red, like a backward pregnancy test.

I'm home alone and can't bring myself to flush the bloody tissue. It has substance to it. I can't close the lid. I press my sweating face into the cold wall tile and breathe out, in, out, in. Condensation circles appear, vanish, appear, vanish.

I leave it in the open toilet bowl. This, I think, is the child Ryan planned to put on his shoulders for the Christmas tree topper. The odor is stale.

I walk away and lie curled around my empty body on the bed where this began, hand over my womb like a pledge of allegiance to the lost ones. When Ryan gets home, I practically beg him to blame me. But he won't, of course.

We watch the red cyclone as Ryan flushes. We hold each other up. He wishes he had been here; I'm glad he wasn't. He says something about tomorrow being a new day, and I stare past him. There is zero comfort in that sentiment. I don't want a new tomorrow—I want a new yesterday. My womb is that much emptier for having been filled. Again.

I wait for relief, expect it, try to conjure it. But the sorrow is as big as a whole life. Around us, the world is cruelly unchanged and I can't escape it, like sunlight through closed eyelids. There are babies everywhere. Waiting to be born. Newly born. Breathing, growing, living.

Then those babies are shrinking. Swallowing their cries. Disappearing. The toilet is sloshing and spitting out blood. I am curling on the bed, uncurling, walking backward to the bathroom, leaning against the wall. My breath mark is appearing on the tile. I am straightening, looking down. Crimson drops on cotton are fading. I am standing in front of the mirror, test in hand, white liquid to red, test in box. I am moaning underneath my husband, pulling the condoms to the front of the drawer. Mrs. Patel's heels are clicking louder and louder. I am taking her baby, backing away fast, hand to my neck. Air is licking up beads of sweat. The baby is touching my face. Men are hanging *Khan Market* on the gallery wall. A woman is staring at me from a street in India. I am closing my eyes, opening them in bed with a man. He snores. My hand is on my stomach like I have something to protect. I am not pregnant. Was I ever?

1972 to 1973

I MET ZACK MELENDEZ AT A MIDSCALE BARBECUE restaurant. It was an open mic night in early December, and he was performing in faded bell-bottoms. He played acoustic ballads about girls and world peace and being misunderstood. His voice was low, luxurious, dripping silk. I sipped sweet tea as we locked eyes. Right after his set, he came and found me.

After that night, he took me out every chance we got. Fresh flowers and the whole enchilada. The attraction was instant, yet Zack was a perfect gentleman. I was saving myself for true love.

On the night of the ceasefire in Vietnam, his band—Zack and the Blacktoppers—played anti-war rock songs under the open Fort Worth sky. Each chord was struck with victorious fervor, and adrenaline galloped through me like a wild horse. I watched Zack's fingers slide across the neck of his Gibson and could almost feel them slide across me. I had decided this was the night. I wouldn't be his first, but I would, according to him, be his "first that mattered."

As if reading my mind, he winked from behind the microphone and gave a shout-out to his girl. Anticipation zipped up me, the girls around me swooned, and I was as done for as those weapons of war.

———

Zack Melendez was worth the wait. Ten months later, no regrets. We had that Hollywood good stuff. Romance in spades. He had an aura, an ability to make life's problems seem conquerable, to make anyone in his sphere feel chosen. It was clear he was going places, and along the way he was doing things like dancing me through parking lots and surprising me after class with chocolates.

The envy of all who knew us, I hitched myself to his glittering dreams. I'd had a tough few years, with one parent's funeral followed by the other's, but this was my coming out on the other side. He was the love of my life, and I chanted this like a mantra when my period was two days late. *The love of my life.* Three days late. *We can do this together.* Four days. *I love him.* Seven days and a doctor appointment. *He loves me.*

I waited for Zack on a shaded bench outside his music appreciation class—a class he considered beneath him. *I'm a musician. Do they think I don't appreciate music?* He said it was a waste of his valuable time. If Mama had still been around, she would've said, *That boy's too big for his britches, Lilly girl.* But she wasn't around, and I happened to like Zack's britches. I happened to think I would have raised my chin and told her so, defending my beloved. Sure, he was a suave and polished type who sometimes sounded like he was delivering lines. But he was also fun and talented and driven and, who knows why, head over heels for me. Not to mention, he was the father of my child.

The Texas Christian University campus was prettier than where I was enrolled at Tarrant County Junior College. Leaf shadows played on my arms as I sat beneath majestic branches, smoothing my gingham dress, chosen for the moment I'd break the news. The dress was old, but I thought it had a maternal quality to it.

I checked my watch. His class should be dismissed any minute. The wind picked up, and an American flag spasmed at the top of its pole.

When Zack emerged from the building, there was a spring in his step. He spotted me, waved, and practically beamed. Good signs. He sat and pecked my cheek and then beat me to the announcement punch: Zack and the Blacktoppers were going on tour.

While this was unexpected, my first feeling was pride. And utter confidence that we could handle the distance. Or the baby and I could even join him on the road. I smiled at the thought of making him or her a little "Roadie" romper.

But before I could get a word in edgewise, Zack hit me with, "I'm sure you'll agree it's best if we part ways."

Part ways. He was sure I'd agree. Right. With him, it was always going to be about the spotlight. I'd known this. But I'd naively thought I might at least tag along in the shadows.

He talked. I listened.

. . . months longer if all goes well . . .

. . . need to focus . . .

. . . Atlantic exec at our Chicago show . . .

. . . lot of sacrifices to make it in this business . . .

Stages and adoring crowds twinkled in his eyes. He had the nerve to take my hand and say, "We had a good run. And I hope you can find it inside yourself to be happy for me."

I nodded downward, thinking about what actually was inside myself. My nausea multiplied, every sweet nothing turned sour. And I swallowed my news back down to the pit of my stomach, where it grew and grew and grew.

1985 to 1986

AFTER THE MISCARRIAGE, ELISE IS ELISE, BLESS HER.
Ryan's still at work when she stops by unannounced with enough pork chops to feed our whole apartment complex. Fresh out of the shower, I have a bathrobe tied at the waist and a towel twisted around my hair. I stuff the pork into the fridge and ask if she'd like something to drink, shaking the towel from my head and tossing it into the bathroom. I hate to be in there with my hollowed body, but I did it. I showered.

"No ma'am, I will not have you serving me." She retrieves two glasses and fills them with water. She pauses in front of Ryan's easel, a more erratic piece with dark reds and slapdash lines compared to the calm realism of most of his work. Saying nothing, she goes to get dish gloves and starts filling the sink with suds.

I accept the inevitability of what's happening and don't try to stop her. We told her about the baby the week before we lost it. I alternate between gratitude and regret that we told her. Right now I feel both at once.

"You know, we do have a dishwasher." I've reminded her of this before.

"Never gets them quite clean." She has given this response before.

45

She nods toward the living room as she scrubs a plate by hand. "Go rest, dear."

I comply and go to the couch; I don't have much choice.

To be honest, I don't mind her company. I know I need this time off work, but it feels like all I'm doing is waiting for blood and tears to stop flowing out of me. Or waiting for Ryan to get home only to wait for him to leave again—we haven't figured out how to talk to each other about this. Or about anything else, now that this exists.

I drift off as Elise tidies the apartment. When I wake up, I've drooled on our brown plaid and Elise is looking down her bifocals at a Danielle Steel novel that she must've brought with her.

Wiping my mouth, I say, "You don't have to stay."

"I know." She marks her page and shuts the book. The apartment is clean, and my water has been refilled.

"Thank you for all of this."

"I'm only doing what your mother would do if she were here."

I nod but don't try to respond. Motherhood makes women ache for their moms.

Elise looks over her glasses at me. "I've been where you are."

I glance at her belly as if that would tell me anything.

"I never told Ryan." She takes off her bifocals and sighs. "Or anyone."

"I'm so sorry." I sit straighter. "Before Ryan?"

She shakes her head as her eyes glaze, just like Ryan when he retreats into memory. "No."

I don't ask anything else. It's not my business, curious as I am.

But then she offers, "It was the day after we left Barton. It happened in a motel when Ryan was asleep. Must have been all the walking. The stress. I carried Ryan a long way. Nobody knew but me." She shrugs. "Funny thing is, that baby's why I had the courage to finally leave." Her voice sputters. "Point is, I think of it all the time. That's normal."

I don't know when, but I've scooted toward her and taken her hand between mine. It's a relief to hurt for someone else. "That's terrible. I'm so sorry you went through that alone." This is the first time I've ever heard her mention leaving Barton. I add, "All of that."

She shrugs. "Well, at least I didn't get stretch marks or spider veins. You can be thankful you escaped those."

It's an awful thing to say. As if our skin is worth comparing to our dead children. But people do this—grasp for at-leasts.

She doesn't stop there. "Just wait. You'll understand someday. Pregnancy can be very uncomfortable and unflattering."

I don't tell her that I already understand, that I won't be getting pregnant a third time. Hopefully she won't hate me. Hopefully Ryan won't hate me.

Speak of the devil, the front door opens. Ryan regards the clean apartment, my bathrobe, Danielle Steel. "Mom?"

"Hi, dear."

I nod toward the kitchen with a tired but grateful smile. "Your mom cooked pork chops."

Closing the door and glancing at the clock beside his easel, he says, "Should I warm them? Steam some veggies?"

Elise stands, putting her book and glasses into her bag and her bag onto her shoulder. "I should actually be going."

"You sure?" We both ask this, wanting her to stay. We don't know how to be alone together anymore.

She's already at the door. "Yes, yes. That pork is for you, and I want you both to rest."

Behind her back, I position my hands in a wide-open gesture and mouth to Ryan, *So. Much. Pork.*

Ryan smiles and kisses the top of her head. "Thanks, Mom."

I squeeze her. "Yes, thank you."

Then Ryan and I are left with pounds of pork and all the things we do not say.

The SG suffers in my absence, but we figure it's no big deal. "A bump in the road," as Ryan calls it. I touch my deflated abdomen. "At least there's a bump somewhere," I joke before I think better of it. Ryan doesn't laugh.

It's not only my absence, though. Our most popular local artist moves out of state. Then we have to close for a week to get up to standard with a new code requirement. The skyrocketing oil industry crashes back down, and wallets close fast. Art is seen as luxury. Plus it's winter, our lowest time for class enrollment, even during a good year. Four classes flatten to one.

Ryan won't entertain the idea of closing the doors, even on days when nobody sets foot into the SG at all. He calls our hemorrhaging gallery alive, and we go to work every day, pretending. I busy myself with meaningless tasks and quietly explore other job options. When people do wander in, Ryan is like a hawk holding himself back. Seeing as none of these wanderers come with tens of thousands of investment dollars, we remain up a creek. Yet when a wealthy restaurateur stops in and asks if the place might go up for lease soon—we're in a prime location—Ryan shakes his head and says, "We plan to be here a long time. Sorry." Afterward, Ryan avoids looking at me.

Resentment settles over each of us like dust. Ryan won't let the gallery die, and I won't let our parenthood live. He mourns the children we won't have, and I mourn the one we did. We say little about any of it.

By the time we get home from these exhausting days, Ryan is always itching to paint. If I suggest we eat dinner straightaway, he has to at least get a spurt or two of color onto a palette—a paper plate or torn cardboard or whatever he can find. I usually heat food as he completes this nightly ritual. Half the time, he carries his food over to the easel and, admittedly, it relieves me not to search for conversation. I watch him mix and stroke and squint and mix again, and I'm aware that there are worse compulsions than art. After a while, I collect his dinner plate, squeeze his shoulder.

Sex is sporadic and detached, every slide of a condom a felt loss. I wonder, in the bowels of night, if he might leave me for a woman willing to make him a father. He never pressures me. Still, being responsible for his sadness feels like a thumb to the throat.

One night, he kisses my neck and I lean into it. I've had four clockwork cycles since the miscarriage. When he dutifully reaches for a condom, I stop him and whisper *just had my period.* I pull him into me, arch my back, and close my eyes. Condom-free sex is one thing I can give him.

A few weeks later, he bakes tilapia. The smell swims up my esophagus. I run to hunch over the toilet, stare at my clammy face in the water-dotted mirror, wipe my mouth with the back of my hand, and shake with fear.

I blot a towel on my face. Then I emerge, mumbling hoarsely into Ryan's chest, "I can't lose another, I can't lose another, I can't lose another." He doesn't know the half of it. I'm angry with him and desperate for him.

The tilapia burns. Ryan, the optimist, calls it crusted. We carry plates of charred fish to our oak table, trying to salvage whatever's left that is good.

Apparently the moon and the bleeding aren't an exact science. No day is a safe day. The first stitch of our daughter is one of the least safe experiences I've known, followed by the second stitch, third, fourth, fifth. Her lengthening bones stretch my tummy flab taut. It's the ultimate hospitality, letting men and children occupy me.

The pregnancy is healthy; I carry her thirty-nine weeks. No varicose veins. A few stretch marks that Ryan kisses, his lips as soft and light as flower petals. He assembles a crib. A whole nursery in our spare bedroom. Pink and white with an azalea painting that takes him weeks of devoted detail. Elise crochets a pastel baby blanket that Ryan drapes over the drop-side of the crib. He gets everything ready, down to a throw pillow for the rocking chair.

I stay outside the room, sneak off alone for appointments, hold my breath, and wait to lose her.

1974

NOW I'M THE ONE WHO GETS TOO BIG FOR MY BRITCHES.
I scavenge maternity dresses at thrift stores while a human balloons in
the sea of my gut. I have a young, round face and a ringless finger. I
ignore speculations and stares, and I nod politely when well-meaning
matriarchs give me advice. I stay away from people who know Zack.

A friend calls me brave and kneads my aching back. She faced a similar situation but made a different choice. She's my emergency contact.

Another friend gives me a *Baby's First Year* book. A card with a stork
on the front.

On his due date, a solid, warm, and slippery baby boy arrives. He has
Zack's jawline and my eyes. He opens his mouth, waiting for me to
fill it.

But I don't get to feed him, only to stare at his tiny features and
wonder how such a marvel could come from two bodies and the failed
latex between them. Then I pass him to a nurse who passes him to an
attorney who passes him to a caseworker who passes him to a new mom.
Alone, I sign the papers.

My milk comes in three days later, and I apply warm compresses to weeping breasts. It's a death without a funeral.

I'm a twenty-year-old orphan eking my way through community college as a nanny, of all things. Each day of work is a reminder that I'm unprepared to be a mom. I couldn't have provided for a child alone when I can hardly provide for myself, right?

But at the end of the day, I can't convince myself it was right. What kind of woman gives away a child? I could have kept him. Or had an abortion, legalized a few months ago. Except I couldn't do that when it came down to it. Sometimes a woman's choice is between impossible and impossible and impossible, and she just has to make it. Survival calculations become more urgent than rightness.

Life has the gall to go back to how it was before, days washing over me like waves over sand, my son a shell carried out to sea. Zack is long gone with his bell-bottoms and G majors.

With copious amounts of Dr Pepper and Joni Mitchell, I work and study and study and work. At the end of each day, I fall onto my second-hand mattress only to be startled awake by too-soon alarms and bills that are too-soon due. I can afford little besides rent and rice.

Sometimes I still feel the baby kick, an entire phantom child. A ghost without a death.

1986

IN MIDSUMMER, WITH THE DRONE OF CICADAS OUT THE window, she is pulled from me like a tooth.

I reach for her weight and throb where she hangs by a pulsing thread, where my body already begins to scab over. I shake from her departure, the bizarre experience of holding a small independent form that was part of my blood and bone.

Ryan catches my eye over her seven vernix-covered pounds, his dark eyes dancing with tenderness. Her cry is dizzying, delightful, worth it. Ryan and I cling to each other. Somehow the thrusting of our bodies made lungs! Flesh! Heart! Future!

This. This is the first moment that I want her. *Her.*

And I get to keep this one.

We settle on the name Georgette, after my mama, gone too soon. Middle name Elise after Ryan's mom, here too long—or so she says when recalling bygone years with a long sigh and a simple, *Oh, time.*

Voices in the room are tinny and unimportant compared to Georgette. I panic when someone takes her so they can sew me up, relaxing only when they place her clean and swaddled beside my pillow, where she still feels too far away, every inch a galaxy.

She wiggles and squirms and shifts, and fear hums beside me as I begin to understand that keeping a child is like keeping the sky—always with me but never mine.

In the blurry middle of our first night home, Georgette cries out in that sudden newborn rhythm. I jolt awake and say to Ryan, "Can you take him a minute? I need to pee before I feed him."

Ryan doesn't correct me. He just clears his throat and says of course he'll take her, subtle emphasis on *her*.

My firstborn hovers in the room, as close as ever.

We call her Jet. I wanted to spell it G-e-t-t-e, but Ryan thinks too many people would pronounce it with a hard *G*. He's probably right.

In many ways, Jet saves us. But salvation is not erasure—it's a redistribution of pressure.

The gallery is barely breaking even and there's an entire person dependent on us. We can't compensate ourselves enough anymore. So, a few months postpartum I return to my branch at the bank, grovel, and gratefully land a position in marketing. Ryan keeps the SG open, but he picks up shifts at Matteo's again. I watch a shadow descend on him, the birth of one dream equaling the death of another. And even though the gain is great, the loss is felt.

Loss is loss regardless of gains that come later. And just like Jet deserves our joy, these losses deserve our sadness. The dying gallery. The unformed baby, buried in the plumbing. If we don't keep our two babies distinct, every emotion feels like betrayal. How can we be happy when we don't have our other one? But how can we be sad when we have Jet?

One evening after an all-too-rare shower, I emerge to find that Ryan has moved Jet's baby seat to face the easel. I pause in the doorway, tighten my robe, and watch them from behind. She is a drooling but captive audience as her dad explains how tricky it can be to master the texture of a piece, how the shading is wrong but adding light *just like so* will help. He asks if he should add a touch of orange to the top right or the bottom left.

She gurgles.

He says, "I completely agree. You're a genius." And he touches a dot of orange to the top right corner of the canvas as I stifle a giggle.

When he turns to kiss the top of Jet's fuzzy head, I'm spotted.

"Sorry, I didn't want to interrupt." I approach them. "A masterpiece."

Ryan lifts a brow and looks at the canvas. "It's hardly anything yet." But I didn't mean the painting.

I smile and wipe drool from Jet's mouth. "Has she seemed hungry?"

"Not especially." He mixes color.

I check the clock. "I should probably try to feed her."

Moving my sop of wet hair from one shoulder to the other, I lift her from the chair. She fusses. Ryan and I glance at each other as I set her back down. She quiets.

"Hmm." I put a hand to my hip and examine whether something might have pinched her. Seeing nothing, I try again. More fussing.

Ryan grins. "She wants to help her old man."

I lower her to the seat once more, where she immediately calms and stares at the canvas as her dad streaks it with emerald. She blows a spit bubble, to which Ryan says, "You're right, too loud," and goes for some white to soften it.

I laugh, and these father-daughter painting sessions become a favorite evening routine.

Having a baby is funny in that you wonder things like, *Did I bite my mama's nipples too?* Babies kill dreams but resurrect family.

Maybe this is why Ryan starts mentioning his dad. *I'm saving for her future, unlike my dad. I'm cooking you dinner tonight; my dad couldn't even work an oven.*

And maybe it's why every new facial expression made or purée tasted by Jet makes me wonder a dozen things about my son.

I click off my lamp and crawl into our creaky poster bed, where Ryan's eyes are already closed. He mumbles, "'Night."

Jet is asleep in her room for the moment, and the privacy that used to be normal feels destabilizing. Entrancing. Afflicting. I should put my fingertips on my husband's moonlit skin. I should trace the dark stubble trailing down his neck and say, *Look at me.* I consider kissing him, but a kiss is too shallow for this need that's low and building like a contraction, all while Ryan is simply falling asleep. It's a tragedy too great to endure, a chasm I can't stand. And so the words spill out, at last and too soon.

"Can I tell you about something?"

"Hm?"

"Um. 1974."

He doesn't open his eyes. "What about 1974?"

I could say, *Forget it.* I could say, *Look. At. Me. Like. You. Used. To.* But that's not enough to pull him from his universe into mine. So I clear my throat, close my eyes, and open my mouth. "I had a baby that year."

I peel back my eyelids as his slam open, his eyebrows like deep-diving caterpillars plunging into a frown. "Is this a joke?"

I shake my head, and sudden hot tears confirm that it is no joke. "Sorry I didn't"—I swallow—"tell you sooner." Am I sorry? Should I be?

He sits upright; I stay lying down. I reach for his side; he doesn't respond to my touch.

Please be the Ryan who feeds the man at the Greek restaurant and does his mother's dishes and strokes the nape of his daughter's neck and—

56

"Is this real?" He asks this like it's not the same question as *Is this a joke?*

I suck in a breath. "It—"

"Wait." He's taking short breaths; I'm taking long ones. He puts a hand on my arm and I can feel the race of his heart through his fingertips. "You had a baby twelve years ago and haven't told me in the seven years I've known you? And married you? And had a child with you?"

I don't correct him. *Two children.*

He sighs from the top of an octave to the bottom of it, and he says nothing else. Only stares at me like I'm a paint color he can't name.

Finally, gentler, he says, "Let's talk in the kitchen?"

I unfold myself and follow him.

By the glow of the stove light, he brews tea and asks questions that I answer honestly. Sorrow colors his face. For me. For himself not knowing me like he thought he did.

I don't share Zack's name, but as I watch Ryan carry my tea bag with a cupped hand, I almost say, *He wasn't good like you.*

It's past midnight when we go back to bed. Jet wakes once. Then Ryan holds me straight through to sunrise. He has remembered that I'm more than who I am to him.

But my confession doesn't deflate my shame—it emboldens it. I regret giving up my first, flushing my second, leaving my third every morning for work. I hold guilt as close as a lover and throw myself entirely into being the best possible mom for Georgette. I don't mean to choose her over everyone else, but it's a choice made deep in my bones. And this is how I manage to miss it as my husband's eyes begin to hollow out like craters.

1987

IT'S AN UNREMARKABLE WEEKNIGHT, AND JET IS DOWN to one diaper. So Ryan makes a late-night store run. He returns with a twenty-four pack of diapers and a six-pack of Shiner.

Confusion spills across my face. "What's this for?"

He shrugs. "I had a drink with some of the artists last weekend. Wasn't a big deal."

I frown. The artists often have drinks. Ryan is usually content with an Arnold Palmer or his signature Shirley Temple. Not only content, but proud. We used to sip Arnold Palmers together at gallery events. But between Jet and my job, I haven't kept up with the SG, which is, against all odds, finding a second life.

He tosses the diaper package onto the counter and grabs a bottle of beer, just like that, after decades of resolve.

He pops off the top and says, "I knew you'd make a thing out of this."

All I've said is *What's this for*, which I'd hardly consider making "a thing." I inhale another frown. "You didn't tell me."

"I just did."

"But you—"

"Well, you're one to talk." The bottle pauses at his lips before he tilts it back and swallows two, three, four times as if emphasizing gulp by gulp that he has no regret. The swallows land like slaps.

I shut my mouth and open it again, a hand on my hip. "Is that what this is about? You needed a secret as some kind of payback for me having a past?"

He runs a hand through his hair. "Me having a drink has nothing to do with your past. Or my past. I didn't tell you anything because there isn't anything to tell."

I say nothing, which seems to compel him to say more.

"Most people who drink aren't alcoholics." A swig to punctuate his point. "And most people—including me—aren't my dad."

He knows good and well that I've never made demands. He was teetotal long before we met. He also knows I have my own reason for wariness. "You know the night *my* dad—"

"I know what happened with your dad. And I know what happened with my dad." He stretches his arms into an exaggerated shrug, Shiner sloshing into the neck of the bottle in his hand. "But I'm not them!" The Barton Edge has crept into our interactions so much that it's just The Ryan Edge now.

He moves toward our sink full of dirty dishes, turns on the faucet, and starts scrubbing a skillet, his beer on the windowsill. He's ending this discussion, which is fine by me.

He is unnecessarily loud as he clanks the pan against the sink, and it's no surprise that Jet starts crying from her crib. I glare at the back of him, exhale hard through the nose, grab the diapers, and walk away.

As bottles and cans accumulate, I fix my focus on our growing baby. An infant is full of need, and being needed is such a big part of love. Ryan doesn't need me. He tells me as much. "I don't need that look." "I don't need you to say anything." "I can take care of myself."

Their milestones coincide. Jet sits up by herself the night of six empty cans on the coffee table. Her dad cheers, smiles, hiccups. The evening she first crawls is also the first time her dad passes out in our recliner. Then, the night of Jet's first fever is the first time Ryan calls late from the gallery and says he shouldn't drive home. Her fever is 102.4 degrees, and I hold a damp cloth to her forehead until she cools.

The night after the fever, Ryan sits down for dinner with his evening drink beside him. I've said very little about the alcohol since he brought home that first six-pack of Shiner. But when he goes for his second beer, I ask, "Why not stop for tonight?"

The immediate eye roll. "Would you leave it alone? It's not hurting anyone."

My stomach drops. I want to take the drink from his hand and chug it and then another and another and another. I want to pass out and not be able to take care of our daughter, or leave and not be able to drive home. I want to do that night after night and then ask him if it hurts.

Jet bangs her palms on the table and squeals. I help her spoon a bite, which she refuses.

Ryan asks me to pass the salt and so I do.

After ten more minutes of Jet refusing food, Ryan puts his hand on mine. He offers to clean the baby and the kitchen so I can go take a bath. I let him.

He doesn't get a third drink or even finish the second one, and we go to bed together for the first time in weeks.

Another day bleeds into another night, and we microwave leftovers as I bring up an overdue conversation about our apartment lease. Jet's asleep, her mushy banana still all over the kitchen. How can half a banana make that much mess? Did any of it get into her mouth? Did we remember to brush her new little teeth? Did I just hear her cry in her room? Cough?

I freeze, listen, and hear nothing. So I open the drawer for a fork, discover that all the forks are dirty, shuffle to the sink, and dig one out to hand wash.

Ryan wants to renew our lease, but I think we should consider a house. I punch microwave buttons to add thirty seconds. Living closer to Elise might be nice. Still cold. I stir my food to mix hot spots and then stick it in the microwave a little longer. Speaking of Elise, I need to confirm that she can still stay with Jet on Thursday. Which means I'll need to squeeze in a grocery run tomorrow. Ryan says we can't afford a down payment, and when I open my mouth to respond, there's a flying flash of darkness. I duck on reflex. Behind my head, a shatter. Shards jump, attaching to my skin like leeches.

It takes me a long, stunned minute to realize Ryan threw a beer bottle.

Ryan threw a *beer bottle*.

Ryan *threw* a beer bottle.

Ryan threw a beer bottle.

At me.

My face.

My Ryan.

Who paints azaleas.

Who sings lullabies to his daughter at three in the morning.

Who once rescued an injured barn swallow on Calhoun Street and nursed it back to health.

I hadn't realized he was upset. Or drunk. My attention was on the baby, always on the baby. What did she put in her mouth and where did the scab on her knee come from and is that sneeze from allergies or a cold because, either way, I should probably call the doctor.

The kitchen gets as quiet as breath.

Then, piercing the silence, Jet cries from her crib.

Ryan's face is sheer terror, his skin ashen.

He's sorry, of course he is.

But I need him to be sorry enough to step backward through time, to fly pieces of glass back together. I need him to hurt enough to never do anything like this again. I need him to beg and plead and make it up to me. I need him to whisper my name, timid like that day in the library a thousand years ago. I couldn't see it then—how need can wound. How it can become an incendiary.

Maybe I should hold on to Ryan Outside Of Time, remembering him as he was or imagining him as he might be. But with glass glinting up at me from kitchen tile like sun from the surface of the sea, I can't see anyone except Ryan The Drunk, who is now ranting about how could I think we can afford a house and don't I know how hard he's working and why won't I ever listen to him.

I don't say, *Because we can* or *Of course I do* or *Because you don't talk to me anymore*. His deflecting from the shattered bottle is scarier than the shattered bottle itself. His implication that this might somehow be my fault.

Jet is screaming in her crib.

With a measured voice and an ice-cold gaze, I say, low, "Clean up your mess." And I step over the broken bottle to go get our daughter.

Another woman in my position might take her baby to her parents' place. Since I don't have that option, I do the next best thing and take Jet to Elise's house. I need space to think.

Elise scoops us some Blue Bell and unfolds the playpen. She knows Ryan's been drinking; she doesn't know he threw a beer bottle at my face.

Jet is ecstatic about the visit to Nana's. Elise kisses the top of her head, takes our empty bowls to the sink, and brings out some blankets for the night, remarking that they were a steal at T.J.Maxx. Then she gives me a long hug and a look that says she's not ready to hear details. Jet is clapping and smiling her cheeks outward like two jumbo marshmallows, and I try to imagine my baby grown and hurting someone.

When I don't hear from Ryan the next day, I worry he might have been drunk enough to forget. But in the evening, he finally calls. Elise passes the phone to me and carries Jet to the back porch. They sit at the wrought-iron table and play.

Watching them through the window, I suck in a breath. "Hi."

Ryan's silence on the line is like a hungry mouth, and I do not fill it.

Finally: "You and Jet can go home."

"Uh, I don't know if—"

"That'll never happen again."

"How can I trust that?"

Outside, Jet covers her own eyes, thinking nobody can see her. She and Elise giggle.

"You can't." He pauses. "So I left."

"Left?" That's when I realize what he said: Jet and I can go home. Go, not come.

"I'm out, okay?" He says this like it's something I wanted. "I'll help you pay to renew the lease, but I'm at Matteo's."

I blink and breathe and soften. "Ry, obviously last night was bad, but don't you think this is extreme? How long'll you be gone?"

Now Elise is doing peek-a-boo, and Jet's laughing like all her tiny body has space for is happiness. I put my hand to the windowpane.

His voice hardens. "Indefinitely. I'll send what you need for Georgette. Talk later, 'kay?"

He hangs up before I can respond. Before I can say, *No, not okay*. Before I can say, *What I need for Georgette is you*. For the second time in my life, I don't even have the chance to say, *Wait, this is your child too*.

Elise cooks comfort food and makes efforts not to weigh in, but I can see opinions on the tip of her tongue like gravy.

She studies her granddaughter. "She looks so much like him, doesn't she?"

I wait.

She turns to me. "I hope you two can work things out. Ryan needs you."

Powerlessness scratches the back of my throat. "We can't work anything out if he's gone." *Indefinitely. I'll send what you need for Georgette.* My eyes sting.

Her expression grim, Elise focuses again on Jet, who's chewing a plastic rattle. She runs fingers through Jet's baby curls and looks toward the painting of Ryan in the red overalls. "Why would he leave?"

The question hangs between us, unanswered. I want to protect Elise from the gaping imperfections of her son. I want to protect Ryan from his mother's disappointment. And I want to protect Jet from the darkness she has yet to see.

All day I've tried to shrink it. Fights happen. It could be worse.

But then I feel the shatter, see his face, hear our baby cry.

Feel the shatter, see his face, hear our baby cry.

Feel the shatter, see his face, hear our baby cry.

I'm short of breath. "It . . . got pretty bad."

Feel the shatter, see his face, hear our baby cry.

Elise's eyes travel from Jet to me, mother's denial and grandmother's compassion in a chokehold. "Bad like abuse?"

Again her question is just out of reach, my breath a marble in my windpipe.

I don't know why he'd leave, and I don't know if it's bad like abuse. Abuse is much easier to identify when it's not in your own kitchen.

I say nothing, and Elise's expression shifts, reminding me of my own mother.

"Oh, Lillian." Her gaze is intent. "Don't let him hurt you."

The marble in my throat melts and heat radiates inside me and it's the first time I've thought to protect myself.

Jet babbles at her toy.

I scoot toward my husband's mother and rest my head on her shoulder. We have no answers for each other about the man we love. We have only biscuits and gravy and this dimpled baby girl who smiles like the sunrise.

———

Two days after our phone call, Ryan agrees to meet me at home to talk. Jet stays with Elise.

I arrive at our apartment before he does, and I discover he was thorough in taking his things. He cleaned up the broken glass and traded it for a broken family. But I foresee him coming through our front door, suitcase in hand, certain he was wrong to leave, ashamed he even considered it. We will put this behind us. On the night of shattered glass, I saw only Ryan The Drunk. But today, I refuse to see Ryan The Drunk at all.

Until he arrives with nothing, saying nothing. Drunk.

My eyes narrow. "So you're giving yourself over to it."

There's a hint of pleading in his eyes, but then it's gone, covered by emptiness. It always surprises me how much space emptiness can take up.

He stumbles to the opposite end of our tattered plaid couch and slurs out, "Say what you need to say."

"What about you? What about what we already said when we took vows?"

"This's how I keep them!" he shouts, as if through a mouthful of cotton.

"What's that supposed to mean?"

"It means," his voice thunders and his eyes drift like clouds, "I don't want to hurt y'all."

I laugh, sharp and bitter. "*Leaving* hurts us!"

"You don't understand."

Before I can tell him to help me understand, his hands are on my shoulders. He shoves me and shouts, "You can't understand!"

What hurts most about his shove is its purpose. He's giving himself permission, proving to himself that this is who he is, his only option is to leave, and we'll all be better for it.

The room spins as though drunkenness is contagious. What else can

I say to him in this state, with his mind made up and alcohol rolling through him like war tanks?

He stands up, looking around at this apartment that's crammed full of us. He mumbles that he'll still help with money, and he swipes his hand across our entry table, awakening miniature dust devils like tiny demons. He bites his lip, opens the front door, and yells to nobody in particular, "God!"

Then he slams the door behind him so hard that our southwestern wall hangings shake. One of them falls, shatters, and spews burnt orange across the room like a spray of vomit. This is how the world ends, not with a whimper but with a bang.

I hate him. But hate is anemic when love hangs around like turpentine in the upholstery. Surely something so good won't end like this. Ryan isn't the monster he thinks he is; the truth is that monsters are myths and men are complicated.

Days later, when Jet and I are back home, a shard of glass gets stuck in her knee. I tweezer it out, and a trickle of red follows. She's more fascinated than upset. I clean it, apply a Band-Aid, go into the bathroom, and cry without a sound.

Hours, days, weeks pass. Over and over and over, Ryan doesn't come home.

I have a recurring nightmare of him shoving me down a flight of stairs, and when I look back toward him, his body is a bottle. Then he explodes. I wake up alone and bury my face in the pillow that still smells like his patchouli shampoo.

1990

STOCK SHOW HUBBUB AND TEX-MEX AROMAS TWO-STEP through our open window. Sunday morning means Jet and I are on the living room floor lost in an abyss of blocks, books, and Cabbage Patch Kids. In the kitchen, leftover pancake batter congeals in a mixing bowl.

Six small knocks on the door. When I don't see anyone through the peephole, I know exactly who it is before I open the front door: Kendall Darnell with his squeaky, hopeful voice. "Can Jet come play? Mommy's making pecan pie."

I look across the parking lot and wave at Shauna, who's supervising from their front stoop. The lot is busy with overflow parking from the church on the corner. Our complex recently started towing unauthorized vehicles, making for some disgruntled Baptists, but weekends remain a free-for-all.

Jet is behind me squealing, "Pie pie pie!" and searching for her shoes. It's mostly irrelevant when I smile and answer, "Sure, she can come."

Little Kendi—the nickname Jet gave him that stuck like sap—waits patiently with his flaxen hair and tugboat pajamas. Jet comes to the door in frilly socks and white sandals with a broken strap. Before I even get the question out, she informs me that no, she does not want different shoes. So I lick my thumb, clean syrup from her chin, and sigh. Pancakes and pie. Oh well, it's Sunday. I'll give her an apple and peanut butter later to make up for it. I kiss her sticky cheek, smooth down her mop of hair, and tell her to have fun and be good.

Kendi says, "Hooray, let's go!" And then he "flies" her toward his apartment in his "plane." At least, that's what I assume is happening when they shuffle their feet, Jet's sandal buckle pinging concrete and Kendi's arms outstretched like metal wings.

Somehow, they'll start preschool this fall. Shauna and I are beside ourselves. I don't remember when Jet crawled for the last time or when I changed her last diaper. One day, it had already happened. Now she sprints and uses the toilet and has long, tangly hair and talks as fast as an auctioneer.

I squint against the sun and watch closely until Kendi "lands" safely and the three of them go inside. Shauna is a single mom too, which is one reason the four of us have become so close since they moved here a couple of years ago. Or as Jet would say, since they moved here yesterday. She thinks *yesterday* means any time in the past and *tomorrow* means any time in the future. She says things like, "'Member yesterday when we goed to that boy's house with that green pool water?" even though that happened six months before. Or in the summertime she'll whine mournfully that, "Christmas is not till tomorrow."

She looks so independent disappearing into her friend's apartment for pecan pie, even though just *yesterday* she gummed my fingers and cut her first tooth and drank the nectar of my chest while her tiny fist tap-tapped my collarbone. *Tomorrow* she'll choose a lipstick shade for graduation, a blazer for a job interview, a wedding dress, makeup to cover sunspots.

One of the most disorienting parts of parenthood is how it can warp your sense of time. Or maybe not warp. Maybe what children do is straighten time out. Like clock hands, they keep us ticking forward even as we try to apprehend the lines and circles of it.

1992

THE NIGHT BEFORE JET'S SIXTH BIRTHDAY, SHE CRAWLS into my bed, fresh off a bad dream. I'm beyond ready for her to outgrow this. I huff and turn toward her in the grayscale dark. Her profile looks exactly like her sonogram, which thaws my exasperation instantly. I curl myself around her, no longer ready for her to outgrow anything.

She points to the cassette player beside my terra-cotta lamp and requests her fall-asleep song, "Diamonds on the Soles of Her Shoes." Her eyelids lower sometime between aftershave and bodegas. The night passes with her musty breath in my face, heels twitching into my ribs. She wakes up six years old and leaps out of bed like life won't wait. As she bounds down the hallway, I call after her, "Slow down!"

When Ryan missed Jet's first birthday party, I thought something terrible must have happened to him. But when Elise got in touch with him, he was hungover. That's it. And that marked the end of crying myself to sleep and asking him to come home. When he called the following day, I rubbed my temple and held the phone to Jet's ear as she pawed it like a cat.

He does occasional visits with her, but he has never shown up for a birthday party. So when he said he "might make it" to this one, my hopes remained flat on the ground. And sure enough. Six for six.

The party's theme is mermaid. Per Jet's specific instructions, I make an ocean cake and we turn on music from *The Little Mermaid*. Ariel sings about whose world to belong to while kids from the apartment complex arrive and don paper hats with elastic under pudgy chins.

Kendi gives Jet a handmade card with an impressive sketch of the Hubble Telescope. He colored it purple, Jet's favorite color. Blue is a close second. Kendi once tried to tell her that blue is a "boy color," to which Shauna rolled her eyes and said, "Oh please. The cardinal doesn't keep red away from us, calling it a 'bird color,' now does it?"

Nervously, Jet asked Shauna what cardinals are like "besides the red part." She hates birds of prey almost as much as I hate dogs in people clothes. Shauna reassured her that a cardinal isn't a bird of prey, so now the two of them are on a perpetual hunt for cardinal sightings. It's their "thing," as Shauna told Jet and Jet told me. Shauna gives Jet a handmade card too, hers with a cardinal sketch on it. Jet hugs her with the full hanging weight of a happy child. She might not have a dad around, but in Shauna she has a loyal auntie.

Our kitchen is packed with small bodies as Elise lights birthday candles, cupping her hand around tiny flames and shushing everyone so we can sing. I appreciate Elise's skill in a room full of children, second nature with all her years as a teacher. We sing in a child-choir's multitude of keys. When Jet dramatically puckers her lips and blows, my brain navigates an obstacle course. Don't think about the husband or three grandparents who aren't here, and don't think about the birthday candles of the baby boy who turns eighteen this summer. Eighteen. Old enough to find me if he wants. It feels like a hundred-year blink since he had hiccups inside me.

Jet blows out six candles and we cheer. I wonder who she'll be at eighteen. Twelve years from now, what will girls be doing with their hair and jeans and eyebrows? Will she still want to be a doctor? She recently saw footage of the L.A. riots after I thought she was asleep. Before I could scold her for getting out of bed, she said, doe-eyed, "So many of them need help, Mommy." Whether she's a doctor or not, she'll be a healer. It's difficult to imagine Adult Jet since Child Jet has yet to master blowing her nose. Still, I know how impatient the years can get.

A small voice knocks me back to the moment. "Miss Lillian?" A tug on my shirt and a concerned little girl. "Kendi's crying."

I don't immediately spot Shauna, so with Elise managing the cake, I rush to find Kendi, who's alone in a corner.

I kneel. "What's wrong, sweetheart?"

He sniffles. "Nothing."

I sit all the way down on the ground, cross-legged. "Want to tell me about that nothing?"

He looks around and says quietly, "Chris said my hair looks like the straw of a scarecrow."

I bite the inside of my lip to keep from laughing. It really does look like that. But when I see his robin's-egg eyes, pure and wet and trusting, my urge to laugh dissipates. "Chris also said it was going to rain today." The truth is that I'm not certain who Chris is, and nobody said anything about rain. "But look there—" I gesture out the window toward the blue sky. "People can be wrong."

Another sniffle. I reach out, and he puts his hand in mine.

"Let's go get cake?"

He nods.

If someone had hurt Jet's feelings, she would have called everyone's attention to the injustice of it. Same with Ryan and even Shauna. But Kendi hides. It's an impulse I share. I give him a hug as Elise's voice calls from the kitchen. "Right, Lillian? It's an ocean?"

I rise to stand, whispering to Kendi, "They're asking about the cake." Then louder for Elise, "Of course it's an ocean!"

I walk back into the kitchen and rotate the cake a quarter to show everyone. "See?" I laugh at my own work. It's blue anyway. Some green globs with yellow gloop above them. Purple dots for shell bras, and dark wavy lines of mermaid hair. Hey, I never claimed to be a cake decorator.

Shauna and Elise tilt their heads to examine my "mermaids" before the three of us laugh so hard that we can barely cut the cake.

Kendi joins the rest of the children as they blink at our laughter and shovel plastic forkfuls of blue dye into their pink mouths. They don't care how the frosting looks; the sugar satisfies.

Sebastian the crab warbles out *sha-la-la-las* from the tape deck as I take a bite of purple shell bra, winking at Jet and whispering, "Happy birthday, love."

1980

ON MY SON'S SIXTH BIRTHDAY, I TRACKED DOWN ZACK'S phone number, called him, and asked if we could meet to talk in person. He was in Nashville and couldn't get away. But I could go to Nashville if I wanted. *Wanted* was not the right word.

I twisted the little round fan above my plane seat and let the air rush out onto my scalp. I was being flown into the past; I needed that swoosh of air like a pinch to wake me up. I breathed. Closed my eyes. Opened them. Still a circle of cold air blasting onto my head. Still clouds beneath me like displaced heavens. Still a man far below who once wrote a song about the curve of my waistline. Still a boy we created together, a thousand symphonies we didn't mean to write.

On solid ground in Nashville, I collected myself and took a city bus to the park Zack chose as our meeting spot. I was an hour early, and the weather was sweltering. He was fifteen unapologetic minutes late, his appearance practically unchanged from seven years earlier. The road had been kind to him. If anything, his jaw was sharper, his physique more chiseled. I rose from a bench to greet him, my body a sudden riot of memory beneath my sundress.

I removed my sunglasses, cleared my throat, and did what I came to do. I told him about the baby, ready for it to be terrible because he'd be upset. But it was terrible because he wasn't. He was indifferent, an option I hadn't considered. He didn't mind that I'd withheld and acted alone. He had moved on. The Blacktoppers had split, but his solo career was taking off and he was engaged to a high-powered music producer, Vivian something-or-other. If anything, he was annoyed I didn't take this with me to the grave.

When he asked if anything was required of him, I shook my head and coughed on the déjà vu. I would have been mad if I weren't so relieved by this proof that I did the right thing in keeping our son to myself.

At least he knows now. There are many fathers out there who don't. Many mothers who dread the day their lost child goes rogue and their lost lover calls saying, *How dare you keep this from me?* Not to mention, Zack's name is on the birth certificate. When the baby was born, I couldn't bring myself to leave that line blank when I knew perfectly well who the father was.

Sitting on that park bench beside a bed of purple coneflowers, I tried to find it within myself to be happy for Zack and his music and his someday children who won't be mine.

With a brusque nod, he went home to Vivian. Their instruments and record deals.

For the first and final time, I considered finding the family who adopted my son. Asking if maybe I could come to his birthday party or something. I wondered what the theme would be, if he'd get icing all over his face, if they were better parents than we would have been. Surely they were.

But he's their son now, and to see that would kill me. I gave him over to the hope of a happy life I couldn't offer at the time. Knowing whether he is or isn't happy would destroy me, either way.

So I tucked Zack and my son into a basement corner of my heart, boarded a return flight, and went home. I was eager to get back to my scruffy, soft-hearted painter. The man who, after some library whispers and baklava, was helping me believe in love again.

1992

NOT LONG AFTER JET'S PARTY, WE SPEND A DAY AT THE zoo with Shauna and Kendi. It's Shauna's birthday gift to Jet because it just reopened after long renovations. There are no cardinals, but there are monkeys and rhinos and onion rings and pulled pork.

Afterward, Jet and I collapse on our couch, where she falls asleep on my lap like a relic of her former self. Her head no longer has that baby scent. It smells like sweat and animals. I can't bear to move her even when my forearm prickles. With my free hand, I pick at the old plaid couch fabric, vowing to replace it this year. No more brown. I rest my chin on my sleeping daughter, not wanting the moment to ever end. But at the same time, ouch. I can't wait to get her into the bath and stretch my aching legs. Holding on eventually becomes more painful than letting go.

When she wakes, we check the answering machine, and the first message is from Ryan. He speaks directly to Jet, apologizing for missing her party on account of "a gallery event." He sings the birthday song, and I put my hand to the machine like I could follow his voice into yesterday, when he was someone else. When he sang to me at the park in exaggerated vibrato and a few chuckling strangers applauded as he dipped me on the final, "Happy birthday to yooouuu."

Jet barely acknowledges his message; she's busy with her new Polly Pocket.

She requests tomatoes for dinner and plucks ripe ones from our box garden, their juice like summer on her lips. When she says that grocery store tomatoes are gross, I tell her not to be a snob. I wish she would have said something about our garden tomatoes last week at her annual checkup, where instead she told the doctor that her favorite food is Kraft macaroni and cheese. I plan to remind her about our garden vegetables before next year's appointment so that I might be exonerated.

As I cook chicken and Jet pops tomatoes into her mouth, she stares down our new thermometer. Last week she said, "Hey, let's invent something to tell how hot it is outside!" I had to break the news to her beaming face that this already exists. She pouted, looking like her dad. And now she's making peace with the thermometer for already existing.

According to our thermometer and wet hairlines, it's still in the mid-nineties the third week of Jet's kindergarten year. We walk to school with Shauna and Kendi. The kids lead the way, looking extra small with their too-big "pack-packs." They kick horse apples off the sidewalk. When Kendi says they look like brains, Jet tells him something she learned about brains from a doctor book.

Shauna and I walk behind them, burning our tongues on Nescafé. Their chatter moves to their upcoming field trip to Casa Mañana for a Disney tribute performance. In the midst of singing Disney songs, Jet's voice becomes even higher than normal as she says to Kendi, "Me and you should get married when we grow up."

Kendi immediately says, "Ew."

"What?"

Kendi explains, "You know what you have to do?"

Shauna and I glance at each other, but curiosity wins and we hold our coffee-burned tongues. Jet gives her best friend a skeptical scowl.

Kendi stage-whispers, "You have to kiss on the *lips*."

"Ew, we do *not*! And besides, we have so much reasons to stay together forever! We both"—she holds up her thumb—"have the same favorite Disney songs." She adds her index finger. "Love jumping on one leg." She adds her middle finger. "Hate pickles." She adds her ring finger and pinky because the pinky won't stay down by itself. "Love Curious George and—" She puts her hand down by her side. "Love doing puzzles over and over times infinity." She lets out an exhale with her whole body like she's utterly spent as she says, "Plus also, you like jets and I *am* Jet."

Shauna and I snicker. Kendi shrugs as if to say, *As you wish.* Then Jet asks if his class saw that *huge* frog at recess the other day, and just like that they've moved on from wedding plans.

It strikes me that somehow Disney is fashioning the marriage story in her mind rather than her own parents, who definitely didn't "stay together forever."

I say to Shauna, "She thinks she wants to be a doctor, but did my daughter just lawyer her way into a betrothal with your son?"

Shauna laughs. "Hey, I'm with her. They have *so much reasons* to get married, and if they do, then *we* can stay together when we grow up, too."

I link my arm through hers like a middle schooler. "Let's please do that no matter what happens with our little Westley and Buttercup."

We giggle as we approach the crosswalk. A school bus squeaks to a stop. The crossing guard waves a group of us across, offering his usual snaggle-toothed grin. We put our hands to our foreheads in salute position. A few clouds drift in front of the big bright orb of the sun like cataracts on an eye. A gust of wind lifts the skirt of a mother in front of us and she battens it down, looking around and letting out an "Oh sheesh" as other women offer chuckles of solidarity.

When we pull open the heavy school doors, Jet chirps to Kendi, "See you at recess."

He waves to her and tugs Shauna's shirt for help with his shoelaces.

Jet skips off toward her classroom as I call after her, "Hey, what about me? See you after school, Mom? Love you, Mom?"

She looks back over her shoulder with a coy smile and wave. Laughing, I smooth my hair, watch her round the corner, and sigh my love into the hall for it to loiter as she rotates between lunch, music, library, and recess with her frogs and her Kendi and her persuading of friends to be patients while Doctor Jet listens to their hearts.

A nearby mom comments on how cute she is and asks casually, as people often do, how many children I have. I let out a small "just one." I've learned to preemptively add the *just*. Otherwise, the asker will respond with it themselves: *Just one?* And I'll have to repeat myself: *Just one.* I lie every time I say Jet's my only child. Not because I want to forget my son, but because this is how I keep him.

As Shauna and I leave the school, a young boy steps in fire ants in the schoolyard. His mother kneels and shoos the culprits from his inflaming ankle. He falls heavily onto her thighs, palms tear-streaks across his face, and burrows into the safety of her shoulder.

1993

I CAN'T SHIELD JET FROM NEWS OF THE WACO BRANCH Davidians.

I try to keep it from her because she isn't even seven years old. But the images are everywhere, a bombardment of smoke and death, like some small punishment for us all.

The night after their compound goes up in flames, Jet has Sparkle Fun toothpaste on her chin as she asks why the "gov-ner-ment" killed those kids. And if any of them were six years old.

Her bluntness and feathery eyelashes and heavyhearted concern stab me as I think of the Davidian children. I open and close my mouth three times before I can speak, silence the only suitable elegy. All I can think to tell her is, "They shouldn't have died like that. Sometimes grown-ups forget to think about how our choices impact children." I kneel and pull her close and squeeze the living flesh of her young arms, burying my chin into her warm neck. The wind howls outside. When I kiss her goodnight and say, "I love you," my voice quakes like the Waco earth.

My sleep is fitful. I dream of my estranged husband as a boy, scared under a table. I dream of my children, ATF officials, David Koresh, his followers, all of their parents and children. I see them outside of time—first steps, last breaths, and the pains and comforts in between.

I get up two, three, four times in the night to check on Jet. Her breathing is soft and steady. The next morning, the air is stock-still. But my chest howls like I've eaten the wind.

1994

RYAN SHOWS UP FOR THANKSGIVING DINNER AT ELISE'S house, and some time passes before we realize he's drunk. When it becomes undeniable, Elise glances at Jet and pointedly back at Ryan, who is "straightening" serving spoons by making them crooked. This might be funny in a college dorm. But tonight it's not. It's pathetic.

Elise clears her throat and says toward her nose, "You need to leave my table."

I can't imagine. It requires strength enough to distance from a husband; it's an entirely different strength to distance from a son.

Ryan doesn't protest. He just fetches his coat with a hard roll of his eyes.

Elise and I look at each other, and I say what we're both thinking. "Ryan?"

"What?" he snaps, looking back at me with eyes like dark liquor.

"You're not driving." I level my gaze, daring him to try to get behind the wheel when he knows what this means to me.

Jet stares at him, her frown knit with concern, and that must be what keeps him from arguing. He looks between the three of us and runs a hand through his hair. "What d'you inspect me t'do?"

Elise scoops sweet potatoes onto her plate, tapping the spoon as she says, "You'll sleep it off in the extra bedroom." She switches the spoon out for a slightly different size and nods at me to help myself.

With a sigh, Ryan drags his feet down her hallway. The red overall painting of him hugging Elise watches us. Our cranberry sauce and empty place setting. Ryan's chair pushed back. I can't bring myself to look at Jet. I miss the days when she didn't understand.

I thought it would be worth it for Jet and Ryan to have a relationship. Sometimes he takes her to the playground and brings her home laughing and trying to tickle him. But he misses more visits than not, and then there are times like this. Part-time fatherhood hurts him, and he's willing to cause even Jet pain if it means he can escape his own.

Once, he showed up at our apartment reeking. I hissed at him for driving, took his keys, and shut the door in his face. Instead of learning his lesson, he went on to later do actual time for driving while intoxicated. Elise bailed him out and checked him straight into rehab with a chunk of her meager retirement. But clearly it didn't work. Ryan Bright is twice the monster he thinks he is.

At her dining table with the empty place setting, Elise looks at me knowingly. She's aware that Ryan's recklessness has transported me straight back to that call on the campus phone.

I'm so sorry. We did everything we could. He was gone within minutes.

The doctor's words bounced off the common room walls and came at me like wasps.

It had only been a couple of years since Mama.

I made it to the hospital and sat alone with the deformed shell of the dad who read me *Dr. Doolittle* and then sat beside my bed when I had monkey nightmares. Who chased fireflies with me in the summers, catching them when I was too short or slow or skittish. He was tall. Fast. Invincible.

It was my second time to face the brutal litany of post-death decisions.

Burial or ashes? Cemetery or mausoleum? Traditional hymns or modern songs? Psalm 23 or Romans 8? Check or credit card?

It was surreal to see it in newsprint: *Theodore Wright, age 53, preceded in death by wife, Georgia Wright, survived by daughter, Lillian Wright.* I rubbed my finger over the obituary letters until they stained my skin like a bruise.

I couldn't leave his body like it was, so I had him cremated and scattered him in the Trinity River. Without siblings, I made the decision on my own. Maybe he and I should have prepared for the event of his death after Mama's, but instead we did the opposite. We assumed crisis would only strike once. We had just gotten on top of the medical bills.

Dad was loud and crass and imperfect, but he was there. At school and sporting events, birthday parties and milestones, rain or shine or the occasional Texas snow. He was there smiling and puffing out his chest and, much to my dismay, pointing me out to everyone around him. *That's my daughter.* Tap tap. *Hi. That there's my daughter.* He was proud of me for no reason except that I was his and he was mine. And even when he embarrassed me, and even when cancer took his wife, he was there like a father should be.

Until a drunk driver T-boned him at sixty miles an hour, leaving me with no family.

Jet and I come home from that strained Thanksgiving dinner to our same apartment. New couch, same place. It's been a long time since Ryan lived here. Still, memories creep under doorways like smoke. I turn the corner after tucking Jet into bed, and I almost crash into one: Ryan Of The Early Years coming toward me before work with morning eyes, a half-eaten donut, John Coltrane playing in the living room, and a scratchy voice crooning, "Dance with me?" Back then he'd turn brown moments golden. The same man could have gone and killed someone today. How many times can I give up on the same person?

Ryan isn't everything, of course—there are many other memories here. Jet running down the hall at two, three, four years old with a bare bottom, giggling and saying she can't find her Rainbow Brite panties. Me asking, "How could you lose those, silly goose?" Then she's hopping down the hall, five years old, the weekend we made an indoor hopscotch with painter's tape during the tornado sirens. We're sharing pizza with Shauna and Kendi as the kids perform "magic tricks" by shoving quarters into their pockets.

Ryan has never filed for divorce or even mentioned it. Though we've never discussed it, he mails a modest check every single month, memo line: *Georgette*. Every month I deposit it into an account for her, and every month I think, *She'd rather have you*. But if he nurses any hidden hope of reconciliation, he must know by now that the years are slippery—coming, going, gone. Future is a finite resource.

Maybe that's why I haven't filed either. I've been on a few dates with other men since Ryan left. This is no Disney movie. There might be someone else out there for me. After all, Ryan was my someone else after Zack. But—and this is the honest truth no matter how I loathe it—nobody holds a candle to Ryan Of The Early Years.

Meanwhile, Ryan Of Today comes to the door in a daze and barely resembles the man I once loved.

Or he doesn't come to the door at all.

The week after Thanksgiving, he stands Jet up for the umpteenth time. Her seeming indifference guts me so severely that I sweep us out the door to the local animal shelter. She wears the Pink Ranger costume that she had on to show her dad. We are going to find a rescue pet. We need someone we can save.

When we see a litter of kittens, I comment on how cute they are. "Cutie-wooties" is my exact expression. Jet instructs me not to get "too attached" because we can't get a cat. Kendi's allergic. So a dog it is.

When we find a border collie mix, we adopt him on the spot. That's what the young staffer calls it, an on-the-spot adoption. Jet looks serious in her Pink Ranger costume as she corrects the staffer. "No, his name's not Spot. His name is Stethoscope."

She still gets tripped up on the word *cinnamon*, but sure, her first pet will be named Stethoscope.

The dog blinks agreement.

I gently encourage Jet to consider calling him Seth for short, and, after deliberation, she agrees. At home, she decorates labels for his bowls: STITHASCOP BRIGHT.

Shauna and Kendi join us for his inaugural walk. We go to the neighborhood park, where mosquitos make dinner out of Kendi's calves and the kids toss Seth a Frisbee that the shelter gave us.

Shauna and I find a bench and discuss the latest news out of school, work, Rwanda. How strange that rays from the same sun fall on the Hutus and Tutsis and violence as fall on us and the dog and the giggle-thrown Frisbee. When we reach our limit of international news, we talk about Michael.

Plenty of men want to be with Shauna, but it's rare for her to return the sentiment like she does with Michael. She's an RN, and—much to Jet's elation—Michael is a doctor. Pediatric oncologist. When he's around, Jet peppers him with doctor questions. He kneels and answers her without a hint of hurry or clipped edges.

The reason I'm not jealous of Shauna is because I don't want Michael, wonderful as he is. I don't want something new; I want something old. The only person I'm jealous of is Lillian In Sundance Square With Ryan Of The Early Years. If there's anything I envy Shauna for, it's not that she has Michael—it's that she doesn't have Patrick Darnell, who died when Shauna was pregnant. Loss keeps a tight grip when there's hope left, and some part of me still hunts for Ryan When He Was Sober And Mine.

Patrick's death allows Shauna the closure needed to let Michael in, and they're getting serious. She's saying the L-word, and she doesn't say that lightly. That's what she actually says: "the L-word," as in, "Lillian, I'm falling in L-word with him." But she's close to saying the real thing.

Kendi has been slow to warm up to Michael, but he'll get there. It helps that Jet likes Michael so much. It also helps that Michael takes Kendi to the Aviation Museum every month.

All Kendi has of his dad are photos and stories and imaginings. I see his face when Jet talks about her dad showing up late or "after too many grown-up drinks." I'm sure Kendi wishes his dad were here, even if only to show up drunk. Some primal place in us believes that having parents at their worst is better than not having them. I would take my own parents in any condition just to have them back here with me. Suddenly, Mama's skeletal last days sear through me like lightning. Okay, maybe not any condition. Maybe there's a world in which being gone is better than being here. But this is far too much for a little boy to carry. I watch Kendi grab the Frisbee from Seth and run, Jet laughing with her whole body and my heart swelling for Kendi.

I nudge Shauna. "Let's play."

I dash up sneakily behind Kendi and steal the Frisbee. I throw it as far as I can, and Seth zooms off after it. Out of breath, Kendi says, "I'm going to get you, Ms. B.!"

"Not if I get you first!" I run at him, Shauna and Jet both cheering for Kendi. But I catch him and tickle his belly until he begs for mercy through peals of laughter.

When Seth slows down and the kids start to yawn, we walk home under a dimming sky, stubborn streaks of pink slashing through the gray like happiness through grief.

Jet's friend Valentina comes over after school. She loves dogs and told Jet all about her dachshund, Chorizo. So we invited her to come meet Seth and play.

I give the girls applesauce with "cimmanin," and then they disappear into Jet's room with the dog.

After Valentina's mom picks her up, Jet says plainly, "I like Kendi better."

I chop onions for dinner. "It's not fair to compare every friend to your best friend. You should have space for lots."

"But Valentina only wanted to play with dolls and hair clips."

My eyes water from the onions. "You like dolls and hair clips."

"Not as much as doctor." She sits at the table, facing me and sporting an adorable pouty face.

"Georgette"—I use my best motherly voice—"you should be willing to play other games besides doctor. You want to be a good friend."

"I asked her to play Guess Who? or turn on my *My Girl* tape."

"And?" The whining and onion and end of day are melding into a dull headache.

"She just wanted to do doll hair." Jet rests her chin on her knee and adds, "Kendi always wants to do what I want."

We're out of garlic. "Well, do you ask Kendi what he wants to play?"

She blinks. "No."

"You should."

She doesn't respond.

As I search for a seasoning to replace garlic, I explain the importance of taking turns, but she goes to the living room, plops down on the rug, and says, "Here, boy. You be the patient." Seth pants contentedly at her side. A train horn yells in the dusky distance. The sounds and smells of dinner at the complex drift through our open window: truck tailgates slamming closed, Latin pop and bluegrass, smoked meat. Seth watches Jet, who has two yellow hair clips in her dark tangles like stars in a night sky.

When I call her to dinner, she tells me some apparently *hilarious* story about how her teacher had a spider *and* an ant in her kitchen sink. So I tell her about my day, how I notarized a home loan *and* a quitclaim deed. We laugh more than either story merits.

If Ryan knew what he was missing, he wouldn't miss it. At that thought, the room spins. Does my son have a cute pouty face? A dog? Friends he likes better than others? Stories to tell until the cows come home?

The phone rings. Elise.

Holding the phone to her face with a food-grimy hand, Jet looks small and big at once. She chats about Frisbees and vowels and bugs with the one grandparent in her life.

I scoot my plate away and lean back as I listen to Jet's side of the conversation. Seth nuzzles my shin. I scratch behind his ears and whisper, "There might be no good men, but you are my good boy."

1996

JET'S FATHER'S FATHER DIED. HER GRANDFATHER, FOREIGN as that is to say. She never met him; I never even met him.

When he went into hospice with emphysema, Elise went to Memphis, where Barton lived his first decade of life, and now his last. She and his estranged brother, Gary, are the only two people to manage his affairs.

Jet wants to go to the funeral. For Nana, she says, which is a mature sentiment and partial truth. It's for her father, too. And her own curiosity, which I can understand.

During most of the seven-hour drive, Meg, Jo, Beth, and Amy rest like a tent on Jet's lap, her chatter occasionally punctuated by reading a page or two. I lose count of bathroom breaks, and her Spice Girls CD laps us at least three times before she lets us change the music. I navigate us to the La Quinta where Elise has reserved a room for herself, one for Jet and me, and one for Ryan.

The Friday-night visitation is Jet's first time seeing a dead body. She approaches the open casket timidly. "I thought he'd look asleep, but he looks dead."

He is dressed smartly. After forty years in the trades, I doubt he would have appreciated the suit. Navy polyester rests against the glossy beige casket liner.

The ceilings are low; the carpet is dark and noise-dampening; the lighting is a dim yellow; and the room is long enough that visitors can congregate at the other end and only have to glimpse the tip of Barton's nose. There are few visitors, though.

I step closer to Barton, whisper, "Nice to meet you," and touch the lifeless hand that so often lashed out at the woman who tried to love him. Barton The Boy who was probably beaten by his own father. Barton The Man who never made peace with Barton The Boy. And now Barton The Body. Sunken cheeks and Ryan's nose. Jet's.

There are two kinds of grief at a wake: grieving the loss of what was and grieving the loss of what wasn't.

A laugh sounds from the far end of the room. Someone is recounting a story from Barton's teen years. It's always jarring to hear laughter near an open casket. But at every wake I've ever attended, it happens. Life is as impossible to ignore as death.

Jet looks up at me. "Can I kiss his hand?"

I nod. "Of course, love."

She lifts onto tiptoes and presses her lips to the rubbery skin between Barton's stiff thumb and pointer finger. How strange, not to feel a kiss.

Two older men are now waiting at a respectful distance, so we trade places with them, exchanging small nods.

Elise is in a far corner of the room beside a table with water bottles and a tissue box covered in gold plastic. Beside the table, a few gruff men shift their weight. People don't know how to act around Elise. She's not a widow exactly, but she's not *not* a widow. She looks exhausted.

I guide Jet over to Elise and ask how we can help. She parts her lips before promptly closing them again and looking over my shoulder with a multiplied exhaustion. I turn to follow her gaze and see Ryan standing between the entry and his father's casket.

"There's Dad." Jet states the obvious, monotone and unsure.

His eyes are like black holes; he hasn't been drinking. He nods at us with his combed hair and then turns toward his father's remains. My bitterness loses its foothold, and my breath quickens as I understand something: it was our pain that pulled us together like magnets, that medicinal click of solidarity between two hurting people. That's what happened in the library, the restaurant, his mother's house. But as powerful as pain might be, it was never going to keep us together. It grew strong enough to flip the magnets, pushing us apart as forcefully as it had pulled us in. The thing that built us destroyed us, and somehow, we didn't see it coming.

Ryan turns away from the casket, his eyes dry.

I excuse myself. In a bathroom stall with a halo of air freshener over my head, I close my eyes and see him. Sober, grieving Ryan. Neither Barton's life nor death can minimize Ryan's wrongs. But this weekend isn't about Ryan's wrongs.

I return to the long dim room that smells of death and cologne. Elise and Ryan are greeting the few visitors. Jet stands between them, her knobby knees turned slightly inward. I am just close enough to hear when someone says, "Oh wow, this the granddaughter?" All three of them look at each other like they don't know the answer.

When a funeral home employee comes to help close things down, Elise and Ryan carry a few framed photos outside to Elise's car. I watch them through the beige sheers hanging in front of the window. There are at least six stilted feet between them, and a fierce impatience rises in me. I want to scream through the window, "Hug!" I want to shove them together and tell them not to carry this alone, all these surfacing memories. Of course that's simplistic. Resentments and wounds are valid even now. Especially now. But time is speeding by, always.

With a nod toward the mother who birthed and fed and sacrificed for him, Ryan leaves and Elise turns to come back inside.

Jet is hungry, so I offer to pick something up and bring it to the hotel. Elise says she isn't hungry, but I disregard this as I know she'd do for me.

Jet and I find a Subway and bring food to La Quinta, dropping off a salad with Elise. She doesn't want company, but she accepts the salad. I remembered extra croutons and dressing on the side, which she notes with appreciation. Even now she doesn't fail to extend her trademark kiss beside my cheek. I squeeze her hand and wish for good sleep.

Jet and I take our sandwiches to our room, spreading out the paper wrappers like plates. She eyes the extra sandwich I got and asks, "You're eating two?"

I shrug. "I thought your dad might be hungry."

"Well, is he?"

"I don't know."

"Should we give it to him?"

"I thought we might see him in the lobby or something. But I'm sure he'll take care of himself."

A smile creeps over her face. "Mom, I know you're old, so maybe you forgot we have these amazing machines called telephones."

I snort-laugh and roll my eyes. "Watch it with the sarcasm, missy." I take a bite. "Besides, we don't know his room number."

"It's 224." She lifts the phone and dials.

I bite my nail. He's almost certainly at some bar and won't answer.

But then Jet says into the mouthpiece, "Hey. Mom got you a sandwich if you want. We're in 221." After a beat, she says, "Okay." Then she hangs up and shrugs in my direction. "He does want it." She takes a sloppy bite of her sandwich and starts talking about how Kendi needs to decide if ten is too old to dress as Buzz Lightyear for Halloween. Someone on his soccer team says it is, but Jet says it's not, that he should be Buzz if he wants to be Buzz. There is mayonnaise on her chin.

A knock interrupts the costume deliberations. Jet opens the door for Ryan, his hands in his pockets. She gives him the extra sandwich as he looks past her to me. "Thanks."

"Sure."

He shifts his weight. Before I can decide if I should invite him in to eat with us, he says, "See y'all tomorrow," and offers that distantly civil nod.

Jet closes the door and is immediately talking about her own costume

92

options: Jasmine or Tinker Bell. But since her hair isn't long enough for Jasmine or blond enough for Tinker Bell she might just be a witch.

I try not to think about Ryan alone and heavyhearted down the hall. I try to think about how much he has hurt us, how mad he's made me for years. But it doesn't work. I want to go to him and reach around his waist and hold him.

"Sound good?" Jet is asking for my approval of something, and I have no clue what it is.

"I'll need to think about it."

She rolls her eyes, mayonnaise still on her chin. "Why? It's just a wig." A wig. Right. "Okay, we can do the wig."

"Yes! Neverland, here I come!" Ah. So she decided on Tinker Bell.

After dinner, Jet turns on *While You Were Sleeping* and is snoring halfway through. The AC fan clicks on and off like trains pulling in and out of a station. I paw through a little care package from Shauna until I strike gold: Hershey's. When she handed me the basket, I told her I didn't even know Barton and it wasn't necessary. She said, "I know. But you're going to your estranged husband's estranged father's funeral. Take the basket."

Flicking off the TV, I welcome the dark and fall into bed with my chocolate. I imagine Ryan knocking on our door again, reaching for me instead of the sandwich, and I let him.

The service is as I expected—somber, uncrowded, impersonal, and fraught with repressed emotions.

Then five of us are left at Barton's fresh grave: Jet, me, Ryan, Elise, and Gary. There's a headstone for Gary, the date of death left blank. Their parents are just to the side. Cemeteries don't care about estrangements. Gary thanks Elise "for everything," shakes hands with his nephew, and makes his exit. Then there are four.

Elise's stomach growls loudly, so I ask if we should walk over to the strip of restaurants by the hotel. Jet says, "Yes, I'm *starving*," which seems to answer for everyone.

Ryan is the last to turn away from the swollen soil. In spite of everything, he's reluctant to let the earth swallow his father. In a way, I can relate. I know what it is to love an alcoholic.

The restaurant we wander into seems undecided with its Southern decor, South American waitstaff, and Greek menu. Ryan orders a gyro as though there's been a glitch in time. But if he thinks about our first date, he doesn't show it.

We eat in tired silence, Jet breaking it every once in a while with a story about school or Kendi or doctors. Her world is our reminder that life remains here in front of us.

I can't help myself when the bill comes. While unzipping my purse and fishing for my wallet, I remark to Ryan, "You didn't spill your gyro this time."

Ryan flashes his surprise and laughs—a sound that erases years. He shrugs. "Things change." The blessing and the curse of it.

Jet and Elise aren't paying attention to us. Elise is handing Jet an unsolicited napkin and saying, "Your face, dear."

I mutter to Ryan, "Some things don't." We smile.

The four of us walk back to La Quinta, discussing the logistics of our travels home in the morning. Jet leads us all into the hotel lobby, delighting in the revolving doors. Once inside, Elise calls Ryan's name. Jet turns to join them, but I redirect her to choose some candy from the vending machine.

"I get candy? Best day ever!"

My eyes dart toward Elise and Ryan, and Jet winces. "Oops."

She gets Skittles and then we browse postcards: Graceland and Beale Street and more Graceland.

It's no surprise that Elise was the one to initiate this sliver of reconnection with Ryan. I shift my position to get within earshot as she's saying, "—with you."

"No." Ryan's sharp tone makes me flinch.

"I miss you, you know."

"Mom." A little softer.

"Just one meeting or session or something, for heaven's sake."

He's silent.

"Fine, have it your way. Just like him."

A hard sigh. "I'll call you."

"Not if nothing's changed."

Silence again. Then, "Sorry to disappoint you." His voice cracks.

"Oh, Son."

Then they're hugging, and my grip on some random postcard is so firm that my knuckles go white. I try to put it back without revealing that I've been eavesdropping, and this is when I notice how many postcards Jet has gathered. I blink at her handful.

"One for Kendi, one for Shauna, one for Valentina, one for Cassidy, one for—"

I put a hand up and stop her right there. "Hold your horses. Let's put those back and just enjoy the candy, hm?"

Her shoulders slump forward. "Okay."

She drops the postcards one by one into their respective slots as Elise and Ryan approach. Elise says goodnight, slips off her pumps, shrinks an inch, and pads away across green carpet with her pantyhosed feet. Part of me wants to run after her, kiss her forehead, tell her we love her. But she is in the elevator, and then there are three.

Jet looks up at her dad. "Can we play?" Her tongue is stained red from Skittles.

Ryan follows her gaze to the lobby checkerboards and says tiredly, "Sure."

I hesitate but then say to Ryan, "Bring her up when y'all are done?"

He nods.

When Jet dashes away to set up, I add, "You don't have to." I lay a hand on his arm. "It's been a long weekend."

He clears his throat. "Think I can manage to beat her at least once."

We both smile, small but sincere. I go upstairs, and then there are two.

Apparently, he does manage to beat her once, twice, thrice, and then she *finally* beats him, or so she proudly declares when he brings her up two hours later. She has remnants of a Drumstick ice cream cone around her mouth. Must have needed dessert after the Skittles.

She hugs her dad in the doorway and goes straight to bed in her funeral clothes. Ryan watches her crawl onto the bed as the Beanie Babies she insisted on bringing tumble to the floor. He emanates adoration as she fluffs her pillow, flops onto it, and falls asleep almost instantly. When I turn toward him, he slides his hands into his pockets.

"Thanks for doing that, Ry."

Softly, "I'm glad she wanted to." He swallows. "'Night."

"Goodnight."

But he doesn't turn to leave. My eyes grab his, and he lets them hold. He takes a hand out of his pocket.

Touch me. It's all I can think.

The AC fan clicks off, and he shoves his hand back into his pocket, drops his gaze, and turns away, not looking back as he disappears across the hall and into his room.

Thirty minutes later, in sweatpants and a T-shirt, I scrawl a note for Jet.

Went to talk to your dad. Xoxo.

I go down the hall to room 224 and knock.

Ryan opens the door and frowns. "Everything okay?"

"Not really."

"Jet?"

"Fast asleep." I pause. "Are *you* okay?"

He looks down. I thought he'd invite me in, but here we stand, shifting weight and clearing throats. Finally he says, "Not really."

Sarah Damoff

There was an openness to him half an hour ago that's gone now. I swallow my pride. "Can I come in?"

He hesitates.

"It's just that you're alone and—" My long-caged words sprint out of captivity like feral animals. "And I love you."

An abject horror darkens his face, the opposite of how someone should look when hearing that they're loved. With a grimace, he opens the door wider and ushers me inside.

It makes sense once my eyes adjust to the lamplight in his curtain-closed room. An open bottle is on the table, rising up and flying at me even as it sits there, piercing me like a thousand shards of glass. Ryan's mistress of choice. Only when I deflate do I realize how much hope had begun to fill me.

I splinter in two. Should I be the Lillian who aches to kiss him hard on the mouth and say, *Who cares? It's only a drink?* Or should I be the Lillian who demands to know what kind of seduction this bottle has that he couldn't possibly resist?

I say nothing, lowering myself to the floral couch. He, also, is quiet.

I glare at the liquor, but it's worse to ignore it than address it. "All weekend it seemed like you weren't—"

"All week, actually."

"If you could go all week, then why now?"

He runs a hand through his dark waves and sits beside me. "You said you love me."

I stare. "Are you blaming me? You'd already started drinking!" I stand and pace.

"No! Sorry, that's not what I meant."

"That's what it sounded like."

"Please."

"Please what?"

"Hate me."

I grind my words between my teeth, but they still come out sharp.

"I do!" I drop back onto the couch. "But I also love you. And I'm not sorry for that." I exhale. "I vowed in sickness and in health, didn't I?"

"And I vowed to protect you, didn't I?" The Barton Edge in Ryan's voice has outlived Barton.

I slap my hands on my thighs hard enough to sting through sweatpants. "I get it!" I lower my voice. "I know sometimes love can mean leaving. But you jumped ship too fast. You chose drinking, convinced yourself you were an abuser, and our lives just became . . . this." I glare past his shoulder at the texture on the beige wall. We're not sitting close, but I scoot further away. "Alcoholics get better all the time. Why didn't you?"

He makes a face like I slapped him, and he says nothing.

"Ryan?"

His expression goes distant. "Alcoholic. Is that what I am?"

"Isn't it?"

"Yeah." He scratches his trimmed beard. "Yeah, I guess I am."

"Well, have you ever tried to stop?"

He scoffs. "Countless times."

Only now do I notice a weathered scrap of paper beside the bottle on the table. It's a note written in a child's effortful hand:

DADEE

TANK YOO FER THA TWUK TOY ITZ THA WUN I WANET YOO R THA BEST DADEE I LUV YOO FWOM RYAN WELLS BRIGHTON YOOR SUN

He is sudden and glaring and unavoidable: Ryan The Little Boy Writing A Letter To His Daddy; Toddler Ryan On Elise's Hip; Ryan The Boy Missing His Dad At The Boy Scout Badge Ceremony; Ryan The Teen Taking His Driving Test; Ryan The Artist Painting Blue Hydrangeas; Ryan The Husband; Ryan The Father; Ryan The Lover; Ryan The Friend.

None of these erase Ryan The Alcoholic. But they do expand him.

I move toward him and can barely get my voice out. "Let me help. I'm your wife."

It's been a long time since I've used that word, and I can tell it affects him like it does me. Breath passes like an electric current between us. Ryan reaches his hand straight through it to the curve of my jaw. It's such a tentative touch that it's almost imagination. He whispers shakily, "Not for a second have I stopped loving you."

I swallow. "I know that. You stopped letting *me* love *you*."

We're an inch apart, his hand on my cheek. I search his desolate eyes, eager for his lips to wash over me like desert rain, for better or worse.

As if on cue, the door handle jiggles and Jet calls out, "Mommy?"

She reverts to *mommy* when she's sleepy.

I close my eyes and inhale the frustration. Ryan lets out a half laugh. Staring at me, he calls, "She's in here!"

I pry myself away from him and open the door.

Jet shuffles in, disoriented. In the checkers victory and sugar crash, she forgot to pee before bed. When she woke up and went to the bathroom, she saw my note.

She has no category for Ryan and me being together without her. And while she's typically excellent at reading a room, her usual sensibilities are at the mercy of youth and sleep delirium. She rambles about a dream she was having, something about a planet where all the food is square. I don't know. She makes herself giggle in her rumpled mourning dress, sheet wrinkle imprints lining one side of her face.

Ryan listens politely. I watch words soar out of her mouth and try to find their place among her parents' words suspended in the air like dust around the room. Not for a million dollars could I recount that square-food dream.

I guess she finishes because she's staring at me expectantly, blinking and saying, "Ready, Mom?" Awake enough to drop the *mommy*.

I repeat, "Ready?"

"To go to our room?"

"Right. Yes. Of course."

Ryan and I glance at each other, emitting want and apology over our daughter's bedhead.

"'Night, Dad." She plods away.

We drag our feet and follow her. Ryan The Hopeful—a Ryan I thought was dead—smiles in the doorway and brushes my forearm with his fingertips, my skin sparking. Glancing back to confirm that Jet's not watching, I bring his hand to my mouth and kiss his knuckles. It's the first time my lips have been on him in nine years.

Then I go into room 221 with Jet, who's already back in bed mumbling, "'Night, Mommy."

I dream of Drunk Ryan and the stairs and the exploding bottle, and I wake up exhausted from the push and pull of it. I don't know if he can stop drinking. I hope. Want. Believe, even. But I don't *know*. Maybe he can't.

Startling me, Jet giggles in her sleep like a lasso tugging me back to this real and concrete place where happy dreams exist.

When I fall back asleep, I dream not of Ryan but of Jet. We're lying on our backs in buffalo grass, tendrils of sun caressing us as we laugh.

In the morning, there's a breakfast tray and a shiny new checkers set outside our door. Jet says she can't wait to beat her dad again, and hope bulldozes straight through my heart.

1997

RYAN VISITS MORE OFTEN AFTER TENNESSEE. HE TAKES Jet for Mexican food and to the Ridglea and to see the majestic performance hall being built on the corner of Fourth and Calhoun. She comes home happy and sings the Beatles in the shower. He is two weeks, a month, three months sober.

I think he lived out in Haltom City for a while. I haven't kept up. But I have his current address in Como. So when Jet is with Elise, I decide to visit. We can continue our conversation from Memphis, especially now that he's doing so well.

When he opens his door, the stench hits me like a brick to the chest. Vodka and filth and shadows hover behind him. Spilled Fritos crunch under his feet with scattered mail inside the doorway. Anger scorches me like a shot of straight whiskey. Two weeks, a month, three months of lies.

I don't say, "You're drinking?" as if I can't believe it. Of course I can believe that. What I say is, "You lied?" His double life feels like the shatter of glass behind me.

How can I trust that? I asked him way back when. *You can't. So I left.* He warned me. I hadn't expected deceit.

I can love someone in a stranglehold with a disease, but I will not love a liar.

101

Standing at his apartment door, he has the nerve to give me a remorseless eye roll. Or maybe it's the vodka that has the nerve, but I can't and won't separate them anymore. I meet his eye roll with crossed arms. Heaven knows why I think now is the time for a confrontation. I'm stupid with rage.

"Lilinin." My name leaks out of him so slurred that I have the urge to shove him and say *faker*. Like when a kid appears so sick that you assume it must be an act to get out of something.

His words trip, try to get at me, make it my fault, like why'd I even come, and my expectations are too high, and on and on. I'm tempted to plow past him and take his keys, because I know he would drive like this. Even after his DWI, after my dad, after Princess Diana. But I keep my feet planted in place.

When he takes a too-heavy step toward me, I'm near a flight of stairs and my recurring nightmare screams like a siren. I back up and repeat myself: "You. Lied." No question mark this time. I pound down the stairs without looking back.

If there's any liar bigger than an alcoholic, it's the alcohol, saying, *All there is is now* and *It won't hurt anyone* and *This is the last time*. Ryan's problem is believing the lies, and I will not do the same.

I don't tell Elise or Jet about the encounter, seeing no reason to heap heartache on them. Ryan's visits grind to a halt, and Jet's shower singing peters out. The amount written on Ryan's monthly checks increases. I'm tempted to rip them up, shred them like I want to shred the memory of him. But they belong to Jet.

Months later, he calls. He received the school flyer about Jet's spelling bee and plans to attend. He acts like everything is normal, forcing me into a corner where I pretend the same.

The afternoon of the bee, the two of us could win Oscars for our performance of normality. Jet gets disqualified on *descendant*. *D-E-S-C-E-N-D-E-N-T*. Ryan gives her roses. We walk out on either side of her, fully immersing ourselves in talk of tricky vowels and silent *p*s. See us, Daughter? Classmates? Teachers? Everything's fine!

I look over Jet's head at this man I wish I'd never met. I honestly believed Memphis was a second wind. Turns out it was a death rattle.

1999

PRESIDENT CLINTON HAS BEEN IMPEACHED, AND OUR country has no scarcity of opinions about it. I won't say a president shouldn't be held to a high standard; I'll only say I don't envy anyone in a position where crowds wait with stones. And I'm in no place to judge a woman for staying beside a husband with a vice.

I follow the news from a computer because we got internet at our apartment. The future is here, and it looks like computers and crossed fingers. It might not survive Y2K.

I log off AOL to go over to Shauna's for Saturday Night Pizza and Play—a tradition we've had for years, as the outgrown name implies.

Shauna, Kendi, and Michael open the door smiling so big that they might as well be shouting, *We have news!*

My gaze leaps to Shauna's left ring finger, and sure enough, she nods and laughs.

Jet and I both say, "About time." Jet beats me to call "jinx." At this point, I owe her dozens of Cokes.

It was the simple proposal Shauna wanted. On a picnic, Michael turned to Kendi and asked if he could have Kendi's permission to marry his mother. Shauna, in her scrubs, coughed on her tuna sandwich. Kendi smiled wide and nodded, all of it prearranged. Michael turned to Shauna, pulled out a ring, and asked her to marry him. When she said yes, Michael hugged them on their knees on the picnic blanket, and then they ate peanut butter cookies while Shauna admired her ring and cried the tears of a woman who has done this before—love and anticipation alongside relief, redemption, memory, fear. A second marriage requires more bravery than a first.

Kendi is happy about all of it except the move. Michael has a house in the neighborhood, so Kendi won't change schools. But we've spent over a decade in this apartment complex together, and I don't blame him for resisting. I'm working to accept that part of it myself. Otherwise, I'm overjoyed for Shauna.

After pepperoni and cheese strings on chins, Jet and Kendi want to go ride bikes. Shauna reaches for Kendi's uneaten crusts. "Y'all drop off that Nintendo game at Blockbuster."

"Mo-om," he complains.

Shauna shrugs, eating his crust. "Up to you. Late fees'll come from your allowance."

He looks to Jet, who shrugs and nods. "One sec." Kendi huffs as he goes to get the game, then to find the case for the game in his room, which is the mirror image of Jet's room. Their apartment has the same floor plan as ours, flip-flopped.

Jet slings her backpack purse over her shoulder, pulling her hair out from beneath the straps. She never goes anywhere without that little thing. Inside are bandages, topical antibiotic, and gauze in case she should come across anyone who needs help. Some people's hearts shrink as their eyes open to the pains of the world, but not Georgette's. I only hope this hurting world goes easy on her.

Once Kendi has the game in hand, the kids head out to get their bikes as Shauna calls after them, "Helmets! One hour! Make sure shoelaces are tied!" When we don't hear a response, Shauna hollers, "Kendall!"

He shouts back from the front stoop, "We know, helmets and shoe-laces!"

Next weekend, we won't have Saturday Night Pizza and Play because the time gods have conspired against us—the kids are about to have their first middle school dance. I didn't even register when Jet started pronouncing her *R*s correctly or stopped calling a "cafeteria" a "cafetortilla," but now she's suddenly old enough to ride a bike unsupervised and go to a school dance and need deodorant and wear a bra, for crying out loud.

Technically, she didn't need the bra. She came home from school frantic one day because the boys were popping straps. She had pressed her back against the wall so they wouldn't know she wasn't wearing one. It was of utmost urgency that we get one *that day*. She simply wouldn't return to school without a strap to pop.

So we went to Target and grabbed a few AAs even though she's still as flat as Texas. I said something about how the boys probably shouldn't pop straps, but she was too busy comparing shades of pink.

I was prepared to be overcome with the *Stop growing up on me* sensation. When I think of bras, I picture red lace and underwire and large cup sizes and sexiness and then maybe even milk stains. But the cute little bras we got were nothing like that. They reminded me more of when we started amassing baby clothes, trying to imagine how something could be so tiny.

Of course, time consolidated into inches and pounds—she grew into bigger clothes like she'll grow into bigger bras. But those teensy bras looked innocently up at me from their little baby hangers with their little baby ruffles as if to say, *We're not so bad*.

In the Target checkout line, Jet tried to appear nonchalant and grown, but she looked as small as ever. Of course, I didn't tell her that. Instead, I affectionately squeezed her shoulders.

She said, "Mom, please."

"Glad to see that even Annoyed Preteen Jet remembers her please-and-thank-yous."

"It's Annoyed *Teen* Jet now, *thank you* very much." Her

pleased-with-herself smile is the exact same as it has been since she was an infant learning to pull to stand. I half expected her to start clapping for herself like she did back then.

Jet is going to the dance with someone named Ben. She hasn't let me meet him yet, though meet him I will. She knows good and well that the only way I'm allowing her to go to this dance is if he picks her up properly and we take pictures.

In the meantime, I serenade her with my best Elton John voice. "*B-B-B-Bennie and the Jet.*" She is not amused. She beg-instructs me not to call him Bennie. *His name is Ben, Mom. Ben.* She says the *n* with an emphatic *nuh*. Apparently, if I *ever* sing my version of "Bennie and the Jets" when he's around, Jet will *die.*

The plan is for Ben to come over with his mother, since these kids are still years away from driving, thank goodness. Shauna, Kendi, his date Cassidy, and Cassidy's mom will come over too. Seth's tail will wag, alert with his *so many humans!* excitement.

Ben will look nice with frosted tips and a cloud of cologne. He and Jet will smile hello, nervously exchange corsage for boutonnière, and roll eyes about their mothers snapping too many photos. I'll subtly tuck in the pale pink bra strap that peeks out on Jet's bony shoulder from behind the red A-line dress we found at Ross. Her hair, same dark waves as her father's, will be in a simple updo, thanks to Shauna. I'll say I'm jealous of Shauna's styling skills, and Shauna will say she's jealous of the Bright women's "big marble eyes" as we help Jet learn to use eyeliner and tweezers in front of the bathroom mirror.

She'll wear thin, dangly earrings that she'll borrow from me even though she has plenty of similar pairs of her own, like when a baby demands food from his mother's plate even though it's the same as his. She'll maneuver earring backs and blush brushes with her first professionally manicured fingernails.

Once, when Jet was a newborn, I cut her nails to keep her from scratching herself. I accidentally clipped the skin of her right pinky finger. She cried, and I cried harder. Ryan rushed into the room thinking something terrible had happened. Well, something terrible *had* happened! But when I showed him the blood blister forming on the tip of our baby's finger, he laughed in relief and said, "Lil, she's totally fine." He picked her up and walked toward the rocking chair, and she stopped crying, Ryan humming and me trailing behind them, repeating through hormones, "I'm so sorry, I'm so sorry."

Not so long ago, Jet was too short to see herself in our bathroom mirror. Then she grew to where her eyes peeked over, button nose level with the rust-colored countertop. Now her twiggy waist is level with the counter, and a boy named Ben will awkwardly encircle that waist and her tiny frame and her beating heart toward himself when a slow song starts in a school gym dripping with cheap, shiny decorations.

At some point, a girl will go to the bathroom to cry about something or other. Jet will follow, trying to help. When the muffled beat from a popular boy-band song drops, they'll rush to dry eyes with paper towels, mascara messes still new to them. Dresses will swish as they hurry back to the pulsing lights, booming speakers, and overabundance of chaperones.

Ben will try to keep his voice from squeaking when a slow song starts and he tells Jet she looks pretty, wondering if he'll get to kiss her later.

Shauna and I will be back home, wondering the same thing. And wondering if it's too soon to get our photos developed. I'll tell her why Cassidy isn't good enough for Kendi, and she'll tell me why Ben isn't good enough for Jet. We'll pull out nostalgia like a deck of cards and trade stories of petty dramas from our own school dances. We'll reassure each other that our children are smarter and more mature than we were. We'll make empty promises that nobody will break their hearts and that they'll be immune to peer pressure and teen cruelties and Columbine-like shootings. We'll hope for perfection; what mother doesn't?

By then we'll feel the spiral tug of that insatiable mother worry, the years at our heels like yipping puppies. So we'll make a snack tray. Jarlsberg, Honeycrisps, crackers. We'll sit on the couch, Seth snoozing at our feet, and we'll turn on *Notting Hill.* We might paint our toenails. Michael will join us if he isn't working. We'll discuss how Shauna might keep her last name, which has to do with the fact that Michael's last name is Titweiler. He is Dr. Titweiler.

But it's not only that. Shauna's last name is the last bit of her dead husband, like ash at the bottom of an urn. Instead of pressuring her to let it go, Michael is considering taking it, allowing all three of them to have the same name: Darnell. They would be hard-pressed to find a man more thoughtful or less self-important than Michael Titweiler. (Also, who wouldn't jump at the chance to shed Titweiler?)

Shauna says she couldn't be happier, and yet her joy doesn't assuage yesterday's grief. *Yesterday,* that undefined past when she walked down the aisle to become a Darnell, or when we ourselves were twiggy girls getting AA bras and going to school dances. How soon will *tomorrow* arrive, that undefined future when Jet is eating cheese and crackers with her friend while her kid is out learning to dance and kiss and become? Time feels as flimsy as the cardboard swirlies that will hang over Jet's head in the school gym while the bass line reverberates in her chest and she wraps her skinny limbs around someone who is not me.

2000

JET HAS HER MOTHER'S EYES BUT HER FATHER'S EYE. SHE photographs a horsefly on dusty blinds as the sun streams through; a young girl holding her mother's hand on the way to school; chocolate chip cookies burned to the cookie sheet; shoelaces in a puddle; Friday-night lights through bleachers; Kendi as he tinkers with intricate model planes. She captures mundane life and makes it look like music. Her backpack purse now always contains her camera alongside her first aid supplies.

I want to tell Ryan about our budding photographer. It'll mean so much to him.

He's been coming by every month or two, barely looking at me, and taking Jet out for frozen yogurt or shopping. I don't think he knows what to do with her now that her interest in checkers has been replaced with friends and AOL Instant Messenger and Chuck Taylors. They talk about music but not much else.

With signature teen enthusiasm, Jet shrugs her permission when I ask if I can show him her photos. As I suspected, she hasn't mentioned photography to him. So I decide to take some of her photos by the SG on my lunch break.

When I open the gallery door and step out of the winter sun, a lump

110

forms in my throat. New macramé light fixtures hang above a cosmo-
politan front desk, yet it's all still as familiar as the old knit blanket I pull
out each October when the weather turns. *Abbey Road* is playing on low
volume. Being here feels like time travel. In front of me, I'm saying *yes*
to Ryan's proposal; I'm saying *I do* in my white dress. I swallow, wiping
an eye embellished with crow's feet. Feelings are valid at the time, and
memories are reconsiderations.

Ryan rounds a corner and stops when he sees me.

To me, this gallery is us. A time capsule. But he's been here, day in
and day out, turning it into what appears to be a charming and successful
business. There's an exquisite painting of three stallions listed for more
than two thousand dollars. I wonder who does his marketing. If he
has a manager who handles things when he's hungover. If he even gets
hungover anymore or if he has mastered spaced dosing. Why he could
commit to the work and art of this place but not the work and art of us.
How alcohol decides what to destroy and what to leave alone.

"Lillian? What's going on?" He's wearing a blue fleece pullover and
sliding his hands into his pockets.

In a back corner, a mother pushes a stroller and observes the exhibit
with toddler-tired eyes. Voices drift from a side room. Ryan waits for
my response.

This is when I notice a small painting. His work, unmistakable. Jet,
sitting on grass and leaning back on her hands, legs outstretched and
ankles crossed, head thrown back in laughter, ribbons of sun coming
through tree branches as they cast a lattice pattern on her skin. Ryan
has always been skilled, but this is breathtaking.

"Wow."

Ryan follows my gaze to the painting and blushes.

"It's gorgeous."

"Thank you."

I force myself to remember slurred words and droopy eyes as I ease Jet's
photographs from my bag. "I wanted to show you what Jet's been doing."

A few women enter. Ryan asks if he can help them. Ryan, in the afternoon gallery with its flood of sunshine and memories.

"No thanks. Just browsing."

He nods at them, ushers me into his office, spreads the photos out on a drafting table, and turns on a high-wattage lamp, bending the neck of it to spotlight Jet's perspective of the world.

He studies them as I study him. I feel the insidious creep of hope and chide myself.

There's a ficus in one corner. In another, a shelf with art books: Georgia O'Keeffe, Norman Rockwell, Eastern sculpture. Tucked toward the back is a small framed photo of the three of us when Jet was a baby. I remember that day. The weather was turning cold, trees reddening like the tip of Jet's runny nose. Elise took the picture. Right after the flash, Ryan rubbed his hands up and down my arms to warm me.

"I can't believe our daughter took these." Ryan's voice snaps me out of that autumn and back to the present.

"I know." I lean over the drafting table with him. "Art begets art." I smile tightly.

We must've been apart too long, because I'm surprised when Ryan turns toward me with glistening eyes. "Can I display any?"

"She knew I was coming to show you, so I'm sure she'd like that. If you have space."

"I'll ask her which ones she'd want to sell."

"Oh, you don't have to do that."

"These are objectively good. Some could go for hundreds of dollars, if she wants."

I smile and say, "Your mom got her the camera."

"Sounds right." His eyes float across Jet's photos. "Mom got me my first camera too."

"Well," I exhale. "You can ask what she thinks about selling. Do you want her new cell phone number?" I realize how close we are in the cramped office.

He jots her number down, and I hate myself for thinking about that once-upon-a-time torn napkin where he wrote his number for me a million years ago.

"Photographer Jet with her own cell phone. Who even is she?"

I scoff. "You'd know if you were around more." I'm not sure if I say this to remind him or myself that he's not.

His gaze grabs mine, undeterred. "Hey, could you and Jet maybe come over for dinner tonight?"

I blink. This is new. We have nothing else to do on a random Wednesday except the usual homework and walking Seth. Flustered, I tell him we'll be there, even as I see flashes of crushed corn chips. I clumsily ask if we can bring anything, sounding so formal that I almost laugh.

"Nope. Got it covered." He gives me the address of a new apartment. "You know it?" He gathers Jet's photos. "It's near Lockheed."

"I'll MapQuest it."

We walk back toward the gallery entrance, across the floor where we had our first dance as man and wife.

"See you tonight," he says, as I step out into the cold, bright day.

Ryan opens his door wearing eyeglasses. Jet and I scrunch our noses in curiosity. Farsighted, he recently found out. He looks older, more sophisticated, the glasses a material reminder that this is how a life goes by.

His apartment is clean and light and airy. A similar aesthetic as the SG and nothing like his old place. Sky-blue curtains frame the window. Beside it, one of his landscapes. The room doesn't smell like turpentine or patchouli but like something new and different. Eucalyptus, maybe?

Ryan serves salad, pasta, and garlic bread. We pass the vinaigrette and eat together, not saying much. Ryan doesn't like vinaigrette; he must have gotten it for me.

After second helpings, I excuse myself. The bathroom is small and crisp with light gray walls. And the new smell is definitely eucalyptus. I splash cold water on my face and stare myself down in the dirty mirror. Ryan obviously cleaned, but he's never been good about remembering mirrors.

What am I doing, allowing us to be here like a family? Setting us up to be wounded? Communicating to Ryan that we're here like a dog toy, waiting any time he wants to pick us up?

Contrary to the loss for words around the table when I excused myself, I return to find Jet with a mouthful of bread, saying, "How can you not think *Abbey Road* is their best? There's no contest. Like at all. I can listen to *Abbey Road* on endless repeat, but *Revolver* is only good for, like, two times through."

Ryan laughs, youthful. "Hey, you're entitled to your opinion. Even though it's wrong."

She scoffs in mock offense as he continues, "Listen, I'm not saying *Abbey Road* isn't great. But *Revolver* their best by far."

They go on to agree, however, that boy bands and *Titanic* are overrated. As the two of them imitate Rose and Jack, I feel my smile down to my toes.

I carry our plates to the sink, snooping under the pretense of cleaning. I check the fridge. Clean. Of course it is; he knew we were coming over. I carry his glass to the sink and sniff it. Not laced with a lie, as far as I can tell.

Ryan got madeleines from a bakery in Sundance Square, so we eat those and fall back into silence. Brushing a few crumbs off my lap, I announce that we should go. Jet still has science homework, and Seth will need to go out.

Ryan clicks his tongue. "Yikes, science. Can't help you there." Like he has ever helped with her homework. How can he say and do such normal things when he's said and done such awful ones? To be fair, how can he say and do such awful things when he's said and done such normal ones?

We collect our jackets as Jet does what I can't—thanks Ryan for dinner.

"Oh!" He palms his forehead. "We didn't even talk about your photos! They're incredible, Jet. Seriously, such an eye. I'd be impressed even if you weren't my daughter."

Jet blushes. "Thanks." She shrugs like they mean nothing to her—her photographs and her dad. But I know better. They mean everything.

"I wanted to ask which ones you might want to sell?" He glances at me and back at Jet. "But I guess we'll have to talk about this another time?"

"Uh, yeah. Maybe I can look through them with you . . ." Her voice trails off, probably due to the same thought I have: When will we see him again, and what is this new family dynamic he has instigated?

Ryan recovers with, "Your mom gave me your fancy new cell phone number. I can call—actually, know what? Think you could come by the gallery after school sometime?"

"Sure. Cool." Jet hesitates, looking between us. "Where is the gallery, exactly?" She hasn't been to the SG since she was a baby. A million no-time-at-alls ago.

"Oh." Ryan grabs a scrap of paper, scribbling the address and cross-streets. "Come by any day next week. Shouldn't be a long bike ride from school." He glances at me for approval, and I nod. The distance of bike ride is fine with me. The dad, I'm not so sure.

"Okay." She pauses, scans the paper, and lets out a barely perceptible giggle.

Ryan asks, "What?"

"Just the name."

"The name?"

"Sundance Square. When I was little, I'd imagine the sun with, like, legs and cowgirl boots, square-dancing across the sky." She giggles again. "Still pops in my head sometimes."

Ryan looks as though the phrase *when I was little* pierces him straight through. I narrow my eyes at him, and he knows what I'm saying: *Yes, you missed it. Don't hurt her more than you already have.*

At his doorstep, he reaches for my elbow and says to Jet, "Give us a minute?"

She looks at me, I nod, and she goes ahead to the parking lot, a slice of moon suspended above her slight frame.

I turn to face my husband.

He clears his throat. "Could you come back for dinner again sometime soon, just me and you? So we can talk?"

Curiosity overpowers all other impulses. "Sure."

Determination sweeps across his face like a sunrise over a field. "Great. How about Friday?"

"Works for me. I get off at five."

"Let's say seven?"

"Sure."

His hands are in his pockets, thumbs out. "See you then."

Back home, we walk Seth and then Jet settles at the kitchen table with homework. I sort laundry. Return a work call. Make a grocery list. Bread (I've given up on the Atkins diet); tortilla chips (the reason I've given up on Atkins); salsa; creamy Jif; bananas; kid and healthy cereals; ground beef; marinara; eggs; yogurt; margarine; Hot Pockets; berries; baby carrots; frozen corn; SlimFast bars.

Jet doodles on her notebook cover. Biology is usually her favorite, but she's distracted. I set my own pencil down and ask, "Penny for your thoughts?"

"My thoughts are only worth a penny to you?"

I roll my eyes. "It's an expression."

She smiles. "I know."

Seth laps water from his bowl. We're okay, the three of us. I don't want Ryan to mess this up.

Eyes on her doodle, Jet ventures, "What do you think Dad thinks of me?"

I set my grocery list aside. "He thinks you hung the moon in the sky."

Her frown increases. "Then why'd he leave?"

"Oh, sweetheart. You know the alcohol was—"

"No, I know the alcohol, okay? But it doesn't make sense. Lots of alcoholics live with their families."

She's a young woman now. I can't give her the vague answers I'd give a child.

"When he drank, he could get . . . aggressive. He didn't want to hurt us."

Her eyes darken. "Did he? Hurt us?"

I exhale, plenty of time to remember but not enough to think. "He came close. That's when he left."

She nods.

"He loves you more than life. Always has."

She refocuses on her doodling. "Doesn't feel like it."

"Well"—a flash of my son's face, handing him over—"love doesn't always feel like we expect."

Jet sets her pencil down with decision. "I'm never going to drink."

Never is so easy for a young person to say. I think about my father's ashes, sunk in the Trinity. And Barton's suit-clad body underground. How Ryan and I both swore off alcohol before we met, carrying our father's stories into our *no-thank-you*s and *just-water-please*s.

"It might come as a surprise, but your dad also swore he'd never drink."

"He did?"

"For a long time."

Jet nods thoughtfully and picks her pencil back up, her doodle a miniature masterpiece.

When she says nothing else, I stand and go load dishes into the dishwasher, still exactly the way my mother did. It's funny what gets ingrained, like which way plates should face. Jet opens her biology book.

"So listen," I say over the running sink water, "Dad actually asked me to come back over Friday evening to talk."

"About what?"

"Beats me." I shrug. "What are your plans that night?"

"None yet. Probably video games with Kendi."

"Need me at home?"

"Uh, no? I'm not a baby."

What a silly thing to say. You don't have to be a baby to want your mom.

Not for the first time, I ache for my own mama. I want her advice about Jet. About Ryan. I've always thought she'd like him. That she'd see the man behind the mistakes even more than I do.

Jet scratches behind Seth's ears as she mumbles to herself about biology. And for the first time, I imagine becoming a grandmother.

2000

RYAN AND THE SMELL OF CURRY GREET ME AT HIS FRONT
door. White T-shirt. Blue jeans. Bare feet. A wooden spoon in hand.
No glasses this time.

His smile widens as he steps aside to let me in. "Hey."

That one little sound from his mouth slings me right back to the Fort
Worth Public Library. My guard goes up. "Hi," I offer, keeping distance.

He darts into the kitchen, asking over his shoulder, "It's butter
chicken. How spicy should I make it?"

I shut the door behind me and steady myself on an antique wingback
he probably got from Elise. His easel displays an almost complete Flagship Hotel. Galveston. I want to jump into the canvas. Spring backward
eighteen years to when the top scoop of my strawberry ice cream fell
onto the pier. Ryan traded cones with me and gave me a sticky kiss before
we returned to licking up rivulets of melting cream.

I set my purse on the wingback. "Very spicy. Need help?"

"It's almost done. Want to set the table?" He's checking the rice and
tasting the sauce and turning knobs on the stove.

I go into the kitchen, forcing myself through these motions of normalcy. With my hand on a top cabinet handle, I pause. Lower myself. Open
the lower cabinet, and there they are. Plates I could grab with my toes.

119

I set the table as though this is something we do. Plates. Napkins. I wonder if other women have done this. If they pretend to like his lower cabinet plates.

I can't bring myself to ask, *How was your day?* That's so normal it feels insane. So we complete our tasks to the soundtrack of food sizzling. I sniff Ryan's water when his back is turned. Pure. Move it to his spot at the table. Find the silverware drawer. Groping for forks and words, I land on, "So, how's work?"

"Good. Oh, and I called Jet. She's coming by the SG on Monday. Her photos actually inspired me to invite the school district to participate in a showcase of local kids' art. They're all about it."

"What a great idea." I set forks on napkins, and a question creeps into my mind. I frame it as a statement. "I guess you've learned a lot about marketing."

His face twists into a surprised laugh. "Oh gosh. Yeah, no. I mean, I did. I had to for a while. But I was pretty pathetic. Kat's been working with me for years now, and she's fantastic." He pours sauce over the chicken and turns off the stove. "I have four full-time staff members, and I wouldn't survive without them. They run the place."

"That's great," I mumble. *Kat.*

He carries our food to the table and swivels his head in a final check to make sure he hasn't forgotten anything. "Ready?" He softens the lighting. He didn't do that when Jet and I were here on Wednesday.

No, I'm not ready. "Sure."

The food is delicious. When we were together, we both preferred Ryan's cooking, but sometimes he'd get so lost in painting that he'd think it was early afternoon when it was nine o'clock at night.

We talk more about the SG. I've been curious for a long time, and especially after seeing it this week. He tells me about favorite exhibits, big sales, media coverage, his indispensable colleagues. I feel a prick of pride for Ryan At The Greek Restaurant, who wanted to paint what he wanted and open a gallery where other artists could do the same.

When he asks about the bank, I say I have no complaints because I don't. The bank has been to me what Stethoscope is to Jet—a dependable constant I don't think about much but would be lost without. I've had numerous promotions. And a small life with a happy child was the grand scope of my ambitions. I feel a prick of pride for Lillian At The Greek Restaurant, for the steadiness she's accomplished in spite of Ryan. In spite of Zack. A small life is a big feat, but I say none of this. Only, "The bank's good. Stable."

Our silence lengthens, and I almost say, *Tell me why I'm here. Don't you know this hurts?* But instead I wait, fork to chicken, chicken to mouth. It's obvious he wants to transition the conversation, but he takes so many about-to-speak inhales that I worry about hyperventilation. I serve myself a second helping.

"So." He scoots his plate a few inches away. *Finally.* "I want to talk about something." *Yes, I am pitifully aware.* He tucks hair behind his ear, heavy on the pepper but a fair amount of salt. I nod my best *Out with it* nod. What is this? Is he moving away? Filing for divorce? Dying?

He wipes his palms on his lap and shifts in the creaky chair. At last, he sits still and focuses on me, resolve pooling in his eyes. "I wanted to tell you that I'm sober nine months."

Oh. "Wow. Congratulations." *Is that it? Why are you telling me? Is nine months enough to break out the Shirley Temples? And where was this ten years ago? Or after Memphis?*

"Lil, that day at my old apartment, most of it is black. Um, did I—?"

I shake my head. "You didn't touch me." His expression awash with relief, I add with a bite, "Because I didn't let you."

"Well, I got help after that. And it's the first time help has . . . helped. I had a couple of early relapses, but my AA group got me back up. They've been like family."

This stings. Why couldn't his family be like family? I cross my arms. "If you're doing so well, then why have you barely seen Jet?"

He pokes at a grain of rice on the table, rolling its stickiness beneath his fingertip. "I didn't think I'd get this far. Nine months since the last relapse and I'm finally understanding I'll never be 'over' it."

"Ryan?" This question has waited stale in my mouth for far too long. "Why did you start drinking?" I hold my breath and brace for blame.

A long inhale. "Fear." A long exhale. "And arrogance." He lets the rice grain stick to his finger and wipes it onto his plate. "I didn't know how scared I was of my dad until Jet was born. I would get stressed and say things to you, little impatient things exactly like he'd say to my mom. And I knew what had come next for them: yelling and bruises. And what had come next for me: hiding under the table and a heartbeat that never slowed down. I would think about that and not even be able to look at Georgette. Every day I got more desperate to prove I wasn't him. To take a drink just to watch myself stop." His eyes are suddenly wet, his voice a raw whisper. "Except I didn't."

I rarely thought about his dad, yet there he was, consumed. I wonder if he would've been better off never knowing Barton. If Jet would've been better off never knowing Ryan. If my son's parents drink.

When Ryan wipes his palms on his lap again, I realize he has more to say.

He scoots close enough that his knee slides between mine, a pleading expression on his face. "I'm so sorry. There's no excuse. All the years and all the—" He looks down and swallows. "You'll never forgive me." He scoffs through his nose, hunting for punishment.

I lean back, giving air to his long-awaited apology. "So what now?" I'm asking if he's cured or if this is just another ascent on the roller coaster of addiction. If that's all a cure can ever hope to be.

He stares down at his fidgeting hands, and I can feel them showing me a brushstroke technique, ushering me to the dance floor, passing me our newborn.

"I'm in therapy with Mom. You know she's asked for years." He shrugs. "It's a start. And sobriety feels really good now that I'm past those early relapses. So good it's almost addictive."

Nine months and AA and therapy with Elise. I let it register, cautious.

Ryan's phone rings and he cringes an apology as he checks caller ID. "It's DJ." One of his four colleagues. "They're hosting a workshop tonight. I should make sure everything's okay. Sorry."

"Of course." I take a swig of water and chew an ice cube as he takes the call.

It sounds like there are materials DJ's trying to locate, and Ryan helps him out.

I stack our plates by the sink, spoon leftovers into Tupperware, and peruse books in the living room.

I send an SMS message to Jet: STILL HERE. MIGHT BE A WHILE. U OK?

She responds immediately: YEP. GONNA CRASH HERE. STAR WARS W/ K + S + M.

K. XOXO :-) Ten cents well spent on sending her hugs and kisses.

Ryan finishes his call. "Sorry." He sits on the couch and tugs a loose thread on his shirt.

I sit beside him, inhaling faint notes of eucalyptus. "You were wrong." He looks at me as I say, "You thought you were him, but I knew you were you."

He winces, my words salt in the wound. If Ryan were Barton, then he doesn't get blame and doesn't get better. But *Ryan* hurt his family. And *Ryan* can get better.

I decidedly add, "You're wrong about something else, too."

"I'm sure I am." It strikes me that the humility I've always admired has self-loathing twisted around it like ivy.

"I can forgive you. If you're honest like this and let me in. That's what I was trying to say that night in Memphis."

"That night . . ." He swallows.

Whether I want it or not, electricity charges through me. We're clearly thinking about the same thing: the moment on his hotel room couch that Jet interrupted.

I study my husband, new fine lines on his face.

I do want it. I want to acknowledge the work of these past nine months. I want to show him that his future can be more than only punishment. I want to lose myself in the best of him, not the worst.

"What are you thinking?" He asks it as he takes my hand ever so carefully, his thumb tracing the back of it like when he kneeled and waited for my yes. When I said yes all those lifetimes ago, I thought I knew more or less what I was saying yes to. But now I know none of us ever can. Now I have no idea if the rabid beast of addiction or some other prowling wolf will bite us in a month, a year, five years, ten.

But now my yes has some teeth to it.

I move toward him. "I'm thinking that I'm still in this, in sickness and health. That I love you. And"—I raise his hand to my lips—"that this time you better let me."

I kiss his fingers, his nails flecked with yellow paint like droplets of sun.

He shivers and moves his hand to my cheek. I lean in, kiss his wrist, tilt my face up. The breathless anticipation of our lips an inch apart is the drunkest I've ever been. I thought I knew how much I missed him, but the full force of it crashes into me now.

Timidly, he closes the gap. Need hammers through me, forgiveness terrifying but firm. Our bodies remember and resist and orbit around desire. I kiss him harder as he slides cautious fingers along the seam of my shirt and inches upward, a blaze spreading across my skin like wildfire. His tongue drags lightly down my neck.

Then he pulls back, asks if this is okay, and swears it wasn't his intention, not even his wildest fantasy. I lock eyes with him and unbutton his jeans.

His eyelids close. When I hesitate, they fly back open. "You okay?"

I lean back, breathless, brushing hair from my face. "I'm . . . it's been years. And. Um." I spit it out: "I'm older."

He laughs so full out that I startle. "Lillian Irene Bright." Oh boy, full-naming me. "I have never thirsted for anything the way I thirst for you right now. For the you of right now."

His fingers float up my side, and I nudge his hand to keep going, to lift my shirt off. When he tosses it aside, his eyes travel down me like an exile returned home.

His gaze halts at my scar, fingers leaping to it, eyes filling with questions like water. "What is—"

"It's stupid." I shake my head. "I was cutting an underripe avocado and the knife slipped weirdly into my stomach. Long time ago. More embarrassing than anything."

Long time ago. He bows to kiss the scar before rising again to eye level. "I'm so sorry for every scar I've missed." He waits for me to look at him and see how he means it. "The years I let us lose."

He kisses my lips, neck, collarbone.

Slowly, he trails downward.

When he tastes me, I hope I'm sweeter than wine.

2001

RYAN IS TWENTY MONTHS SOBER. THROUGHOUT THE
past year, there have been hard conversations, soft kisses, raised voices,
lowered expectations, therapy sessions, tears of hurt and of hope, and
not a bottle in sight.

We still live in separate apartments, though I'm not sure how much
longer this will last. Most evenings, he comes over for dinner. Jet wants
him around, as do I.

His affection makes me feel like I'm Jet's age. It surprises me to look
in the mirror at the sagging and softness of age. I'm no longer bleeding
every month, yet butterflies still flutter in my rib cage for the man I love.
Time is funny. Bodies, too. What fades and what doesn't.

Suddenly we're in the bungalow with the blue ceiling, and I can smell
the sea. We're at the beginning. It can be anything we want.

It's Jet who reminds me that beginnings are relative.

When she was young, she would ask question after question about
my childhood, so I deemed her Curious Georgette, which led to a hat
made of yellow construction paper and a mother-daughter Halloween

costume. She is fourteen now and still has questions. "What were you like when you were my age?"

When I was fourteen, my best friend had broken my heart.

Lisa Ballard and I were joined at the hip. Two peas in a pod. We had sleepovers on weekends and study sessions on school days. That is, until Susan O'Malley invited Lisa to her party but didn't invite me.

Soon after, I watched Lisa wear the same shoes as Susan and use the same words as Susan and part her hair like Susan. Every time I invited Lisa over, she gave excuse after excuse until she finally asked me to leave her alone. She said *please* and her face turned red. I went home and sobbed my eyes out until Mama said, "Lilly girl, come outside."

In the backyard, she had me choose a tree. It was drizzling. I walked over to the magnolia. Mama pulled out a pocketknife and my eyes widened. I watched her kneel down and carve *GW + LW*. She struggled with the *G*, an unfinished rectangle. I didn't offer to help, and I wondered if Dad would be unhappy about this act of vandalism. When the *G* was as good as it was going to get, Mama leaned back against the trunk and patted the damp earth beside her. "Sit."

I obeyed.

"I'm not saying not to cry about Lisa." She sighed. "I'm saying there will be other Lisas."

At that, I started to cry.

"Oh, just listen, will you?"

So I did.

"You have parents, friends. Someday you'll have lovers and maybe kids." That's how she spoke to me then. Lovers. "It's not that you don't need anyone—just that you don't need everyone."

She pointed to her fresh engraving, the thin lines of stripped wood. "Know what this is?"

I shrugged.

"It's where you started. Georgia Wright and Lillian Wright. First love." She put her hand to the bark of the tree. "There's something permanent about where you start." I watched her touch our initials and I nodded, trying to understand what she was telling me: beginnings aren't blank canvases.

"Listen"—she looked pointedly at me—"I'm the first person you needed, but I'm not the only or the last. Lisa was a good friend for a time, but she's not the only or the last." She cupped my chin in her hands. "You can't control anyone else's choices, but you start with what you're given and then you make your own."

Part of me thought, *Obviously*; the other part thought, *Huh?*

As we walked back toward the house, Mama pulled a peppermint from her pocket. For as long as I could remember, she'd given me a peppermint whenever I felt bad. I took it and looked up at her, drizzle dotting her hair like gemstones.

I lost track of Lisa Ballard. Last I heard, she was a social worker and a mother. And Mama was right: I chose to need other people.

I don't know what became of our magnolia. But I know that it never had to be Lillian and Ryan. It could have been Lillian and anyone. Love is time shared, and we make our choices. I'm looking at one of mine in her tender round face.

"I was a lot like you," I answer Jet's question. "Delicate. Loyal."

She scrunches her nose at the implication that she's delicate. I run my finger down it like a slide, and she scrunches it more, swatting at my finger and smiling.

Shauna knocks on my front door. We're going out for Saturday lunch to review my matron-of-honor duties and details for her wedding weekend. Since Michael and Shauna both work in medicine, nearly two years have slipped by as they've planned their wedding between MRI results and medication protocols and recording vital signs and on-call weekends and Kendi's student council meetings and science projects and Shauna's race to keep up with how fast a teenage boy outgrows his shoes. But the date is finally set.

I open the front door and ask her to hang on a minute. I pop an Advil for a headache and then peek into Jet's room to let her know I'm leaving. Seth is at her feet with a chew toy.

"Hey, I'm headed out with Shauna. What are you and Kendi up to today?"

Jet pulls headphones off barely long enough to answer. "No clue what he's doing, but I'm writing a paper."

Something's going on with them. I have theories but don't want to pry, so I simply say, "Well then, good luck with your paper." I make a kiss sound in her direction and add, "Keep your friends close, love."

Her headphones are back over her ears.

Part Two

JET

2001

MOSQUITOS ARE EATING THROUGH OUR DEET, AND MY
sandal strap just broke. But Mom and Dad are, like, seriously in love,
and we're together to celebrate my birthday week. And America's.

Fireworks pop along the Trinity River. Kids in patriotic face paint
cover their ears, smudging little American flag cheeks. Shoes frame
dozens, maybe hundreds, of picnic blankets. Flip-flop tan lines make
people's feet look like they're smiling. I can't stop taking photos. Plus,
I have the inside scoop on what's about to happen, and it's going to be
awesome.

Mom's first hint is Nana's arrival.

"Hey?" Mom throws her hands out like, *What are you doing here?*

Pop boom pop.

"I wanted to watch fireworks with my favorite *fifteen*-year-old." Nana
winks, kisses me, and spreads a small blanket next to ours. Color whizzes
into the sky as a firecracker swims upward like a tadpole.

"Well, glad to have you, then." Mom stretches to hug Nana and, over
her shoulder, gives me a look of shrugging apology for the unplanned
intrusion. I try to look surprised. My armpits are wet with nervous
excitement.

Pop whizz boom. Michael, Shauna, and Kendi arrive.

Mom jumps up. "Oh my gosh, what a surprise!" Michael and Shauna are two weeks into marriage. Last time we saw them, we were throwing rice. Mom turns to me. "Looks like everyone wants to celebrate you."

My voice comes out in a catlike screech. "Yeah!" I've never been good at lying to Mom.

We all do our best to swallow giggles as the three Darnells sit beside Nana—the only one who is successfully keeping a straight face. Michael tries to turn a snicker into a cough. This is when Mom whips her head to the side and shoots exclamation mark eyes straight at Dad, who is reclining on the blanket and staring at her like the rest of us aren't even here. In an exaggerated voice, he says, "So nice of everyone to join us. Let us watch this finale, shall we?" He pats the blanket beside him. "Lil?"

Crackle whizz pop pop pop. Nana pulls something out of her Mary Poppins–esque purse. A baggy of her patriotic puppy chow: white-frosted pretzels, red and blue M&M's, and Chex dusted with powdered sugar. "Snack, anyone?"

Kendi and I dive toward it. Nana's puppy chow is a long-standing favorite.

Mom laughs. "People! What is going on?"

Boom crackle crackle pop.

We ignore her, wipe our powdered-sugar mouths, smile at each other, and watch the sky sparkle. Dad kisses Mom's shoulder as she mumbles something about us being up to no good and reaches for an M&M.

Then, something low in the sky. A soft "oooh" from the crowd.

The horizon lights up with the word *Lillian*.

Murmurs splash through the crowd along the riverbank.

Mom stares in confusion as the bright letters become smoke.

Dad's cheeks are wet.

Boom. Boom. Boom.

In an explosion of heat, a lancework question appears: *Re-marry me?* Above it, a lopsided heart.

Heads all around us bobble like they're on the dash of a car that took a corner too fast. People nearby spot the happy couple because Dad is rising to one knee, his re-proposal suspended above the river.

Mom's hand flies to her mouth, and I'm certain she's telling herself, *Hold your horses, Lillian.* She rises to her knees and faces him.

There are gasps and squeals and shushes. I adjust my camera settings and click click click.

Dad says something to Mom that nobody can hear except her. His question in the sky fades into vapor like their first try at marriage. Mom finally answers him with, "Again and again."

They kiss and add a new ring to her finger. I think about my friends with married parents. Holiday cards and family road trips and conversations with teachers where one parent looks at the other with a squeeze of the knee as if to say, *That sounds like our kid, all right.* I'll finally get to have that stuff. Better late than never, I guess.

Cheers ripple through the crowd. Toddlers who were frightened by the fireworks get distracted by the applause. One of them bounces his knees like the claps are music. He smiles with tears still wet on his squishy red cheeks.

Shauna hoots and hollers. She's more protective of Mom than anyone, so the fact that Dad won *her* over this past year is saying something.

Mom and Dad are still kissing. Kendi once told me that a kiss on the lips was what made people married, and I believed this for way too long. When I was eight or so, I asked a random teen boy where his wife went after I'd seen him kissing a girl. He looked at me like I was certifiably insane.

The applause fades, and the sky quiets. People turn away, gathering trash and blankets and sweaty children. Stragglers lean toward us to say congratulations as they walk to cars with arms full of patriotic gear. Dad says something to Mom about "becoming less independent this Independence Day, if you know what I mean." He's the king of jokes that barely pass as jokes, and also of saying "if you know what I mean" when everyone knows what he means. Mom leans her head on his shoulder as they talk about whether to have a second wedding. Mom does the thing where she claims it's too extravagant but clearly wants someone to argue that it's not.

When Dad first told me his firework plan, I scrunched my face and said, "Wait, are you secretly rich?"

Laughing, he buffed his nails and said, "Art world connections, baby." No surprise. Fort Worth adores Ryan Bright.

We schemed about how I'd tell Mom I wanted to go see fireworks "for my birthday" and "to try a new camera thing." Mom is so camera illiterate that we knew she wouldn't ask for details. And I figured it would be cool to share my birthday celebration with my already married parents' engagement. *Weird,* but cool.

Kendi elbows me congratulations. I hug him, not used to how tall he's getting. I don't say, *Sorry I got my dad back and you didn't.* Michael's better than Dad anyway.

The two of us make gagging sounds as our parents flirt. We're like backward chaperones for some old-person double date. When we tell the parents to get rooms, they look at each other and nod, and that's how Kendi and I end up spending the night at Nana's. I make him watch *Coyote Ugly,* he makes me watch *Star Wars,* and Nana makes popcorn with a sprinkle of Parmesan before she says, "'Night, kids," and retreats down the hall. We finish off my birthday cake and fall asleep somewhere between dances on bars and intergalactic space invasions.

The first time Dad stays with us for a long weekend, I start to wonder if this engagement and remarriage thing will work.

It's a Thursday night, and he's grilling hamburgers and hot dogs. When he tosses Seth some beef, I look at Mom and Mom looks at Dad, who says, "You don't give your dog meat scraps? Look how he likes it."

Seth gobbles it up.

We all look between each other until Dad says, "It's ready if y'all want to get out the fixings?"

Mom and I blink at each other. It's not that any of this is wrong; it's just different.

Mom says, "Of course," and she opens the fridge for the relish.

She gives me a look over her shoulder, so I reach for tomatoes to slice while announcing, "I'm *not* doing the onions."

Dad stretches past me for a knife and says, "I will."

As we all move around each other and get food ready to serve, I say the Preamble to the U.S. Constitution. I have to recite it in history class tomorrow, our first assignment of the fall semester.

As I finish, Dad turns from the chopped onion with tears streaming down his face. "It's just so beautiful." He sniffles. I giggle. Mom playfully shoves his shoulder.

We squirt mustard and rip lettuce and take our first bites of Dad's perfectly grilled burgers, and he surprises us by reciting the Preamble right back. Then he takes a man-sized bite and says, "Things from childhood really stick."

I notice Mom's pained expression. She looks from him to the fridge to me and finally into the bag of potato chips, which she reaches for as she rearranges her expression to a purposeful blankness. I saw it though.

After dinner, Dad washes dishes. Mom says something to him about which cabinet to keep the plates in and they chuckle. It's so weird that he lived here before and I don't remember it.

Dry dishes usually mean that Dad is going back to his apartment, but this time he's staying all weekend. So I take my math homework to the table while Mom and Dad clear throats and wipe palms on pants, and it's so uncomfortable that I can't look away.

"Mom?" They both look over at me like they forgot I was here. "Can you help?" I wave my math paper.

"Of course." She grabs her own stack of paperwork and sits with me, our evening routine. I want to tell Dad that dinner was enough and he can go now. No offense to him, but it's my turn with her.

He stands there in the middle of the kitchen like the last kid picked for the team. "I'm decent at math if you need—"

"No thanks." I show Mom the problem I'm stuck on.

Her face pinches as she says over her shoulder, "Hey, did you bring paints?"

His expression is full of regret as he says no, he didn't. "But I need to do SG paperwork for an upcoming exhibit." He goes into the living room, pulls out some papers, and begins to click his pen like a metronome. Click pause click pause click. I look at Mom like, *Seriously?* And she gives me a small shake of the head, a silent instruction to let it go.

Seth ambles over to Dad and whines. Seth never whines. I look at Mom like, *Double seriously?* She only sighs. Around the corner, click pause click pause click pause click.

I make it through homework and go to brush my teeth before bed. As I'm spitting out toothpaste, Dad appears at the open bathroom door and clears his throat. "So a buddy of mine has a darkroom and we're going to do some developing tomorrow afternoon. Want to come? Maybe we could meet your mom at Chili's for dinner after?"

"Really?" I've never told him I want to learn how to develop film. Or how much I love Chili's cajun pasta.

"If you want to. No pressure."

"Yes!" It sounds perfect.

"Okay, I'll pick you up from school, then." He taps the doorframe. "Sweet dreams."

I'm so excited that I almost forget to rinse my sudsy toothbrush, which I'm waving around as I say, "You too!"

He smiles so big that I want to hug him, but for some reason I don't. He goes. I rinse my toothbrush, wash my face with the new soap Mom got me for acne, and think about the Preamble and film exposure and going to a restaurant with not one but two parents.

The next day, the darkroom and cajun pasta are as perfect as I imagined, a world away from Dad's missteps with Seth and the clicking pen. Instead of feeling like he's in the way, I'm excited to go home together after dinner. Maybe he'll help me with my camera lens questions.

Back at home, I change clothes and take my camera lenses into the living room, where Mom and Dad are on the couch. His arm is around her in a way that makes her look different. Young, small, I don't know. Her leg is draped over his. They're talking in hushed tones and stop when they notice me. Mom smiles at me, her face lit with warmth. Dad says, "Come sit?" and gestures toward the chair. He is welcoming me to my own living room.

A candle is flickering, and I don't like any of this. I should like it, but I don't. "Oh, uh, I was just going to call Kendi and then go to bed." I wave awkwardly and leave the room. "'Night."

I wasn't going to call Kendi and then go to bed. But now I am. Now I'm going to call him and ask why it feels like I'm losing them both, like I do want Dad, but on my terms. Like maybe this isn't as easy as holiday cards and family road trips and two parents to conspire with teachers.

Kendi says he sometimes feels like a third wheel with his mom and Michael, too. Then I feel bad because at least I'm a third wheel with my own dad. So we stop talking about parents and instead laugh about how Mrs. Cohen always farts during study hall, like, every day. I fall asleep on the phone, my parents down the hall trying to figure out if they can be something both old and new.

Kids at school are calling Kendi and me lovebirds and making kissing sounds. He's staying with us while Shauna and Michael are in Napa Valley, finally taking a honeymoon two months after their wedding. These stupid kids don't get that we are seriously like brother and sister. Kendi doesn't seem bothered, but he's not the type to stand up for himself. I, on the other hand, am determined to prove them wrong. So I make plans with other friends pretty much every night Kendi is staying with us. I'll show them. No birds here.

The third night Kendi is at our apartment, I stay out late at a basketball game. I don't care much about basketball, but at least I'm proving I do *not* have a crush on Kendi. As a matter of fact, I have a crush on Clarke. Point guard. We've been passing notes in third period.

When I get home after the game, Kendi's still up, eating grapes and reading *The Fellowship of the Ring*. I close the front door behind me. Seth stirs before dropping his head and snoring again. I slip off my sneakers, pop one of Kendi's grapes into my mouth, and look toward the kitchen for Mom, eager to brag about getting home ten minutes before curfew.

Eyes on his book, Kendi says, "She's asleep, I think."

I pat Seth and peek at which chapter Kendi's on. "Liking it?"

"So good."

"Told you."

I look around again and frown. The dishwasher's running, the stove light is on dim, the mail's on the counter, the peppermint bowl is full, and Seth is kicking his back paw in a dream. Everything is as normal as can be.

Except no way would Mom go to sleep before I got home.

But sure enough, her bedroom is dark. I shuffle blindly toward her old orange lamp. Her mantra of *Why use an overhead light when you can use a lamp?* is so ingrained that I don't think twice.

Crossing her bedroom in the dark, I stumble into something with my foot and let out a yelp.

The overhead light gets flipped on behind me, and my heart slams into my chest.

Mom is at my feet in gray-striped pajama pants and a T-shirt from the bookstore. She is folded into an unnatural position, colorless, hair draped across a crooked neck.

I drop. Touch her. Jerk back. She's cold.

I croak out something about 911, but Kendi is already on the phone.

I vomit on the floor.

Then somehow Dad's here, stricken as we watch paramedics hunch over Mom, her finger swollen purple around her new engagement ring.

They pronounce her gone. A couple of hours already. Signs point to cardiac arrest, but an autopsy will confirm.

Twenty minutes ago, everything seemed normal. I took off my shoes. Straightened them the way Mom likes. Ate a grape. A grape! While she was dead on the floor on the other side of the wall.

I enter a trance. Do I answer questions? Ask questions? Do they take her? Do I sleep? Cry? Eat? Pee? At some point, Dad is replaced by Nana. And later, Nana by Shauna.

An obituary is written.

A funeral comes and goes.

Time is broken glass, and I'm stuck in one piece of it—the piece where I still have her.

Dad and Kendi ate dinner with her. I was gone, watching a striped rubber ball bounce back and forth. Nobody realized lasagna would be her last meal. Did she get extra Parmesan like she likes? How could anyone be paying attention to basketball instead of whether Mom got extra Parmesan? Dad went back to his apartment after dinner; he's been busy packing to move in with us. Then Mom told Kendi she was going to rest because one of her headaches was coming on. She asked if he needed anything, and he said, "No, ma'am. Thanks, Ms. B."

That was the last time anyone saw her alive. Dad and Kendi.

It should have been me. It should have been my voice she last heard. If I'd been home, then I might have found her sooner. I might have saved her. I'm furious at Kendi for being there, and for being the reason I wasn't. I can't stand the sight of him.

I saw her that morning and said goodbye as usual. Or did I?

The night after the funeral, I squirt soap onto my toothbrush in my exhaustion. Start brushing. Startle. Gag. Spit. Keep spitting. Make myself throw up. Again. More. As much as I possibly can.

After rinsing, I open the bathroom window. Air—I need air.

Wind slaps me in the face.

No stars. No moon. Just the pitiless wind, and darkness.

2001 to 2002

I WISH DAD DIED INSTEAD.

I move in with him by default, though it soon becomes clear there's no space for me with the alcohol that fills the fridge, his gut, my nightmares. I've never seen him like this. Mom did though, and I can't believe she said yes a second time. Love makes people stupid.

Each bottle cap seems to release the fizz of anger. He wouldn't normally care about the butter being gone or a cabinet handle breaking or my needing a paper signed for school. But now he's impossible to predict. He might shout at his car keys or send a tissue box flying across the room or go completely quiet, barely managing to sit and grunt and nod. I can't keep up, so I keep away.

After a few months of this, Nana takes my chin between her hands and tells me she just got new sheets for her guest room. Jersey knit, my favorite.

The next day, Dad watches me take Seth and leave. His expression reminds me of someone who had a flying dream only to wake up disappointed that it wasn't real. What's real is gravity and a dirty apartment and a daughter zipping her duffel bag.

At Nana's house, she hands me the yellow notepad from beside the curlicue cord of her phone and instructs, "Make a list of what you like to eat and your favorite Blue Bell flavors. Oh, and what kibble to get Seth."

When I give her my list, she puts on her glasses and whispers each item to herself as she reads them over, her chin tucked into her neck. Then she promptly sets off for the store.

A lamp is left on in the guest room. There's a neat stack of towels on a wooden stool beside the shelf with trinkets from her students: a wooden apple, a needlepoint A+, and a WORLD'S BEST TEACHER mug with pencils in it and a lace doily beneath. An extra blanket that smells like laundry detergent is folded at the foot of the bed.

I heave my suitcase onto the bed and welcome Seth to our new home. He blinks at me as if to agree that this will be better than Dad's apartment, where it was always dark. Where the pantry consisted of ramen and expired Cheerios. Where he would barely even look at me.

As if Mom weren't enough, this greedy earth devours, like, three thousand more lives in one gulp when planes crash into the World Trade Center. One of those lives is the aunt of a boy from my school. She was a nurse and probably not an alcoholic. All of these people, but Dad's still here.

The thing about living with Nana is that she makes me go to therapy. Gag. We try one session with Dad and I want to die. Guess I shouldn't talk about death like that, but I kind of think I have the right to talk about it however I want, being bereaved and all.

Okay, I don't want to actually die at the therapy session. But I wouldn't mind digging Mom out and curling up inside her casket, clinging to her rot rather than trying to talk about feelings with a therapist and Dad.

144

He won't talk about her, is the problem. He talks about anything and everything else. Nana says there's an elephant stampede in every room he enters, but he denies that he's getting trampled.

I pass my driving test. I look like Dad in my license photo. Our noses. Nana gives me her Corolla and buys a "new" used one for herself.

I wish Mom were here to criticize my driving and "worry sick." I would bring her back for a day, an hour, a minute, even for just a few screechy seconds of *Georgette Elise, ten and two!* as I grip the steering wheel. I must be selfish—I must not love her enough to let her go. And she must not love me enough to haunt me. She doesn't rattle tables or make doors creak open in the night. She's dead silent. Ha.

Sometimes I fantasize about being careless in the car and letting the crunching metal of traffic pull me under like a tide so that, even if I can't be with her, I won't have to be without her.

When school's out, I sleep all day and night and day again. Nana tries to lure me out of bed with banana bread or a walk with Seth or a documentary about cameras. But I just want sleep. One day is nothing. Even if I wanted to sleep for one week. One month. The thought slides through my brain like a runny egg: one *life* is nothing. Nobody needs me—not during this nap, this day, this lifetime . . .

But then I think of Mom and shake my head into my pillow because no, one life can be everything. Jeez. She makes me want to die but forces me to live. Like, make up your mind already.

From my bed, I can hear Nana in the kitchen. The suction of the refrigerator door. Water running. A fork or something clanking into the sink. I guess I could stand a slice of banana bread. I sit, kick my feet over the edge of the bed, and push myself up.

On the one-year anniversary, I go alone to Mom's grave. It's midday and the sun fries me. I feel my cheeks burning within minutes. There's an anthill near her flat headstone. Do caskets keep bugs out?

I wonder what her hair is like now. When I touched her that night, only her hair felt normal. Not cold or stiff. Just hair. I raked my fingers through it over and over and over. I should have cut some and kept it.

A young tree grows near her grave. Oak, maybe? Not big enough for shade yet. It watches me with my sketchbook like, *Is that all you think I'm good for? Paper?*

Who even decides when and why something dies? A human says, *Okay, tree, enough of your shade and sap and seed, I need you to be paper now.* And something stronger than a human says, *Okay, human, enough of your work and love and life, I need you to be fertilizer now.*

On a dead tree, I sketch the living one. It's only a baby. This paper could be its mom or sister or friend. I rip out the drawing and bury it and wonder if maybe I'm going a little crazy.

2004 to 2005

I LIKE WATCHING THE OAK GROW FROM MOM'S GRAVE more than I like high school.

My grades drop like acorns.

Teachers try to extend due dates, but their sympathy makes me irate. When Ms. Collier offers me a test to retake, I rip it up in her face. Her horrified expression and manicured appearance reveal how fresh she is from the sorority house. She gapes like I'm a gorilla loosed from my cage. All I want is to be treated the same as kids who don't have dead moms.

One day, I come home to milk and freshly baked sugar cookies, and I know something's up.

Nana scoots a chair out for me and pats the seat. "Georgette, I don't want to tell you what to do."

She says this when she's about to tell me what to do.

"You're too smart not to finish high school. You used to want to be a doctor, you know."

I wish people wouldn't tell me about myself like I need a reminder. I'm not saying I haven't forgotten; I'm saying let me forget.

But Nana's too good to me. She does things like notice a hole in my sock and then leave a package of new socks on my dresser the next day, the Big Lots price tag carefully torn off. She cooks brisket with corn on the cob every weekend because she knows it's my favorite.

"Okay." I wipe milk from my upper lip and swallow. "I'll finish."

I go back to Ms. Sorority and ask how I can graduate. She sends me to the guidance counselor, who talks to my teachers. I'll need to do an economics paper, a calculus test, and a physics project. The counselor says I won't get to walk in the spring graduation ceremony but that I could get everything done in summer school and graduate in August.

I don't ask, *Then what?* I don't say that watching other people's college acceptance letters fly around like confetti makes me never want to go to class. I didn't apply for college. I don't have the grades or the will or the money for that. Medical school was a pipe dream. There's nothing I want to learn now except how to rewind the world.

Seriously, what would that be like? I don't think it would go very well. Take, for example, people. Everyone got up in arms when Justin accidentally showed Janet's boob for a split second; meanwhile, hundreds of thousands of people die from AIDS and tsunamis and things like cardiac arrest. Maybe we'd all still focus on the wrong things even if we could go back in time—covering boobs instead of unbreaking hearts. I wonder how far forward we'd need to go to know what we should have done differently.

No, school won't do anything for me because there isn't anything I want to do. There's no point in finishing. But—for Nana—I learn about scarcity and derivatives and refraction, how light can bend.

It's senior picture day. I wear my black V-neck dress and Mom's silver necklace with the drop-down thing. Sully calls it a "beautiful choice."

Sully's my boyfriend. He has a smattering of freckles across the bridge of his nose that I secretly play dot-to-dot with when he talks. After pictures, he comes with me to the cemetery. The sky is an uninterrupted blue. This is a bad idea, but he asked so sweetly. Bringing him to my mom's grave feels more intimate than bringing him to my bed. Which I also did because he asked so sweetly.

He kisses me with my mother's cadaver a few feet below. He touches her necklace as if he knew her. As if he knows me. His finger on the silver on my chest is like an IV of pity I want to rip out. Instead, I let the freckles center me. I imagine tracing a long line from one nostril to below his other eye. I tilt my head. I've made an almost-complete drawing of a lizard across his face. I try not to smile about the freckle lizard as he says something trite but sincere about Mom.

At long last, I drive him home and speed back to the cemetery, hundreds of quiet histories, quiet mouths, mine to sit with. No boyfriend with his never-ending stream of kisses and platitudes.

The school counselor says I'll get my diploma on August twentieth.

My insane first thought is that Mom will want to celebrate and make a big thing of it.

Then, in the split second it takes for a stomach to drop, I remember.

On August twentieth, I sit at Nana's wrought-iron table on the back patio and show my diploma to Seth. He pants and nuzzles me, a deviation from his usual lick-bark-lick greeting.

Nana joins us, lighting a citronella candle. We eat brisket tender enough for no knives, and she says, "Your mom would be proud."

I smile weakly. Even if it's true, I cringe when people speak for the dead.

As for the living, Dad leaves me a message and says he knew I could do it. I delete it.

Swallowing a bite of brisket, Nana also says—more to herself than me—"Need to schedule you a dentist appointment this summer."

There are two things my grandmother seems to need in life: ice cream and to manage details the way she wants. So I don't say, *I hate the dentist* or *My teeth are fine.* I nod submissively if only to avoid the circle of anxiety disguised as logic that she'd lead us around before eventually getting me to the dentist anyway. Little things become overly important to her when she can't control them, so I resign myself to my dental fate and tell Nana that the brisket is delicious. Besides, with all the ice cream we eat, I probably do need a dentist appointment.

Spearing little yellow holders into the ends of my corncob, I watch Seth romp in the sunny spot near Nana's vegetable garden, where he keeps a pile of drool-soaked tennis balls. He snaps his jowl and clamps down on air, inches away from any ball. He's struggling with depth perception.

Later, I decide to let him sleep in bed with me. Mom would never approve. Too bad for her, she's not here to tell us no. She should've thought about that before she went and died.

I slide my diploma into a drawer and snuggle up beside my good boy.

Shauna has invited me out to lunch every month since Mom died. I can count on one hand the number of times I've gone. I always expect her to say something like, "So Kendi tells me you look away when you see him at school." But she never mentions him. Kendi and I have said little more than "Hey" in passing. Once, at my locker, he asked if I had the study guide for our Spanish exam. I didn't.

But high school is over now, and Shauna's lunch invitations continue. Aren't I—a high school graduate and legal adult—now mature enough to see her without getting moody about Mom or Kendi?

There's one other reason I accept Shauna's invitation this time: she invites me to Kincaid's. She knows perfectly well that I can't turn down a Kincaid's burger.

It always surprises me, the flood of comfort when I see Shauna. Her frizzy hair and bold clothes and loud laugh. Her hug and how, even though she's a talker, she's also a listener. Over fries and ketchup and juicy burgers, we cover graduation and Nana and Seth. A little about Sully, his kindness and how he for some reason adores me. I tell her about applying for jobs even as I scan the restaurant for a hiring sign. Discounts on cattleman burgers? Yes please.

I don't tell Shauna how often I make myself throw up; I don't tell anyone this.

Pat Green sings to us from the restaurant speakers. Shauna and Michael are doing well. They went to Mexico over the summer. A little beach time while working at a medical clinic in Chihuahua for a month. She recounts a story about Michael being propositioned by a highly medicated patient before she noticed his wedding band, turned beet red, and promptly fell asleep. Shauna, having heard the whole thing, sashayed over to give Michael a dramatic kiss and sing "The Boy Is Mine" to the unconscious woman. I really do love her.

Despite my affection—and relief when she doesn't prod me to talk about Mom or Kendi or even Dad—when she calls me again the month after Kincaid's, I make an excuse. And the next month. And the next. She's a wave in an ocean of reminders, and I am quietly drowning.

I should be over Mom's death by now, but some piece of me is stuck in that night. I wade through time even while trying to turn into her bedroom and tell her I'm home before curfew. Listening for her laugh to bubble up. For the teakettle to whistle on a rainy morning. Or for the weird good-morning song she sang. Did she make that song up? How can I not know this? One death is a thousand others—the death of songs and tea and rain. If she had to go, I wish she'd go already. She's nowhere but everywhere. In the sky and the kitchen and Shauna. And Dad.

I miss him too, but that's different. When I'm away from him, I want to see him. When I see him, I want to get away from him. He's as drunk as ever. I have no idea how he maintains his job. I pulled my photography from the gallery. He doesn't get the daughter's work if he doesn't want the daughter. If he decides he wants me, I'm right here. All he has to do is not drink.

His problem is that he loved Mom too much. When I do see him, he can barely look at me because his eyes overflow with her, crowding out everything else. Her absence blinds him. She's haunting me after all, but instead of knocked-over furniture it's a knocked-out dad. Seeing him makes me think that maybe it's not alcohol I should be swearing off. Maybe it's love.

2005 to 2006

SULLY'S IN TOWN FOR THE HOLIDAY BREAK, AND COLLEGE in New York looks good on him.

We sit outside Cowtown Cup, where I've been working for a couple of months now. I zip my coat as high as I can, teeth chattering. Sully's cheeks are nicely rosy, the cold weather making him look even hotter than usual.

He breaks a cinnamon scone in half and holds the halves out for me to choose. "Have you ever thought about coming to New York?"

I pick a half and don't hesitate. "No. My least favorite things are crowds and cold." The scone is warm and delicious.

Sully chews slowly and gets uncharacteristically serious. Then he says the distance is too hard. I focus on his freckles. He becomes distraught. It takes me a minute to understand what's happening.

I act sad, kiss his cheek, and think about kissing Mom's cheek.

Oh, poor Sully. He never had a chance.

It's over once he runs out of deliberations and apologies. It all seems unnecessarily dramatic. He can't possibly feel this deeply when I feel so little of anything.

———

153

Nana drags it out of me the next day when Sully doesn't come over. She cooks chicken pot pie and says, with mitts on both hands, "No harm in some comfort food." She tells me there are "plenty of other fish in the sea." I'm not worried about other fish one bit, but the flaky pie full of bird is a nice gesture anyway.

When she suggests, "Maybe you should try something different with your hair," I fire back, "Or maybe Sully should. All that well-groomed red was really hard on our relationship." She sighs, raising her fork to her lips.

For Christmas, it's just the two of us. I give her a Miles Davis record, and she gives me a photography book. I fake gratitude. Photography is another thing in my life that's dead and buried forever. Nana tries to wrest it out of its grave, but that's not how life works. Or, I don't know about life, but that's not how death works.

She leaves a message for Dad. He doesn't call back. I don't know why she tries.

With Miles on the Garrard, we bake cinnamon rolls and half-heartedly check what movies are playing and never change out of the red-and-green pajamas Nana found on clearance at T.J.Maxx.

The day after Christmas, Shauna calls me. The Darnells are planning a "small" New Year's celebration at their house. Dinner, sparklers, noise-makers, champagne, sparkling grape juice for kids, that sort of thing. Can Elise and I come?

"Let me get back to you." I don't plan to get back to her.

But Nana overhears and says, "We should go!"

"Not interested."

"Why not?"

"Because I won't know people and don't like staying up late?"

"Jet."

"Nana."

"You need to get out more."

"It's not a good night for it. Seth hates fireworks. He'll need me."

"Seth'll be fine."

"Oh my gosh, you need to drop this like the ball in Times Square."

She laughs but says again, "We should go."

After two more days of this, she is scrubbing a skillet and asks me to look at her. "Forget the party, dear. I have something to say, and I want you to listen."

I raise my eyebrows.

"The living have living to do."

Jeez, if it means this much to her.

I call Shauna and say we'll be there. Only at this point do I find out she invited Dad. Great, Shauna. Invite the alcoholic to a party where people will be toasting the New Year. Whatever.

Nana buys me a "new" secondhand dress for the occasion, which is beyond unnecessary. She's ecstatic that I'm doing something besides serving coffee or reading in bed with Seth.

The dress is very not me. It's New Year's Eve–y: short, tight, and shiny black with gold loopy stitching. I wear sneakers with it because I must draw the line somewhere. It gives me a hit of satisfaction when Nana complains about my shoe choice.

I straighten my hair, swipe on mascara, and sigh at my reflection. Let's get this over with.

When we walk into their doctor's-salary house with the soaring ceilings, Shauna grabs my shoulders and examines me up and down. Her raspy voice is animated with party and booze. "You look hot, girl!"

I blush. Michael steps forward with a knowing look and generously shows me to the appetizers. After filling my plate with mozzarella sticks,

I scan the room for Nana, who hasn't progressed far from the foyer and is being a social butterfly.

If she's a butterfly, then I'm a slug trying to slink unnoticed along the border of the room. But Nana calls me over with, "Oh, Georgette dear, have you met the Calloways?" and, "You know my granddaughter here is a talented photographer," and that sort of unbearable thing. She's a modest woman, but she's of an age when everyone talks like that in social settings, their noses lifted like they're pulled by puppet strings.

It doesn't surprise me that there's no sign of Dad. I am surprised, however, that there's no sign of the main reason I tried to avoid this party in the first place—Kendi.

My relief at his absence turns into curiosity. I find myself watching doorways and people rounding corners. Shauna, who knows me too well, sneaks up behind me and says low, "Your dad or Kendi?"

"What?"

"You looking for your dad or Kendi?"

Both. "Neither."

She looks at me pointedly, so I say, "Both. But not because I want to see either of them."

"I know, honey." She lays a hand on my shoulder. "Well, I can't speak for your dad, but Kendi won't be here."

"Oh?" I try to sound casual.

"When I told him you were coming, he thought it might make you more comfortable if he made himself scarce."

"He didn't have to do that." I'm certain he'd be annoyed that Shauna told me.

Before she can respond, we see Michael escorting Dad in from the foyer. Knots of dread form instantaneously in my shoulders. He doesn't appear rip-roaring drunk, so at least there's that.

Wow. My New Year's Eve—my life, really—is trying to avoid the best friend who was there when Mom died and the dad who wasn't there when she was alive.

Before Dad sees me, I disappear into the bathroom, make myself throw up my half-digested mozzarella sticks, rinse my mouth, swipe under my eyes, come back out, and beg the gods in charge of grandmothers to make Nana ready to leave soon. But then I spot her, mid-conversation and holding a plate loaded with black-eyed peas and stuffed mushrooms. That's when Dad approaches me.

"Hey, Jet."

"Hey."

At the same time, we both ask, "How are you?"

We both look down and mumble until I look up and say, "I'm fine. Wild parties with Nana. You?"

He laughs, and I'm pleased with myself for that. Maybe I can keep him laughing instead of drinking.

"You look beautiful, by the way. So grown-up."

Heat dots my cheeks. I shrug and fidget and look around for Nana or anyone to save me, but nobody's paying attention to us. "Thanks. Uh, so how's the SG?" That's always safe.

He lights up the faintest bit, like somebody raised a dimmer switch. "It's good. We had our big annual fundraiser, and it was the best turnout we've ever had. And we're about to get a cool anime display that I think will draw in a younger crowd. It'll coincide with a new exhibit at the Kimbell, so we expect traffic from all over the metroplex."

"Cool." *Yeah, I can't do this.* "Well, Nana's probably getting tired. I'm going to find her." I walk away without waiting for a response.

I keep Dad in my peripheral vision as I tell Nana I'm ready to go. It seems like she's fixing to argue, but then she looks at me and stops before she starts. We say goodbye to the Darnells and make our way to the door. Nana turns. "Shoot. Forgot my shawl. Be right back."

"I'll wait out front." It's not a cold night.

I sink to the porch step between deflating balloons that are bobbing like silver phantoms. There's a round of bottle rocket blasts, and I turn away from the fireworks. When the door opens behind me, I stand, expecting Nana. But it's Dad pulling the door closed behind him. "Jet?"

"Dad?"

"I don't care about New Year's Eve."

"Uh, okay? I don't either. That's why I'm leaving."

"I didn't come here because of New Year's. I came because of you."

"Not really sure what to do with that. Plus, it's getting late."

"It's ten thirty. On New Year's Eve. You're eighteen years old. Don't you—"

"Nineteen."

"What?"

"I'm nineteen. Like, six months now." My eyes bore holes into his absence, so present between us.

"Right." He brushes past it. "You're nineteen. It's not that late. We're both here. You should stay."

"Why? So I can keep hearing all the things you don't know about me?"

"I knew you turned nineteen. I just . . ." He pushes away the air in front of him like he can't be bothered with birthdays or oxygen or finishing sentences.

"You could have been there on my birthday. That might have helped you remember." The only birthday he's ever celebrated with me was my fifteenth, with the puppy chow and proposal.

I look past him toward the house, craning to peer through the window and aware by now that Nana did this on purpose. A gecko slithers up the window, intercepting the glare meant for my grandmother.

Dad looks pained, which is like kerosene to my fire.

"Okay fine," I concede.

"Fine what?"

"Fine, I'll stay." Hope colors his pain. "If," I add, "you can tell me when you last had a drink." Words are leaping to my mouth like a lion to prey.

His jaw tightens. "It wasn't today."

I slow clap, rage wanting out like vomit. "Oh, good job!"

He holds eye contact. "I won't lie. I drank last night. But not today, because I wanted to come here and see you."

I can't overlook the *I won't lie*. "I appreciate your honesty. But I'm just . . ." I pinch the bridge of my nose. "I'm . . ." I exhale. "I'm tired and I'm going to go. I've got a dog and"—I gesture toward the house with Nana somewhere inside—"a grandmother."

He lets out a "Ha!" Then he says, "Your grandmother is also my mother, and no matter how old she is, she shuts parties down. If y'all are leaving before midnight, then it's because of you, not her. If we're being honest, let's be honest." There's a bite to his words. Neither of us has the long temper Mom has. Had.

"You're right. I'm a young woman out on New Year's Eve. I should be enjoying myself." My feet inch backward while my words creep forward to the bleeding edge. "But I'm not. Because I'm tired. Exhausted, actually. And that? Is because of you."

I see on his face that this cuts like I want it to. Satisfaction and regret fistfight within me, but I can't stop now. "I'm not Mom. I'm not going to give you chance after chance and pretend there's not a problem."

Actually, maybe I'd regret that more if I didn't say it. I keep my chin high.

"Georgette Elise Bright." My full name doesn't belong in his mouth like that, but it still quiets me. "Your mother didn't pretend there wasn't a problem. She just"—his voice breaks like her heart—"loved me anyway."

"Whatever." I cross my arms and look away. "I'm not her, and she's not here."

Fireworks bang the sky like a drum. We look toward them, remembering Mom's sky-held name as though its flaming letters are licking up our skin, branding us as hers whether we like it or not. We belong to the unending loss of her.

The front door opens, and Nana steps out. Breezy, she says, "So what are—"

"Took you long enough. Let's go." My clipped words hit staccato against her.

I walk away, ignoring whatever look they might exchange. I'm not the long-suffering wife or the loyal mother. I'm the daughter he didn't want. Twice.

It's almost eleven o'clock when we get home. Nana kisses the top of my head with a doting, defeated exhale that says there's no point in staying up now. She has the good sense not to talk about Dad, and she patters toward bed, mumbling about how it seems like just yesterday she was reading me Little Golden Books in the playpen at bedtime. *The Poky Little Puppy* or *Tawny Scrawny Lion*.

On the East Coast, it's already 2006, another year ready to come and go like a tidal wave.

I take Seth out back. He's jittery from the fireworks and keeps looking back to make sure I'm nearby. I flip my phone open and scroll down. Mom's still there, my last *M* contact. I scroll back up a little. Kendi's still there too. Our moms took us to pick our first cell phones together. A navy Nokia and a silver one. We were so excited that instead of hanging out, we went home just so we could call each other. Then we hung up to add contacts and play *Snake*.

My fingers stall at his name, moving of their own accord: HEY. HAPPY NEW YEAR.

Almost immediately: HEY. THANKS. U 2.

That's it?

I send another: YOU CAN GO HOME NOW BTW. I'M GONE.

A few minutes later: DIDN'T WANNA RUIN YOUR NIGHT.

Ha. Dad took care of that.

My phone buzzes again: I'M AT OUR PARK. PARTYING WITH SNACKS AND A BOOK.

I gnaw my lip and follow my impulse: CAN I JOIN?

I'll have to face him eventually. Might as well be now.

But he doesn't respond. He might have been considering my

comfort when he fled the party, but I'm sure he doesn't want to see me either.

Then a buzz: BRING ICE CREAM IF U HAVE IT.

I smile. I live with Elise Brighton. Of course I have ice cream.

I take Seth inside, whisper goodnight to him, and grab a pint of Blue Bell Homemade Vanilla from the overcrowded freezer. I open the dishwasher and yank out two spoons.

Kendi is exactly where I pictured, sitting on the old picnic table.

As I approach, he does a barely perceptible double take. Oh, right. I'm still in my party dress and it's been a while since we've seen each other. I hope he doesn't think this is how I normally dress now.

He looks different, with fuller muscles where there used to be lanky limbs. He still dresses the same though: jeans and a T-shirt. Despite the time and pain and change, this is the boy I grew up with. We don't have to fake pleasantries. By way of greeting, I hold up the ice cream. "Provisions."

"Sweet," he says intentionally, before adding, "Nice kicks." I glance down at my sneakers. Without saying anything else, we dig into the ice cream, silence more comfortable than the words waiting beyond the bottom of that cardboard pint. Our childhood ghosts toss a Frisbee in front of us, our moms beside us on the bench that's now a slab of cement with a Comanche historic plaque.

A group of kids shoot a firework. Spooning a bite into my mouth, I ask through frozen cream, "Hey, remember that one New Year's?"

He grins.

"With the pistachios!" we say at the same time, laughing.

My hair blows in my face, so I clip it back as I say, "There was also the one before Michael, when we thought we could set your mom up with that famous actor guy. What was his name again?"

"Totally forgot about that. Dave Mercury?"

"Dan! Dan Mercury. We wrote, like, five letters and sent a picture of her and everything."

Kendi shakes his head. "She'd kill me if she knew about that."

"I'm sure some staffer just threw it in the fan mail stack with all the rest."

"All the rest? I never thought he was one of those heartthrob types."

"Oh, Dan Mercury was *so* hot."

Kendi chuckles and shrugs. "I don't see it. Besides"—sincerity infuses the moment—"only Michael deserves Mom."

I face him. "So things are good? With your family?"

The ice cream is gone. I shiver, lick a sticky finger, and drop my spoon into the empty container, which makes it topple over.

"They're great. He still thinks Mom's an angel straight from heaven." The sheen of memory draws him in a different direction. "There was also the New Year's with Ben and Cassidy."

"Oh, man." I bite my nail.

That year, our moms let us go to a party at a friend's lake house. The "supervising" parents were having their own party in the house while we were all out by the lake with our middle-school, braces-mouthed, hormone-filled flirting. Kids were sneaking alcohol from inside, but Kendi and I didn't see the appeal. We were laser-focused on our plan: we were each going to kiss someone at midnight.

Earlier that day, Kendi and I decided over AIM to kiss each other for practice. Neither of us had ever kissed anybody *like that*. When he suggested the practice kiss, I responded with, "Wouldn't that make us married?" We LOLed and then, a couple of hours later, we did it. Warm, wet lips. No tongue. That year, I was taller than he was, so I bent my knees a bit. Embarrassed, we both said, "Good job" and "Good luck tonight." Then at midnight, he kissed Cassidy, I kissed Ben, and later we compared notes. Ben tasted like pepperoni, and Cassidy tasted the way margaritas smell. Ben used tongue, and Cassidy didn't. We both found braces and the post-kiss moment to be unpleasant.

"We were so dumb." I laugh.

162

Wind blows the empty ice cream container off the table, the spoon clanking on cement below.

The kids across the park start shouting. I check my phone and wave the screen at Kendi. Midnight. 2006. "Happy New Year."

"You too." He pauses. "Hey . . ."

No, Kendi. Don't do it. I scan the catalog of my brain for another fun memory to keep the others away. Laughter is so nice. But I come up blank and can only say, "Yeah?"

He pauses long, stares at his feet, then looks straight at me. "I'm sorry I didn't save her."

My eyes prickle, and I shut them tight. But eyelids are no protection against the screaming sight of it: bumping into her, dropping down, touching touching touching her hair, her blue-gray skin, her bent neck, Kendi behind me, my own vomit in my hair, the room filling with an assault of light and people.

I look away from Kendi and try not to hyperventilate as he continues, "I'm sorry I was there and you weren't. I'm sorry I didn't sense anything was wrong." He swipes a finger under his nose and sniffles. "I want nothing more than to bring her back. My dad, I never had to lose him. But your mom, she—and you—" He presses knuckles into the corners of his eyes.

A mascara-tinged tear drops from my chin to my knee. I hadn't realized I was crying.

This is the first time I've considered Kendi's pain. Was I seriously upset with him? Was it the only way I could make sense of Mom's death? By landing blame on one of the only people I trust?

The past can't change. But memory can, which is almost the same thing. I suck in air and say, "You couldn't have done anything differently." It's the first time I've believed this.

He stares at me raw, eyes like glass, allowing me to see his regret. He has needed this absolution for years. "Still." He hauls a heavy breath across the air, searching for where to set it down. "I wish it were different."

I let out a bitter fraction of a laugh and wipe my eyes, leaning back and away from the weight of it all as I quip, "Title of my memoir."

He chuckles, sad. The kids and fireworks have quieted.

I exhale. "Saw my dad at your house."

"How is he?"

"Same."

Kendi crinkles his nose. "That sucks. Sorry."

I shrug. "Hey." I nudge him. "I haven't heard about school. Tell me."

Kendi just finished the first semester of an aerospace engineering degree at LeTourneau. He left our world for one behind the Pine Curtain where he has both money and motivation for an impressive degree. This is when the lives of childhood friends diverge.

"School's good. Basic classes for now. But the cafeteria has decent food, and my professors and friends are cool."

"Any *special* friends?"

He raises an amused eyebrow as I hear myself, laugh, and explain, "Too much Nana."

He does have a special friend, in fact. Leah, who's also working toward an aviation degree. They've been together for two months.

I tell him about the breakup with Sully, but that it was never serious.

He hesitates, searching for something else to ask me. I'm sure he knows enough: no college, living with Nana, barista even though I don't like coffee. Soon our lives will be so different that we'll have nothing to talk about at all.

He asks, "Still taking photos?"

"Not really."

"You should."

I sigh. "Nana says that too."

He puts his hands up in surrender. "We know how talented you are."

I hop down, picking up our trash and spoons. "Hey, thanks for hanging out. Maybe I can come visit your dorm sometime or something?"

"Yeah, sure thing." He gathers his stuff, and we walk quietly to the parking lot.

"Well." He shrugs. "'Night."

"See you soon?"

He smiles. "See you soon."

I toss the empty ice cream pint into a trash can and watch Kendi leave.

Mom's still dead. Dad's still drunk. But I think I got my best friend back.

2007

WHEN I ARRIVE AT SHAUNA'S HOUSE TO PICK HER UP
for lunch, she waves me inside.

"Sorry, lost track of time."

I step into her house, where she's in a hot-pink bathrobe. There are three garbage bags labeled GOODWILL on the foyer tile, with a pile of clothes beside.

I set my keys on the entry table and step over a bag. "No rush. I'm off all day."

She throws back her last sip of coffee and says, "Let me run up and get ready. Makeup is a necessity at my age, but I'll be lickety-split."

I laugh. "Don't worry about it."

She notices me eyeing the clothes and says, "Finally cleaning out clothes Kendi left behind. Good riddance to his whole only-wear-black phase, right?" She takes her mug to the kitchen.

"He had an only-wear-black phase?"

She pops back around the corner, pulling her hair out of a messy ponytail and frowning. "You don't remember? It must have lasted almost a year in high school." She clomps up the stairs as she adds, "The same year he refused to cut his hair."

I'm left to wait with sunshine pouring through the front windows, illuminating every speck of lint on the black oversized clothes that apparently were Kendi's. I squat down and riffle through them. I have a vague memory of his hair being long, but I honestly don't remember him dressing like this. A year of grunge from predictable and clean-cut Kendi? Then again, I hardly remember how I dressed in high school. I wore whatever Nana gave me or whatever I'd slept in, my personal little revolt against a material world that no longer included the mother who used to dress me in matching jumpers and bows.

Shauna hollers from the top of the stairs. "How do pancakes sound?"

"I'm always up for pancakes."

"Ol' South?"

"Sounds great."

"Two minutes!" I hear a door close upstairs.

My stomach growls, and suddenly I want to run to the bathroom and purge it entirely. I want to call Kendi and ask if he's okay, if he was okay, what the black was about. I want to go to my ninth birthday party and tell Mom that I'll never outgrow our matching outfits.

Shauna finds me holding one of the black shirts, and I set it down. "I don't remember him dressing like this."

"You had a lot going on."

"I guess." I had nothing going on. That was the problem.

She rummages for her purse. "Kendall lost himself there for a while, but everyone has their journeys."

"Lost himself?"

Makeup now on her face and purse now on her shoulder, Shauna studies me as if assessing my level of frailty before confiding, "Along with his appearance, he abandoned all things aviation. He quit soccer, and he didn't go out. All he did was play video games."

I shake my head in disbelief, missing him sharply even though I was with him in East Texas just last month. "But he"—I borrow her language—"found himself?"

"Michael sat him down and talked about the choices in front of him, choices from Michael's own past, I don't know. After that, Kendi looked into aviation programs and started playing soccer again. It was still months before his wardrobe showed any hint of color." She looks down at the old black clothes in her foyer. "It's not like we wanted button-ups and khakis. That wasn't him either. But the first day he came down in plain blue jeans again, I squeezed Michael's arm in relief."

My stomach resumes growling.

"Goodness, I've made you wait long enough. Ol' South, here we come." She claps her hands together and ushers me out through the maze of donations.

We walk to my car, and I don't tell her that I disagree. That I hear her relief, but I would never say good riddance. I'd say, *This is you too* and *Don't forget any of it* and *I see you* and *Tell me everything.*

Later, I text Kendi: REMEMBER YOUR GRUNGE PHASE?

His response: HA. YEAH. REMEMBER YOUR K-CI AND JOJO SHIRT EVERY SINGLE DAY PHASE?

I smile wide. Sixth grade.

I wonder what phases are still ahead. And in this moment, it doesn't exhaust me to imagine the future.

2009

I STUMBLE ACROSS MY CAMERA IN AN OLD BOX LABELED
BOOKS. I get it out to sell, but one thing leads to another.

Neither Nana nor Kendi gloats. They temper their gushing about my new photos. Well, Nana tempers it. Kendi toes the line, saying stupid stuff like, "I've never seen such an incredible photo of dough," and meaning it. That dough photo did turn out pretty okay. It's of Nana baking bread. Dough fills most of the frame, but the focus is on her floury, kneading fingers. The morning light through the kitchen blinds made perfect highlights.

A few months after my camera's resurrection, I find myself getting hired for jobs. I do end up selling my camera—to buy a new one. A Cowtown Cup friend helps me set up a website. When a well-known company commissions me for their annual paper calendar, I barely rein myself in before saying, *People still make those?* I also barely rein myself in before saying, *You want* me *to do it?*

I take the calendar gig. It will be good money, great for my portfolio, and a fun break from making espressos. I need a series of nature-themed photographs from anywhere in the state, so I call Kendi and suggest Palo Duro. We're already planning a trip to celebrate his graduation from college, so I propose a two-birds-one-stone trip. We'll hike and celebrate, and I'll take photos for the calendar.

"Never been," he says. "I'm in."

Leah and Kendi have been on-again-off-again all throughout college. They're "on" when we plan the trip, so we invite her. I like Leah. She's a great fit for Kendi and easy to talk to.

But the night before we hit the road, they're "off" again. Kendi texts me after midnight that it's "going to stick this time." I don't know whether this is good or bad, but I'm sure I'll find out.

The closest I've been to a relationship since Sully is with enchiladas from Joe T. Garcia's, and I'm perfectly happy with this. Kendi is different though. Every time he and Leah break up, he gets all introspective and withdrawn.

Our trip is four days, and the first three are perfect. Cool but sunny. Wind isn't bad. Clear skies, ideal for photos. We take beautiful hikes at both golden hours. Seth would have loved this. When Kendi says he's sorry I had to get Stethoscope put down, I thank him. I don't tell him how desperately I made myself throw up that night or how every death intensifies every other death. I don't want to think about death on this trip; I want to think about shutter speed and camp breakfasts.

Waking before dawn on the second day, we hike the Lighthouse Trail and get to the iconic rock formation as the sky yawns awake, the sun like a yellow tongue. I click furiously to capture the iridescent rock. It's a gorgeous morning, the canyon a brassy, brightening place. One of these photos will be the calendar cover.

Kendi and I oscillate comfortably between silence and conversation. We admire road runners and aoudads. Once, we come around a bend to a clearing where four deer look up at us not five feet away. They stare without moving, one with magnificent antlers. Then they go back to grazing. I take no pictures of them.

We crawl through percolation caves, red-flowing streams, and prickly pear. The trip feels like my first exhale in years, the power of earth and air and friendship.

Kendi is reluctant to talk about what happened with Leah this time. I drop it because I don't want anything to exist besides us, the canyon, subdued breezes, red clay, sunshine, my Canon 5D Mark II, and the deer.

Kendi camps often with Michael, so he brought cooking gear. When it gets too dark for photos, we head back to our site, peel off shoes and socks, and lament bug bites or sunburns. Kendi cooks dinner under the branches of two juniper trees. I give him aloe vera for his pink nose and athletic tape for his sore ankle. When he asks if I still always carry this first aid stuff around, I shrug and say, "You know me." And the truth is that he does.

I doubt anything in the world could be better than campfire, photography, and Kendi. I never think about throwing up, and I sleep hard each night—I'd say like a corpse except it's very different from a corpse. It's the sleep of life.

After open-air hammocks the first few nights, we unpack Kendi's tent from the bed of his Ranger and set it up for our last night. Rain's coming.

In that tent in the middle of the last night, I bolt upright, frantic, sweating, breathless. It wakes Kendi. I whisper-apologize and say it's nothing, even as I try to catch my breath.

He scoots toward me, concern radiating through the dark. The silhouette of his hair sticks up in all different directions, and his sleepy voice pulls itself toward waking. "What's wrong?"

Rain patters the tent.

I swallow. "I have nightmares sometimes." Embarrassment adds to my disorientation. "The night with Mom or when I lived with Dad after. I just need to catch my breath. Sorry."

His hand draws calming circles on my back, and he offers me his water bottle. "How often do you have them?"

"Every month or two." I guzzle water. "Used to be every couple of days." I screw the lid back on the water bottle.

It's quiet except for the rain. Then he asks, "What was it this time?"

I sigh, still shaky. "Mom. The way she looked."

"I have nightmares about that too."

I turn to face him in the dark. "You do?"

He drops his hand to his lap. "Only a few hours before she died, she was humming while loading forks into the dishwasher." He takes a slow breath like a cigarette drag. "And then she . . . I didn't know if . . . just . . . her face was so . . ." He swallows the ends of those thoughts like knives.

Of course it was terrible for him. Obviously it's not the same, but she was a second mother figure dead in front of him while his best friend retched out her metastasizing realization of what was happening. He was a kid. He was there. He lost something too. I remember the pile of black clothes in his mother's house.

Handing his water bottle back to him, I ask, "What was she humming?"

"Oh," he exhales. "She was straight-up humming Kenny G."

I burst into laughter. Kenny G! I used to hear her listen to Kenny G when she'd do her makeup in the bathroom. At first she tried to pretend it wasn't true, that I'd misheard. But I guess she grew into her own skin because eventually she would just shrug and say, "What's wrong with enjoying a little smooth jazz?" And now I've learned she was humming it in her last hours of life.

My heart seizes a new thought: maybe she died happy. Maybe she was okay without me, and I can be okay without her. I shake my head. "Of course it was Kenny G."

I feel sheltered by Kendi and our tent and this perfect trip. I hug him long. His presence on the night of Mom's death used to feel like a betrayal, but now it feels like a gift. Time can wash dirt off a memory until it is revealed as something else entirely.

I lie down. We're planning one more hike tomorrow if the weather agrees. Kendi lies close and tells me to have sweet dreams.

This time, I dream of being with Mom in the canyon. We ride majestic Clydesdales, no saddles. She looks back at me and smiles. I tell her that I dreamed she died. But she assures me, "I'm right here," and our horses break into a canter.

Rain falls steadily through dawn. Kendi is awake early, reading by the light of a colorless sky. *The Name of the Wind.* The sleeve of his gray thermal is dotted with campfire ash. I sit up and slip a damp Cowtown Cup hoodie over my head. "Still want to do a hike if it lightens up?"

"Sure. Even if we don't pack up until after lunch, we'll still get back to F-Dub before sundown." He keeps reading.

I look closer. "You okay? Sorry again about waking you."

He rests his book upside down on his lap. "Don't apologize. Nobody chooses a nightmare."

I move a scrunchie from my wrist into a sloppy ponytail. "You didn't get much sleep though, did you?"

He looks down and mindlessly runs the corner of his book underneath a fingernail. "It's okay."

I know he's sleepy and it's storming, but there is some other cloud hanging over him. "Hey." I wait for him to look up. "What's on your mind?"

"Nothing."

"Leah?"

"I'm fine. Just tired."

"We don't have to hike. You can sleep right now." I think about the drive home and mutter, "Wish I could drive a stick."

He waves me off, looking down again.

I have a decent read on people in general, but I am very literate in

173

Kendall Darnell. Something is definitely off. I sit cross-legged on top of my sleeping bag, and thunder rolls like the sky is placing a wager.

"Kendi." I wait for him to look at me again. "Tell me what's up."

He closes his book decidedly, holds my gaze, grinds his teeth, and inhales. "Remember when those kids called us lovebirds?"

I half frown, half smile in confusion. I had blamed those kids for that night too, back when I blamed everybody because it was too hard to blame nobody. I don't know why in the world he's bringing them up now. "Yeah?"

"They weren't totally wrong. I did have a crush on you."

I blink. "I mean, lots of friends have crushes as kids. Wh—"

"Leah dumped me because of you."

"What? Why?"

"She felt like nobody could compare to my best friend."

"But Leah and I got along great. I never knew she had a problem with me." The rain crescendos. "Is that why you guys broke up any of the other times?"

"Every time."

"Wow, I had no idea." I frown. "It's not really fair to put that on me, though."

"That's not even close to what I'm trying to do."

"What are you trying to do, then?"

There's fire in his cheeks, an edge of impatience in his voice fueled by having to yell over the rain that's now pelting our nylon dome. He sits straighter. "I'm trying to tell you she was right. I'm trying to tell you . . ." He stares straight at me for one, two, three exhales. ". . . that nobody can compare to you. That I love you."

I can hardly breathe. All I feel is fear. I can't lose Kendi again. He's just hurting and confused from his breakup. I measure my words. "It makes sense that you feel this way. We're like siblings. We've grown up together, so of course we love each oth—"

"No, Jet." He rises to his knees. "I'm in love with you." He inches closer, cheeks as pink as a sunset. He's doing that thing people do when they sound mad even as they say nice things. He gets close enough that the heat of his breath hits my face in warm waves. "For years I've told myself exactly what you're saying now, but I was wrong." He puts a bold hand to my cheek, his thumb grazing the corner of my mouth.

I freeze. *No no no.*

His eyes are on my lips. "I can live with unrequited. I *have* lived with it." He backs away. "But I can't live without *you.*"

I pull my knees to my chest and cross my arms around them like a shield. "I don't get it. You tell me this and want us to ignore it? Stay friends like you didn't say it?"

He clenches his jaw. "Obviously I don't *want* to just ignore it and stay friends. But I know you don't feel the same way." He flicks his sleeping bag zipper back and forth. "Right?"

He stares unblinking at the zipper, and I half expect it to answer instead of me.

I lick my lips, chapped from the dry canyon air and the panic. *I know you don't feel the same way.* But he must have believed in some chance or he wouldn't have said any of this. Kendi isn't impulsive and definitely isn't famous for letting people know how he feels. As a kid, he'd get sick at school and go home with a burning fever because he didn't want to tell the teacher he felt bad. He has never liked drawing attention to himself, especially if he's anything less than okay.

I know you don't feel the same way. Right? It takes a small eternity for me to answer. How can I break my best friend's heart?

Finally, I look away from the plea burning in his eyes, and I say quietly, "I'm so sorry."

He nods in quick little *I knew it* bursts, nostrils flaring with each breath. He unzips the tent and goes out into the rain as I sit staring at my ankles.

After several long minutes, he calls toward the tent, "Rain's letting up. Let's hike."

Our last hike is intense, conducive to avoiding conversation, all focus directed toward scrambles and securing our feet between slippery crags. It's drizzling, and we're lost in the race of our own thoughts. Kendi doesn't look at me once.

Afterward, we busy ourselves breaking down camp.

We get in his truck wordlessly and drive past the longhorns, over a pothole, and out of the canyon. We drive past sprawling fields; cattle and pump jacks; wind turbines like colossal, cartwheeling children; and a warning sign that reads HITCHHIKERS MIGHT BE ESCAPING INMATES. We drive past yellow grass and dilapidated mailboxes and roadside stands with signs for Tacos and Ammo. Saddles and Tack. Bail and Bonds.

The air inside the truck is suffocating. I crank the AC as we force normalcy into stilted silences:

Bathroom break?

Can't wait to see how the calendar turns out.

Whataburger?

Looks like we'll beat traffic.

Beef jerky?

So many McCain signs still up.

Seen the latest Wes Anderson film?

When he pulls up at Nana's, I say, "It's not going to be the same anymore, huh?"

With a vacant expression, he stares straight ahead and grips the steering wheel. "I don't know."

I'm itching to get away from him but not sure what words to leave behind.

Trip was great? No.

Talk soon? No.

I gather my camera stuff, clean trash off the floorboard, and settle wheel.

on, "See you later." I close the passenger door as he nods curtly at the
steering wheel.

It rained here too. Water runs along the curb like a miniature Red
River. I grab my wet backpack from the truck bed and sling it over my
shoulder. The truck idles as I walk the never-ending path to the house.

As soon as I open the front door, Kendi steps on the gas and speeds
away.

2009

NANA NEVER COMES RIGHT OUT AND ASKS ME TO STAY,
but we both know she doesn't have anyone else. Dad sometimes comes
over to do yard work and eat rhubarb pie, but we can't count on him.
And, as Nana likes to say, she's "no spring chicken." But she's not the only
one who's glad I still live with her. Truth be told, I'd be hard-pressed to
find a better roommate than Elise Brighton.

It's my night to cook dinner. I'm at the kitchen table googling a
broccoli-rice casserole recipe on my laptop when an email arrives. I
skim it. Nana is across the room, knitting. When I see Mom's name in
this stranger's email, the floor drops out from under me.

Nana's as good at reading people as I am, and it's been hard enough
to not tell her what happened with Kendi on our trip. I close my inbox
and try to focus on ingredients. The walls *broccoli* are caving in *rice*,
but no way *butter* am I going to *onion* share this *milk* with Nana *cheese*
before I have time *flour* to think *paprika*.

Somehow I make it through our whole dinner. And shortbread cookies with a scoop of Blue Bell. *And* a conversation about different types of
flour. All of it at a pace so leisurely that a sloth would become impatient.
After we clear dishes—bowl by sloth-speed bowl—I pack my computer

in my fake non-hurry and casually tell Nana that I'm going to Cowtown Cup to do some photo editing.

"Haven't you spent enough time at that coffee shop?"

"I'm only taking shifts every week or two now." I kiss the coarse gray hair on top of her head. "I haven't had their Lavender London Fog in way too long." I try to speak with a calm smile in my voice, to make her believe that's what this is about. Tea.

She pulls her knitting back out. "Okay, dear. Drive safely."

"Always do." I grab my keys and get into the older of our two Corollas. Fi-nal-ly.

At Cowtown, I do in fact order a Lavender London Fog because it has in fact been too long. I find a corner table. Now that I'm free to reread the email, I put it off. Sip my tea. Open other emails. Look around. Then I force myself to do the thing I was so eager to do.

I hover the mouse over the sender's name: *Davis Condie*.

My heart races.

Click.

Georgette,

I hope this is the correct email address. It has been difficult to track down. My name is Davis Condie. I live in San Antonio and work as a foreman for a construction company. My birthday is June 19, 1974. I'm married to Bekah, and we have two children, Liam (7) and Marigold (4). I don't know the different things scammers do these days, but I've tried to figure out the best way to demonstrate that I'm not one. Here's my LinkedIn and MySpace. I'm also attaching a photo of my family and me in front of our home.

My parents are Gus and Mary Condie. They adopted me as a baby and have given me a wonderful life. My birth mother is Lillian Wright, whose married name, it looks like, is Lillian Bright. Your mother, if I'm not mistaken.

My research on my family of origin has produced some gaps. I found relatives on my father's side, and you were the only other child of Lillian's I could find. I know it must be shocking to find out that your mother had a child she placed for adoption, if you don't already know. But it seems we are half siblings. I apologize for any distress this might cause.

I should say that Lillian's obituary came up in my search, so I'm aware she passed. There is nothing material I'm seeking. My lack has only been knowledge of where I come from. I thought I should at least let you know I exist, so you can do with this information what you will.

If you want to delete and ignore this, I won't blame or bother you. But I write in hopes that you might be willing to meet. No ulterior motives. Just interested in meeting my little sister. And learning about my mother and family, if you're willing to share. I'm putting together a family tree on one of those genealogy websites. And my kids are starting to ask questions about ancestry. Liam has a grandparent project at school.

If you're open to meeting, we could do so whenever and wherever you're most comfortable. Please take your time considering this. You can reach me at this email or the phone number below, and I'm happy to answer any questions. I hope you are well. I hope your life has been good. I hope I get to learn more about it.

Best,
Davis

2009

I REGRET COMING TO DAD'S APARTMENT BEFORE I EVEN knock on his door. I knock anyway.

There's a shuffle inside. He opens the door with good posture and alert eyes. "This is a pleasant surprise." His speech is intelligible, each syllable falling in line like baby ducks.

I look past him to an artist-tidy apartment. A landscape on the easel. A dinner of sodium-filled clumps inside black microwavable plastic. *The Brief Wondrous Life of Oscar Wao* upside down on the table. The television flickers muted news: a murder and a warm spring.

A glass of what appears to be water sits beside Dad's microwave dinner. I'd like to be encouraged by the clean apartment and the fact that he isn't drinking at the moment. But if there's anything I've learned about him, it's that a good moment is only that.

His iPod fills the small apartment with Coldplay, which gives me an unwanted jolt of satisfaction—I introduced him to their music.

He turns Chris Martin down and says, "Come in, come in."

I cross my arms and stay outside. "We need to talk about the baby."

His eyes fly to my stomach, and I blush. This is the first time I consider that Dad might not know. Davis didn't say who his birth father is. I assume it's not Dad, but surely Mom would still have told him? Or maybe I should go back to my first theory: Davis is nothing more than a skilled scammer.

Still looking between my face and stomach, Dad asks, "The . . . baby?"

"Just," I huff, flustered, "who is Davis?"

Dad's face is blank. "Uh, I don't know? Who *is* Davis?"

I push past him, go inside, and sink into his wingback.

As I study him and say nothing, he adds, "I honestly have no idea what you're talking about."

I take a deep breath. "I got an email from someone named Davis Condie who says he was born to Lillian Wright in 1974. That's Mom!"

I wait for Dad to refute it, to say it's not possible, to provide evidence that it's a scam, to tell me what Mom was doing in 1974 that was *not* having a baby. Then I can go back to pining for her rather than wondering if I even knew her at all.

Dad drops to the couch across from me. "Oh," he sighs. "That baby."

My heart hammers. I knew it the minute I saw Mom's eyes on Davis's face in his photo; I just tried to convince myself otherwise.

Dad asks, "Tea?"

"No, I don't want tea! I want answers! Do I have a brother?!"

"A half brother, yes. It was before your mom and I met. She never knew his name, and we only talked about him once."

Questions volley in my brain like Ping-Pong balls, and before I can pluck one and volley it to Dad, he says, "Hang on," and he disappears into his room.

Chris sings about someone's love going to waste, and I whisper, "What is happening?" The electric guitar gives no answer.

Dad returns with a weathered envelope.

I immediately recognize Mom's loopy cursive on the front: *Georgette Elise*.

"What is this?" I snatch it from him.

"It's from your mom."

"I can see it's from Mom." I stand. "What is it? Why am I just now getting it?"

He sighs. "I found it when we cleaned out the apartment."

"So Mom had some whole other life that you knew about. And not only did you not tell me, but you kept whatever this is"—I shake the envelope at him—"from me? Just decided that, despite my name being on it, you'd keep it until what? When?"

"Jet—"

"No." I walk out the door.

He follows me onto the landing. "What does he want from you?"

"What?"

"What does this guy want from you? Why'd he contact you?"

"I don't know." I shrug, exasperated. "To know his sister and where he came from? I mean, I don't know anything. Did Mom abandon him? You two think you can just go around having children and leaving them?"

"That's not—"

I shake my head and put my hands up like they can stop sound. They can't. Dad makes his defense anyway. "I left you and your mom for your sake. And your mom—"

Faster than thought, I cut him off. "Actually, you chose alcohol over us, bottom line. It was for your own sake."

A long blink and his typical bypass. "Just be careful with this guy."

I scoff. "You're suddenly concerned about me?"

Disbelief moves through me like venom, and I storm down the stairs.

As much as I hate myself for it, I pause at the bottom in case he follows.

But then above me, his door clicks closed.

I flee toward my car. I don't know what's in this envelope, but I know what I need to: Mom left a child just like Dad left me. And she lied. Memories flash through my mind—the countless times she called me an only child. I throw the envelope on the floorboard, check the rearview, back out, and pull away.

What else don't I know about my mother? I can't relearn someone who isn't here. My heart pounds like it's in one of those bands where the drums are too spotlight thirsty. For once, couldn't my stupid heart need a little less attention? I don't know if it's pounding because of Mom or Dad. It's not anger, exactly. It's volume. Like the only space I had left in me was paper-thin and this new information simply won't fit.

For the first time, I understand the urge to drink.

A stoplight blinks to red. I reach over and cram the envelope into my glove box beneath the user's manual, a couple of tampons, and a packet of Chick-fil-A sauce. Then I slam it shut and drive.

2009

Dear Davis,
You're right. This does cause distress. Delete.
Your family is lovely. I can't believe I'm an aunt. Delete.
Are you as mad at our mom as I am? Delete.
I don't think you want to know about the Brights. Whoever
adopted you is better. Delete.
I'm sorry for what Mom did. I know about being left behind too.
Delete.
You might be the only family I want anymore. Delete.
I don't think I can meet you. You look too much like her. Delete.
If you have other sisters, then just stick with them. I'm a mess.
Delete.
Are you planning to hurt me? Rob? Murder? Hold hostage? Delete.
Yes, I'd like to meet. I can come your direction. I work most Sat-
urdays, but let me know if there's a Sunday that might be good.
Keep.

Sincerely, Delete.
Love, Delete.
Warmly, Delete.
Best, Delete.
Georgette Send.

2009

WE MEET AT THE RIVER WALK.

Davis sent me the name of a restaurant. I see him before he sees me. He's at a table near the river, flipping through a menu. The pixelated version of him didn't prepare me for seeing him in person. It's like looking into a shadowed mirror. He's me with darker hair, eyes, skin. Same facial structure: big eyes, thin lips, pronounced cheekbones. Unlike me, he seems to have the good fortune of naturally thin eyebrows. He is wearing blue jeans, boots, and a white button-up. I didn't send a photo of myself, but when he looks up, I know he sees it—himself, a couple of shades lighter.

He stands, wiping his palms on dark-stain Wranglers. "Georgette?" He reaches a hand out to shake mine and says, "Sorry, this is weird. I didn't know how to greet you, so I settled on a handshake and acknowledging that it's weird." He sounds exactly how everyone thinks a Texan sounds. A straight shooter with a drawl.

I resist the urge to run. At the same time, I resist the urge to hug him like he's Mom back from the dead. Instead, I return the handshake. "You can call me Jet."

He gestures toward our table and we sit, adjusting chairs with little scoot-scoots. Two glasses of water look as sweaty as I feel. I busy

186

myself straightening my napkin through the awkward silence. So far, I've learned that this guy is Texan, polite, and nervous.

He clears his throat. "Thanks for meeting me. Was your drive okay?"

"Yeah, not bad!" I sound overeager, so I drop my voice a half octave. "A spot of traffic but not bad."

Globe lights click on over our heads as the sun sets. A child whines that he wanted fries, not fruit. And I am sitting at the River Walk with my *brother*. Half brother, granted, but half of something is still something. What if we had grown up together? Would we have fought over the remote? The bathroom? Walked to school playing I Spy? Would I have been less lonely? It's an endless mental game. If Mom had kept Davis, I might not have been born. Mom and Dad might never have met. Everything would be different. Still, I spiral into the infinite fiction of what-ifs and could-have-beens.

But Davis is here in front of me, in San Antonio, with Jimmy Buffet on the restaurant speakers, asking whether I want anything else to drink. I shake my head. "Water's great. Thanks."

The waitress takes our order. She's one of those who doesn't write anything down, and we can only wait and see.

I sip my water and try to return Davis's pleasant yet direct demeanor. "So which of us should tell our life story first?"

He laughs an easy laugh. "I'll go."

Hands in my lap, I'm ready as I'll ever be to find out who he is and what he wants.

"I always knew I was adopted. My parents were gracious toward Lillian and sensitive to what I'd lost. They knew my loss didn't mean anything about them as parents. I'd ask about her on holidays or when someone commented on how different I looked from my parents. But they couldn't tell me what they didn't know.

"My big brother, Howie, was adopted too, which helped. Our parents couldn't have biological children, so I think in the same way we knew their sadness over that didn't make us any less their children, they knew our sadness over our birth families didn't make them any less our parents.

"Let's see. Mom's a librarian, and Dad works in tech. Still married. Other than how our family came together, I had a typical childhood: school projects, tee ball, summer vacations to Colorado to escape the Texas heat. And a big extended family to spend holidays with, cooking and arguing about who forgot the green beans."

We chuckle. He tells me to stop him if I have questions, and I nod as he continues.

"I went to college for business because I did whatever Howie did. He works at a big investment firm up in the panhandle now, by the way. Divorced with two strapping teen boys. We're still close. Anyway, in college I started working on a construction crew because a buddy got me the job—I was a temp who needed cash for tuition. Turned out I had an aptitude and liked the work, so it stuck." Davis looks down, shrugs, and says, "Boring, I know."

"Not at all."

"Bekah and I are coming up on ten years." Her name lights a fire in his eyes, subtle but unmistakable. "Liam is going into second grade. His favorite things are outer space and Pokémon. And Marigold's our little wild child." He chuckles. "Starting pre-K and a head of untamable curls." He shows me a few pictures and remarks with reverence, "Family is my world."

The first emotion that skitters to my surface is jealousy. I'm jealous of Howie for getting Davis. I'm jealous of Davis for getting such glowing stability.

"They're beautiful." I swallow. "Now I'm sure you want to hear about my . . ." I backtrack. "About . . . Mom."

His nervous face returns, and I realize he must envy me too. Because I got her.

He says, "You know, I've wondered about her my whole life. I should have started searching earlier."

Sarah Damoff

I pull a stack of disorganized photos from my bag. The one on top is from Shauna and Michael's wedding, the whole big group of us. It's one of the last pictures taken with Mom. Davis points right to her and mutters, "That's my mother." She's one in a crowd, but somehow he immediately knows it's her. A memory surfaces: I was small, sitting on our brown plaid couch as she read me book after book. Her voice suddenly got funny, and I looked up to see that her eyes were wet. I got alarmed, but she blamed allergies. The book in her hand was P. D. Eastman's *Are You My Mother?*

I swallow. "Yeah." I look down at the photo that Davis is still studying. "That's her."

Our waitress arrives with a loaded burger and a grilled chicken salad, unwritten orders spot-on, even my side of ranch.

I show Davis more photos, tell stories, and answer questions. He wants to know about holiday traditions, her favorite foods and movies, her medical history. He's the only one in his family who can do the tongue roll thing, and I tell him he got that from Mom. With that one bit of trivia, I hand him a puzzle piece he has sought for decades. He asks if she liked cilantro. I laugh because she said it tasted like soap. Same as Davis, apparently. Another puzzle piece. (I can do the tongue roll thing but love cilantro.)

I tell him that I never knew about him. That I have no idea why she didn't keep him, but I'm so sorry she didn't. He says it's not like he would give up the family he got. He just wishes he knew her story, which is also his.

We discover that our birthdays are only weeks apart, so I flag down our waitress and order a slice of triple chocolate cake. Two forks, one plate. I remember kids complaining when they had to share birthday parties with siblings. Maybe Davis will eat more than his share of cake and I'll get a taste of what those kids could have possibly been complaining about.

He asks me about Dad, hungry for any scrap of Mom's life. When

I give him the overview of Dad, he lets out a sympathetic descending whistle and remarks, "Orphanhood sure can take many forms."

I bite my lip at this surprising insight, feeling seen in a way I haven't felt since Mom.

We don't talk about what it was like for me to lose her. We don't have to. Our experiences weren't the same, but the effect is closer than expected. We're concentric circles.

Davis leaves me the last bite of cake. Insists. Turns his fork over and tosses his napkin on the table in surrender. He's not too full; he's just being kind. This clinches my decision that I would have given up *The Little Mermaid* for him. We would have done monster trucks or Batman or whatever he wanted, and I wouldn't have complained about sharing like other kids did.

When I ask if he has been able to connect with his father, his face darkens. "I tried recently. For a while, he didn't respond. I wish it had stayed that way so I could assume my email didn't reach him. But then he wrote back." Davis shakes his head and grimaces a little. "He has a life. It doesn't have space for me."

As curious as I am about this man of my mother's past, I ask nothing more.

The waitress drops off the check. Davis grabs it fast, saying it's the least he can do. My long-lost brother could be anyone—a serial killer or nudist or fire-eater. But it turns out he's a construction foreman and father and genuinely nice guy who pays for our meal, has my jawline, lives only a few hours away from me, and wants nothing more than to know where he comes from. I wonder why Mom missed out on him and how many times he has wondered the same thing.

I glance at the tip he leaves. Generous.

We mosey down the river, lights reflecting in the water like stars underfoot. He asks if I always wanted to be a photographer, and something inside me stings. I confess, "When I was little, I wanted to be a doctor. Silly childhood dreams. You have any of those?"

He chuckles. "Mine was musician, believe it or not."

"Wow, so are you musical at all?" I picture him as a Garth Brooks type.

"I can carry a tune." He looks as if there's something he isn't saying. "I wrote a song once in high school, but who didn't?" He shrugs.

Nearing our cars, I pull out my keys and notice that the Corolla needs updated registration. I should check Nana's, too.

Davis stops beside my car. "I'm glad we met."

I nod. "Me too."

We're both quiet. Then we're both not.

"Maybe—" I start.

"I don't know if—" he starts.

We laugh as he says to go ahead.

"I just thought maybe if you're ever in Fort Worth—"

"Yeah, I do want to visit Lillian's grave sometime with Bekah and the kids."

I don't know why this short-circuits my brain a little. Maybe because I want her grave to stay mine. Or because it hits me that she has grandchildren. I have a niece and nephew. Something about this feels good and bad at the same time, like a sneeze.

I hold my hair down as the breeze picks up. "Y'all could come over sometime, and from there I could point you toward the cemetery. I mean, if you have time."

"That'd be great." He pauses. "No hurry though." He keeps being so thoughtful.

"Thanks again for dinner. You didn't have to do that."

"Oh man, of course. Thanks for making the drive and being willing to meet. I know it's not easy."

I look up at him. "For either of us."

A boy rolls by on a skateboard, and I unlock my car.

Davis steps back, thumbs through his belt loops. "You drive safe now."

I step forward to give him a side hug like some middle-school crush.

191

We laugh because what else can you do with the ever-shifting composition of a family?

I drop into the car and exhale as I back away from the river for my drive north. Mom's envelope throbs in the glove box. For the first time, I don't fantasize about burning it. I even wonder if I should open it, for Davis's sake. But I still don't want to know what's in there. Or what's not in there.

I stop at Buc-ee's and fill up on gas and wonder what kind of music Davis listened to on his drive home, what kind of song he wrote in high school, if he played sports or won awards or went in a limo to his senior prom.

Passing through Austin, I click on my radio. Pussycat Dolls. Switch. Brad Paisley. Switch. Zack Melendez. Switch. Sports radio. Switch. Kenny G. Don't switch. I have to admit, the satiny saxophone is kind of nice.

2009

IT'S TWO THIRTY IN THE MORNING WHEN I GET THE call. My ringtone volume is set to loud. I bolt awake for a photography job that's a first for me: a birth. I don't understand why anyone would want to preserve pain like this. But since they do, I'm glad to have the job.

Peach trees and boxwoods frame the birthing center. The wraparound porch looks inviting even in the dead of night. Inside, the lights are dim. The walls and floors are dark wood. There's a massive poster bed in the center. Two armchairs to the side. A mini fridge and a cradle. A corner with machines, medical supplies, sheets, oils, and diapers. Beyond the birthing room is the biggest tub I've ever seen.

The mom and dad are in the armchairs, talking in hushed voices. She seems calm. Mildly uncomfortable and cramping, but not too bad. A midwife and assistant are methodically moving around the room, setting up equipment, checking the baby's heartbeat, and offering the mom ice chips. This continues for some time, and it seems they know the drill. It's this couple's third child. "Third and final," the mom told me when we met a few months ago. She gave her husband a chin-down, eyebrows-up look when she said it. He smiled, their two girls pulling on him to go play outside.

Her groans intensify. He presses fists into her lower back hard enough to leave red marks. Beads of sweat form along her neck and face. I adjust my settings to capture that detail. She removes her oversized shirt, leaving only a sports bra. The sports bra seems fitting—if this isn't athletic, then nothing is. Stuff is coming out of her that is not a baby. I focus my lens on her face instead of the stuff, which the assistant cleans as fast as it comes out.

The contractions begin to rack her. I fight the urge to shout, *Someone do something!* The midwife is attentive and calm. Smiling, even.

Between contractions, the mom catches her breath and sucks on ice. Soon, the pain hits so hard that she throws up and is no longer allowed ice. I watch her lips chap like a time-lapse video. It makes me thirsty just to look at her. I don't know why anyone would want to do this, let alone have pictures of it.

I stay in motion at the perimeter of the room, letting the medical professionals work and clicking away. I position myself for the most dignifying angles possible, and I have to admire the dance between parents. She stares into his eyes as she contracts, gripping one of his hands while the other dabs her forehead with a cool cloth. Her skin gets pale and clammy, her noises otherworldly. Three times she has done this. Three! People always say not to forget because then history will repeat itself. But maybe history will repeat itself anyway, and forgetting is how we bear it.

How can her husband stand this helplessness? A hundred things could go wrong. It's so intimate and agonizing that I have the impulse to look away. Except this is precisely why they've hired me—to memorialize their anguish. To document their work, the pain between passions.

I don't know how long it is before the mom rolls herself onto all fours. As the baby's head emerges, the mother roars like a lion. Her husband weeps. Her power beside his softness makes my breath catch. A few more pushes. Shoulders, and then the dad tugs a slippery child out of a woman's body that doesn't want to let it go. A son.

My thoughts are as frenzied as my clicking. How can they bring this fragile being into this savage world?

The baby cries, sudden and shrill and frantic. The mother pants relief, and the midwife guides the father to cut the cord. A protest twists inside me: *No! Let them stay together!* But this is where it starts. We begin to say goodbye as soon as we say hello. Death is a corollary of birth, and to welcome life is to guarantee loss.

The bloody creature writhes in discomfort, his feral lungs shrieking, *Put me back in the place before breath!*

I document his pain. His raisiny nakedness. The slimy, veined placenta that nourished him. We hear his cries and shiver with awe because to cry means to live. Which I guess answers my own question: they want to preserve this pain because they want to preserve this life. This baby has already survived more than many of them do. And in spite of the pain that was and is and is certain to come, happiness blankets the room like a sunbath. Even I am not immune.

I keep my camera working as the baby is put to the breast, mother and child finding their way back to each other. A little noise escapes me. Something like a laugh of awe rising from a long-forgotten garden.

When I drive away from that birth room, I go straight to Mom's grave and yell at her. For lying, for going through all that birth stuff with Davis and then throwing it away, for hurting alone, for dying, for not yelling back. I ask her a dozen angry questions about men she loved and childbirth and if Dad cried when I crowned. If death hurts as much as birth.

Eight years have passed, and time is no healer. A mother stays even when she's gone, like a muted moon in the daytime sky. And the existence of Davis warps everything. You'd think being upset with Mom might appease my grief, but it compounds it.

Quieter, I tell her my plan. I'm going to apply to school to become a nurse-midwife. Not a doctor exactly, but exactly what my doctor-heart craves. This is what I want to do more than anything, become a doorkeeper to this hard and hardy world. I am fully decided, and the decision feels like the click of solving a mystery when it seems I should have known the whole time.

I'm aware that it won't always be like today. Some babies won't make it. Some moms won't keep the ones who do.

It starts to rain. I lie on my back beside Mom's headstone in a sudden downpour. The oak tree at her grave is twice the size it used to be. I close my eyes and open my mouth, swallowing clouds whole and glutting myself on being alive.

2009

SHAUNA TELLS ME KENDI IS ENJOYING HIS NEW JOB IN Houston. She doesn't say much else about him, and I don't ask. I assume he hates me. We haven't talked since Palo Duro eight months ago.

In December, I cave. I text him and ask if he'll be home for Christmas. He will. I say it would be nice to catch up. He agrees.

Surely we can forget the storm-soaked tent.

The day before Christmas Eve, we meet at Cowtown Cup and order hot drinks surrounded by glittering garlands, poinsettias, and Mariah Carey not wanting a lot for Christmas. The holiday crowd whirs like a coffee machine. Snippets of conversation fill the air, people talking about ski trips and ugly sweater parties and whether Obama deserved the Nobel Peace Prize.

I order a hot chocolate while Kendi orders coffee. He checks his watch and adds, "Decaf please." Then to me, "Coffee still not your favorite?"

"Shh." I look around. "Sometimes I still work here, you know."

He chuckles.

Too crowded, we go outside. Too cold, we walk the block. I didn't even have to ask; Kendi knows I hate crowds and cold.

I tell him about Davis and applying to nursing school. He's shocked and excited, respectively. He shares about work, how every day he looks forward to his entry-level aerospace design job and couldn't ask for much else. He's renting an apartment with his friend Jerome, who's about to get married and move out.

This seems as good of an opening as any to ask if he's seeing anyone.

He looks down and nods. "Anna."

Huh. Not Leah. Well, this is good. If Kendi is dating someone, we can get back to normal.

He doesn't say much about her. Instead, he tells me Shauna and Michael got a puppy. A lab. It's an early Christmas present that he says they're annoyingly calling their grandbaby as they point eyes accusingly at Kendi and say things like, "Since we don't have any others."

This knocks me off-balance, the thought of Kendi as a father. He's a little boy making *zoom* noises with toy planes and scoring his first soccer goal and skinning his knee at Saturday Night Pizza and Play. He can't be a father.

I steal a glance at him. He is almost twenty-four years old. He absolutely could be a father. Actually, he'd be a really good father.

I stutter, "Are you, I mean, is that something you want?"

"Kids?"

I nod.

"Eventually. Mom and Michael actually tried after they got married, but it was too late for them. Guess that's when I realized it's something I want someday." He pauses. "Don't you?"

"Want kids?"

"Mmm-hmm."

"I'm not going to have any."

"You don't want to?"

"That makes it sound like I don't like kids, but it's not that. I love kids. I just don't think I could handle loving my own kids, if that makes sense." I stare at my paper cup. "All the suffering."

Understanding washes over him. "Makes sense."

We've drained our drinks past their dregs. Our walk around the block has brought us back to Cowtown Cup three or four times now, having averted our eyes from armadillo roadkill every loop around.

He doesn't ask if I'm seeing anybody, which is fine because I'm not and it doesn't matter. Kendi can go on with his coffee and his career and his Anna. I'll go on with my hot chocolate and my grandmother.

It's getting late, so I veer toward our cars. "Oh, I actually have a job near you in March. A wedding in the Woodlands. Maybe we can grab lunch or something?"

"You got a wedding? Congrats!"

I forgot I told him how hard it is to break into wedding photography. "Thanks. I've done a few and am starting to get some referrals."

"That's great. Yeah, let's do lunch." He unlocks his truck. "Where are you staying?"

"Don't know yet. Plenty of hotels, though."

"Jerome's room will be empty then if you need to crash at my place. Might be too far from your site, though."

"That could work." I consider and say, "Yeah, can we plan on that?"

"Sure thing, just text me dates."

"Will do."

He opens his truck door. "Talk soon."

"Tell your mom and Michael I said 'Merry Christmas.'"

We don't hug goodbye, but that's okay. I still inwardly celebrate our progress in navigating the rocky terrain we brought back from Palo Duro. When I go stay with him in Houston, it'll be like old times.

Then, as he climbs into his truck, without thinking I check out Kendall Darnell's ass. When I realize what I'm doing, heat floods my face. I look around, mortified that someone might have seen, like anyone would care.

It means nothing more than this: I'm a woman. He's a man. He looks good. (Yes, he looks good! Lots of people do!) But we're reestablishing our friendship (again), and I will not jeopardize that (again). So what if Kendi's old enough to be a dad? So what if he's surprisingly muscular underneath his Levi's? This means nothing to me. Nothing.

2010

WHEN MY ACCEPTANCE LETTER ARRIVES, I'M ALONE. Nana's asleep, Dad doesn't even know I applied, and things with Kendi still feel precarious. So I text Shauna: GOT INTO NURSING SCHOOL!

Minutes later: OMG, I KNEW YOU WOULD! CONGRATS!!! SO PROUD OF YOU!!!!! LIL IS SMILING!

Within the hour, Shauna brings over an envelope and instructs me to open it later. Whatever it is, I'm told it was all Michael's idea. When later comes, I find a sizable check. Squeezed onto the memo line, it reads, *For my favorite future medical practitioner.* Beneath the memo line, *A gift, not a loan.* All the doctor questions Michael has put up with over the years, and now this payment toward my tuition. I press the envelope to my chest and wonder how I can ever thank him.

I whisper to nobody, "See how easy it is to hand me an envelope, Dad?"

I zip the check safely into my wallet. Come to think of it, I've been assuming there's a letter inside Mom's envelope. But it could be money. A photograph. Legal papers. The deed to a castle in Timbuktu. Anything, really. The possibility of another surprise only makes me want to open it less.

Nana's still sleeping. I leave my acceptance letter on the kitchen counter, imagining how she'll pick it up, her puzzled frown shifting toward a dawning smile.

While Davis isn't on the list of people I alert with life news, he happens to be the person I think of next. So I text him: HI. SORRY IT'S BEEN A WHILE. YOU AND YOUR FAMILY ARE WELCOME IN FORT WORTH ANY TIME :-)

Five minutes later: HI THERE. GOOD TO HEAR FROM YOU. HOW ABOUT EARLY FEBRUARY?

I didn't tell Nana about Davis until after I met him. Her jaw dropped. "No," she insisted. "Lillian would have told me."

I shook my head. "She barely even told Dad."

Thoughts raced across her eyes like horses. "Oh, Lil."

"You've got to see his picture. He looks just like her."

She shook her head and mumbled, "She let me put my foot in my mouth so many times."

"It's her own fault. I mean, she could have said something."

Nana exhaled. "Must have been a shock for you."

I shrugged. "Yeah."

She looked to the ceiling. "Damn, I miss her." She then started straightening everything within arm's reach. "Whose turn is it to cook tonight? Should we order takeout?"

I couldn't remember ever hearing Nana cuss, and she definitely had never suggested takeout.

We ordered Szechuan and split the sweet-and-sour chicken. I showed her the picture of Davis, and she shook her head some more.

When I told her that Davis is bringing his family over, she offered to scoot. Take care of errands to give us space. I told her absolutely not, that Mom loved her like a mother and we both know it. Nana was a mother when Mom's was gone, and Mom was a daughter when Nana's son was gone. Plus, I live in her home. As far as I'm concerned, she's as related as I am. When I made this argument, she touched her own cheek and said, "Good heavens, I'm old enough to be a great-grandmother."

To Nana's amusement, I clean the house until it shines. I polish sconces. Scrub grout. Move furniture. Try not to streak mirrors. Make an overdue handyman list. Knock cobwebs from the crucifix. Wipe down frames, careful with Dad's art. Clean wainscoting and top shelves and corners and corners of corners. Our dusty baseboards have more layers than Jennifer Aniston's hair, but I remedy that.

None of this is to say that Nana's sitting around. Oh no. When I tell her she should get off her feet, she won't have it. "There's far too much to do for me to sit idly by and twiddle my thumbs, dear." I don't know why I bother. Nana's love is composed of practicalities.

She cleans the kitchen and bakes poppyseed muffins and puts on makeup in front of her little magnification mirror that makes her pores look like moon craters. She remarks that she's "running low on rouge" even though I've repeatedly told her we call it blush now. She purses her lips at her moon crater mirror, and we both shake our heads at a strange generation. She goes back and forth for ten minutes about which shoes to wear. "A woman should always consider both fashion and comfort." She calls this out as though I need the tip while shaking Borax into the bathroom sink.

After lunch, we wait in a cloud of Pledge for the doorbell. Nana decided on her black loafers.

The Condies arrive right on time. At the front door, Liam stands beside his parents and looks shyly around, which only now makes me realize how few kid activities we have. Marigold steps toward me, reaches her finger upward, and says, "I need a Band-Aid," as though we're old friends.

Bekah jumps in, "Marigold, say *please*." Then to me, "So sorry."

I smile. "We have Band-Aids, no problem."

Bekah whispers, "It isn't even bleeding. But if you have one, it might spare us from continuing to hear about it."

I laugh and lead them to the kitchen. "I'm Jet, which is probably obvious."

Bekah says, "I'm Bekah, which is also probably obvious." I like her already.

Nana, for all her gravitas, gets teary-eyed as she meets the children. She apologizes for being a blubbering old woman. Marigold's face creases with worry, but Nana explains that they're happy tears. Marigold says, "I didn't know happiness could feel sad." Then she hugs Nana's leg and asks, "What's your name again?" The rest of us chuckle.

Davis helps Marigold take off her jacket. Nana dabs her eyes, claps her hands together, and asks who wants sweet tea. The kids look to their parents, who nod permission. Marigold beams and hops a little. "I do!" She looks at her mom and adds, "Please!"

At the table with tea and muffins, Liam tells us about a rocket launch he saw in Florida. He thinks my name is "so cool." I have a niece and nephew. Two living, breathing mysteries who need Band-Aids and like outer space. And I admit I hadn't given much thought to Bekah. It's clear why she fills Davis's eyes with sparks. She has a temperament as soft as her curls, like Jane Bennet. As nervous as I was to see Davis again and meet his kids, I only now realize that maybe I'm gaining something of a sister.

Throughout the afternoon, there are times when we're all chatting about the muffin recipe or a recent documentary and I learn some basic fact like Davis's middle name (Paul) or that he has a nut allergy (tree), reminding us of what we're trying to do. Most people would give up. They'd meet once at best. Get busy with their lives. Send holiday cards, thinking, *Shame they live so far* or *It's just too weird* or *We have nothing in common.*

Something different is happening here. There's a magnetism stronger than blood, and I wonder if this is similar to what Davis and Howie have. Or what I have with the Darnells. Or what anyone who falls in love has—family forming from scratch.

It turns out that Davis and Nana both love gardening and have much to discuss regarding how to get rid of nutsedge. Bekah minored in photography, and we both treasure our Sally Mann books. We also talk for half an hour about midwifery and birth stories. I won't pretend there aren't awkward silences, but still. A kindred spirit isn't something that can be manufactured.

At one point, Davis says something incidental in support of a politician I loathe, and a thrill zings through me. Everyone talks about avoiding politics at family gatherings, and now I have that too. Maybe someday we'll even be close enough to argue.

As the afternoon unwinds, Marigold chirps on about her favorite bird (mocking) and favorite book (*Peter Rabbit*) and favorite color (all) and favorite potato chips (barbecue, the wavy ones) until she falls asleep mid-sentence on Davis's lap while Liam and I play Mexican Train. Liam has a triangle of white at the corner of his lips—he has discovered the joy that is Nana's puppy chow. Davis lays Marigold on the couch, where her little body coils like the ringlet across her face.

Nana takes Bekah to the kitchen to show off some Le Creuset cookware she found at a garage sale. Liam goes for more puppy chow. When everyone else is occupied, Davis confides in me that he writes letters to Mom. "Since I was old enough to hold a pencil. Silly, I know."

Then Liam is tugging Davis's shirt and whispering, "Potty?"

I point the way and watch him go, one shoe untied and a cowlick on the crown of his head. Davis was younger than Liam when he started writing letters to my mom. Our mom. His unknown mom. I close my eyes and hold my breath as waves of sorrow crash over me. All I can think to say when Davis turns back toward me is, "It's not silly. I'm so sorry."

I look around the room for Mom like I did in those early months.

If she is ever going to float around a corner or crash into the room and knock over the mantel clock, now would be the time. But nothing. She remains only in us.

I tell him how to find her grave. They'll go to the cemetery soon.

When Liam returns, Davis kneels to help him double-knot his shoe. Somehow, despite his unsent mother letters and a father whose life doesn't have space for him, Davis bends low and patiently maneuvers his son's fingers to the tune of *Bunny ears, bunny ears, playing by a tree.* After his laces are tugged tight, Liam reaches a hand out toward his dad, who helps him up.

2010

NANA HAS A BLADDER INFECTION, SO I PICK UP HER prescription from the pharmacy. Two days later, her pain is worse. She tries to downplay it, but I take her straight back to the doctor. The antibiotics didn't work; the infection has moved to her kidney. I'm told I did the right thing by bringing her in.

They give her a different antibiotic. When I ask if she should be at the hospital for surveillance, the doctor says she'll be fine monitored at home. She's lucky to have me, he says. I want to say that he has it backward, that I'm the lucky one and would be lost without her. Instead, I thank him for his help and squeeze Nana's hand.

When we get home, she isn't hungry. Just tired. She goes to change clothes but falls asleep without having put on—as she calls pajamas—her "night duds." I slip the shoes off her feet, drape a blanket over her, click the lamp, and kiss her forehead. Her breathing has a slight rasp. I frown and spend the evening googling medications and side effects and infections and complications. I jot questions on the yellow notepad by the phone. I'll call the doctor tomorrow.

Nana sleeps a lot even when she doesn't have a kidney infection, so I don't want to disturb her. But when I haven't heard from her by lunchtime, I tiptoe into her room. I immediately catch the berry scent of her lotion, which is open on her nightstand beside tissues and rosary beads and a booklet of crosswords. A stub of a pencil.

I knew it when I moved in, when I watched Nana move slower and tire faster, when she climbed past her seventy-fifth birthday and then her eightieth. I knew I might have to find another dead person.

Here are things that are different from Mom: Nana is still warm and supple, appearing to be serenely asleep. Sun streams into the room and across her bed, making her look celestial.

I rush to her. No breath. No pulse. I kiss her leathery face, gravity pulling my tears through the grooves of her wrinkles like a maze. I stay there long enough for the light to shift, the warmth to leave.

Then I call Dad, who arrives twenty minutes later, blinks at me with puffy eyes, and walks stiffly to her bedroom. I close the door to give them privacy, mother and child in the sunshine and death. This is a first for him. Yes, he lost a parent before, but not one he loved.

Here are things that are the same as Mom: I wonder what I could have done differently. I worry Dad will drink. I grieve a woman who raised me.

The grief surprises me. Not that she doesn't deserve it; I simply didn't know I still had it in me. But grief is no respecter of past griefs, and grandmothers are underrated. Nana was, when it came down to it, the world's best. Any amount of years would have been too few.

I'll do anything for Nana, even plan her funeral with Dad. So we back-burner all the hurt between us and go browse caskets and flowers. I keep thinking about Dad at Barton's funeral and Dad at Mom's funeral, and I hold my breath for his inevitable disappearance.

Davis and Bekah send white roses. Kendi comes to the service, staying in the periphery with Shauna and Michael, their presence a balm.

When Shauna pays her last respects, she cries. I blink in realization that she must have cared about Nana. And in realization that I remember nothing about how she handled Mom's death. She must have been devastated. Gosh, she must have cut her honeymoon short. I didn't give it a thought at the time. I had folded in on myself, the immaturity of my sorrow, the all-consuming totality of sudden disaster. I find her after the service and tell her as much. I thank her, for the first time, for being family when I had so little of it.

"Oh, darlin'," she says, as her fire-engine-red nails pull me in so she can plant a firm kiss on my head. "Love you."

Later, I watch her pull Dad aside. She hugs him long, and his shoulders start to shake. He is sobbing. I look away quickly, a memory surfacing. An almost identical scene from Mom's funeral. I don't remember forgetting it. I remember Dad being nothing besides gone and more gone. I remember nobody hurting like I was hurting. And maybe that's all accurate. But at the same time, there's this. Dad and Shauna consoling each other, then and now.

I don't look back at them. I don't want to know what other omissions my memory has made. I don't want to see Dad like this and be tempted to make excuses for him. But the sight of them behind me—here and nine years ago—pokes at me almost as much as this question: What's the difference between an excuse and a reason?

Despite myself, I do look back. Dad is wiping an eye that's as red as Shauna's nails. She's handing him a tissue.

"Nana was such a force."

I startle at the nearby voice and turn to see Kendi. Nodding, I exhale through my nose, the way people do at memorials. "She was."

He notices where I was looking. "He okay?"

"Who knows." I search for something more positive. "Glad he has your mom."

"And glad she has him."

A small snort escapes me. "Why?"

Kendi's expression scrunches. "The obvious? They really helped each other get through it after Lillian. Mom's always been thankful for that." *The obvious? Dad helping someone? Shauna's been thankful for him?*

I raise a skeptical eyebrow. "I don't know if it's fair to say he got through it." This has too much bite, and I look up at the swirly white ceiling. I should be kinder at Nana's memorial.

"He's here." Kendi shrugs. "And not drunk."

I look back at Dad with Shauna, both nodding at someone I don't recognize. "Here and not drunk is a pretty low bar."

"Is it?"

I open my mouth and shut it again.

Then Michael appears behind Kendi and moves his lips into a thin line that I'd call smile adjacent. It's the Funeral Acknowledgment, careful not to appear too emotional one way or the other. I return the Acknowledgment by pulling my own lips into a thin line. I'm not sure when I learned this unspoken etiquette.

Shauna approaches and asks Kendi, "You ready, kiddo?" She loops her bangle-covered wrist around Michael's elbow. The living have living to do.

Kendi hesitates and says to me, "I assume you're not coming to Houston?"

Right. That's next weekend. I'll need to find a replacement photographer. But I've worked so hard to get weddings. Plus, Nana would almost certainly say, "Go to the wedding, dear! Take your photos! Wear something elegant!"

I say that I'll let him know soon. Then the Darnells hug me goodbye, Michael intentionally hanging back to tell me that I was one of the most beautiful parts of Elise's life. His words settle as a lump in my throat, a film in my eyes. I nod my gratitude and hug him. Expressing gratitude for anything anyone says is another part of Funeral Etiquette, but with Michael, I mean it.

Guests continue to trickle away, many of them leaving behind stories about Nana's stubborn particularities or her strength of character or the constant thoughtfulness she hated to be thanked for. Neighbors and former students and even Nana's manicurist, who keeps blotting her eyes.

Nana rests at Greenwood now. Her affairs were unsurprisingly in order, every *t* crossed and *i* dotted. She left me the house, which is not a surprise but still a shock. I don't know how I'll stand the emptiness.

When the guests have gone, it's just Dad and me. His eyes are blood-shot, and it does something to a girl—even a grown girl with an awful father—to see her father hurt. Maybe that's why I've looked away. Kendi's question echoes through me: *Is it?*

Dad stuffs his hands into his suit pockets. "There's a Braum's across the street."

I frown. ". . . Okay?"

"Want to go?"

No, I don't want to go. I look around and sigh. "Sure."

So after everything is done at Greenwood, we slide into a Braum's booth and eat sundaes in our funeral clothes.

Dad looks down his nose at a spoonful of ice cream. "These haven't changed. Nana used to get them for me when I was boy."

Now there's a wild thought. Dad as a boy. He never talks about his childhood.

"Really?" I spoon a bite and press my tongue to the roof of my mouth to prevent brain freeze.

"Every week after mass. She'd say, 'Sundaes on Sundays.'"

I cough and pretend it's from my mouthful of cold. They went to mass? I fill up with a hundred questions about beliefs and family, and suddenly there are a million things I should have asked Nana but didn't.

Across the table, I see Dad as young as Liam and as old as Nana. I shiver and swallow and say, "Tell me more."

"More what?" He eats a spoonful.

"What else did you do with Nana when you were little?"

So he tells me. And as it turns out, Dad and I have some similar childhood memories. After all, Elise Brighton raised us both.

We keep the table for hours.

He's here. He's not drunk. I can at least give him a chance to stay this way.

2010

"WHY IS IT THIS HUMID IN MARCH?" I DROP MY OVERNIGHT
bag on Kendi's floor and set my gear on the table, unzipping, checking,
sorting, and re-zipping. It's Friday afternoon, and Houston traffic got
bad early.

Kendi chuckles. He took a late lunch to come let me in, but all I have
time to do is pee and reapply deodorant. He eats a sandwich as I rush
around his apartment. I apologize and slip my shoes on to leave not ten
minutes after arriving. He asks if I'm hungry. Starving. He plates the
other half of his sandwich, passes it to me, and tosses me a water bottle.
When I eye the sandwich, he says, "There's no pickle."

I give him a quick *Right, thanks* look and heave my bag strap onto
my shoulder. He gives me the extra apartment key since it'll be a late
night, and I scurry out.

Rehearsal dinners are a delicious perk of the job. Spanish tapas at this
one. I usually eat later or squeeze in bites when I'm not photographing
toasts, dabbed corners of eyes, forced embraces, or glances stolen across
twinkling table settings.

I don't know the story, but the wedding planner informed me that there's no father of the bride. As the bride laughs with her bridesmaids, I feel indignant on her behalf. Wherever he is, she shouldn't have to do this without him.

My job is observant by nature. Wedding weekends are stressful, and I notice moments people think are hidden. Tonight, it's the groom's parents. When the focus isn't on them, they speak in clipped sentences, their gestures abrupt. The groom doesn't seem to notice; he's focused on his bride-to-be with her long sentences and regular breaths and graceful gestures. The contrast between the young couple and their parents does not recommend marriage.

As the evening wraps up, I realize I made the rookie mistake of misplacing a lens cap. When I'm about to round a corner to hunt for it, I hear hushed voices. I pause. The groom's parents again.

His mother sighs. "You should have at least apologized to the caterer."

"It wasn't my fault."

"Well, you know what is your fault?"

"I'm sure you'll tell me."

"You gave me these kids just to marry them off. He's the last one, and now I'm losing them all!"

I risk a peek around the doorframe.

He's pulling her into a hug, chuckling like they weren't just fighting. "That's why you're upset?"

She leans into his chest like a teenager with her boyfriend, and she pout-mumbles, "Yes, it is."

I back away, shaking my head. I can't keep up: Family's worth it or it's not?

Kendi is awake and on the phone when I get back to his apartment. I wave a silent greeting. He mouths *sorry*, then says, "Yeah," into his phone. I head to the extra bedroom to change clothes.

I was such a tornado of activity when I spun through earlier that I didn't get a chance to look around. This is my first time here, and it's quintessentially him. Everything is in order and simple but with thoughtful touches: a model plane, a picture of his dad, a potted cactus, the first film photo I took of him, and shelves lined with books. It's minimal without being minimalist. In the extra bedroom, I find an inflated air mattress with a tidy stack of blankets.

When I come back to the kitchen in my sweats, he's off the phone. I search cabinets for a water glass and ask, "Anna?"

He looks at me with confusion before shaking his head and exhaling a light laugh. He opens the correct cabinet for me. "Jerome." Kendi waves his hand dismissively. "He just had a question."

I fill a glass. "I have a question too."

"Hmm?"

"Do you fly?"

"What?"

"I mean, I don't know much about your job. Airplane design, right? Do you fly?"

Amused, he looks at me like I'm a kid on career day. "I have my pilot's license, yes."

"Come on. I want to know more about what you do."

"Computer modeling. Grounded." One side of his mouth ticks up in a half smile. "But I fly on my own time."

"Do you like it?"

"Do I like . . . flying?"

"Some people are scared to fly, you know. But I guess you wouldn't have gone into aerospace engineering if you were one of those people."

"I love it. The adrenaline and freedom."

I smile and guzzle half my water; I always forget to hydrate on shoots. "I hate flying." I involuntarily shiver.

"Wait, what? No. How have we not talked about this?"

I shrug and finish off my water. "Always more to learn about some-one, I guess."

"Sure, but you grew up playing airplanes with me. We've known each other for decades, and I'm just now finding out you hate planes?"

"Not planes." I point to him. "Flying. The planes are fine. The flying is nerve-racking, gut-churning, unnatural, why not drive where you want to go, why go up above clouds like it's not a *huge and heavy chunk of metal*?"

He laughs in disbelief. "The flying is the point of the planes! Plus, statistically"—he points back at me—"people die from car accidents way more frequently than air travel."

"Yeah, you won't convince my fear away with stats. I've heard that even if you're safe up there, people have panic attacks, claustrophobia, motion sickness, turbulence . . ." I shiver again.

"Hold up. You have flown before, correct?"

I watch him survey his own memory for when I might have been on an airplane, and I wait with a sheepish expression like Lucille Ball.

All of his fingertips fly to his temples as if trying to force the truth into his brain. "You've never flown?! I have utterly failed you. And how can you be afraid of something you've never done?"

I laugh. "You haven't failed anyone. And most fears are of things people have never done."

He tilts his head. "I guess."

"Anyway, it's seriously cool that you're doing what you've dreamed of since we were snotty-nosed kids."

Laughing, he says, "Yeah." Then, "Should I start some water for tea? I have decaf."

"Sounds heavenly, but I should turn in. Big day tomorrow." I put my glass in the dishwasher. "Do you have plans on Sunday? I'll be done working and not in a rush to leave."

"Sunday's great." He takes my hand. "Hey," he adds. "I wasn't trying to give you a hard time. It's just that flying is life-changing. You feel small and strong at once. I just want you to experience that. And how can you know unless you try?"

"Maybe someday." *Never.*

"I'll take you."

I smile and give him an acquiescent nod. *Truly no chance.*

The truth is that it has become difficult to concentrate because heat has rushed to my hand where Kendi's touching it. What is wrong with me? This is Kendi's hand. Kendi! We've thumb-wrestled and played slapjack with these hands. I've seen him pick his nose. I taught him *Here is the church, here is the steeple, open the doors and see all the people.*

Maybe I'm affected by the wedding festivities or something. I try to talk myself down. *It's Kendi, it's Kendi.* But every time I think his name and remember whose hand is on mine, I heat up more.

Trying to be casual, I pull away. "Well, goodnight! Thanks again for letting me crash here!" I escape toward the extra bedroom.

"Sure thing. Sleep well."

I hear him start the dishwasher and turn off lights and then close his bedroom door. I read a few chapters of *The Hunger Games* before going to sleep, but Effie and Katniss and Peeta apparently aren't enough to stop me from having a dream about Kendi—a steamy one. I wake up confused, frustrated, and trying to grope my way toward some solid denial. In the darkness of night, when Kendi's dream-lips were just on me, the best I can do is whisper-chant to myself, *He has a girlfriend, he has a girlfriend, he has a girlfriend.*

Kendi makes us breakfast on Saturday: scrambled eggs with Tabasco, avocado slices, and buttered sourdough. I lock my dream in the "Do Not Touch" compartment of my brain, and we settle into the safe territory of music and analyzing the Grammys. Beyoncé dominated; we've both been meaning to check out more Taylor Swift; and Lady Gaga's voice is a thing of wonder.

After breakfast, I shower and put on my black nice-enough-for-a-wedding dress with my black comfortable-enough-to-be-on-my-feet-all-day shoes. It cooled off so much overnight that I'm going from sleeveless on Friday to a jacket on Saturday. Which is fine by me. The cooler the better. I don't know what got into me last night, but thank goodness that's over.

My work today begins when the bride starts the process of hair and nails. I'm in the background making myself invisible enough to capture candids. Photographers never know what we're walking into, but this particular wedding day is thoughtfully planned and well-organized.

When I photograph weddings, I'm running all over, chasing people and angles and light. It doesn't leave much time for contemplation. In the rare still moment, divorce stats run through my mind beside the stern face of Judge Judy. It feels like I know a secret nobody else knows: most of these glowing couples won't make it until death do them part. And whatever it is that parts them will be excruciating. I smile to cover up the fact that I don't exactly believe in this whole thing.

When it's time for vows, this bride tries to start twice and can't get words out. I've never seen a wedding fall apart at the altar, but better now than later. The room is quiet except for some scattered coughs and a baby's cry, which is quickly stoppered with a pacifier.

The bride bites her bottom lip. Finally, she shakily speaks. "You met me when I'd sworn off marriage." There's a soft wave of reminiscent laughter and some nods from the wedding party. Camera gold. I click as she continues. Maybe this isn't falling apart after all.

"Over the years, you've been patient and undemanding. You and most of the people here"—she looks out at the crowd, many of them nodding strength in her direction—"know that my past taught me not to trust anyone." Her voice cracks. The maid of honor sniffles. The bride looks to the maid of honor and back to her groom.

"But I know I can trust the promises you're making today because you've already kept them, already loved me so well for so long." The groom sniffles. The bride checks her notes. "It's my greatest fear, losing you. I might not survive it." Her voice wavers again, but she pushes on as though turbulence is to be expected. "Nobody can promise me it won't happen, but now I understand that this isn't a risk to eradicate. It's a risk to embrace."

I can hardly hold my camera up, like it's weighed down by her words. "Thank you for being so patient with me. Today I wholeheartedly commit to the risk of it all. I choose to say yes, and I do, and I will." Her voice smooths out like a plane touching down. "Because you have shown me that love is worth the losing of it."

Silence holds the room captive, hope curled inside every throat. I have never heard vows that address reality so head-on.

I shift my camera position as the groom clears his throat for his turn, and suddenly all I see is Kendi. Kendi throwing the Frisbee and letting me on his bike pegs and cooking over a camp stove and knowing that I don't want crowds or cold or pickles. Kendi at Mom's funeral. Kendi's hand on mine.

This is not good. In one fell swoop, this bride has chopped down my delusion like it was a sick tree. I do not, as it turns out, have a monopoly on pain. It's not some secret knowledge of mine. These people have heard the stats too. Have felt the stats. They know it hurts whether promises are broken or kept—they make them anyway. *I'm* the one left out of a secret. And for the first time, I want in.

The groom says his vows. I adjust, click, adjust. The baby cries again, and his mother takes him to the back, where she bounces and sways. Where a man sits alone with his walker and oxygen tank and whatever losses he's survived.

The couple exchanges rings, and I fight off the image of Kendi and me. Even if Kendi didn't have a girlfriend and were still remotely interested, even if by some miracle we could "make it" without anyone being drunk or abusive or unfaithful, one of us would eventually lose the other. One way or another, the risk is a certainty.

I could never set myself up for that loss. And I definitely couldn't set Kendi up for it. Is this how Dad felt when he left? Like it was the best of bad options? Like he had to choose one pain to prevent another?

The bride comes back down the aisle, this time beside her husband. I follow the wedding party toward wine and cake and music, and I take hundreds of photos. Feasting. Toasts. Dances.

Mother and groom: Guns N' Roses, "Sweet Child O' Mine." A surprise choreographed piece. The crowd erupts into cheers.

Uncle and bride: Bruce Springsteen, "When You Need Me." Unlike the previous dance, they're crying more than dancing.

Husband and wife: Etta James, "At Last." They smile so big that everyone else disappears in the glare of their joy. They don't notice when the song ends. I raise my camera and freeze time, their foreheads touching as the dance floor fills around them.

I get back to Kendi's apartment near midnight and am beyond relieved that he's asleep.

It's quiet, one small lamp left on beside the cactus. I slip off my shoes, set my camera bag down, and go change into pajama pants and a T-shirt. I tiptoe back out and accidentally bump into a kitchen chair, cringing at the shot of loud in the quiet. I fill a glass of water and tuck into the corner of the couch by the little lamp, restless. *The Hunger Games* is beside me, but I mindlessly scroll piled-up texts.

"Thought I heard you."

I jump a bit. A groggy-eyed Kendi stands in the doorway.

"Sorry," I wince-whisper, "I bumped a chair. I'm about to go to bed though. You don't need to stay up or anything." *Stop being weird, Jet. This is Kendi, your best friend. Yeah, but this is Kendi, your best friend.*

220

He sits beside me. He has no shirt on, because of course he doesn't. Because it's only me and he was asleep and it's no big deal, so I need to cool my jets, as Mom used to say. But my somersaulting heart doesn't cooperate.

I turn toward him. The soft lamp highlights the definition in his shoulders and arms and chest. I refuse to look lower—ab ogling is off-limits.

"Jet?"

"Hm?"

"I asked how the wedding was."

"Tell me about Anna."

"What?"

"Just tell me about Anna right now please."

"What? Why?"

"You haven't talked about her! What's she like? Is it serious? Tell me how wonderful she is and how in love you are!"

"You're being weird. What's going on? Did something happen at the wedding?"

"I need you to tell me about your girlfriend right this second or I am going to kiss you."

Great. I squeeze my eyes shut and grind my teeth at myself. Now I'll lose him again. Probably forever this time. He'll tell Anna, and they'll chuckle and shake heads and pity me as they get engaged and married and have the babies that will make Shauna and Michael stop this ridiculousness of calling their dogs grandbabies.

"Have you been drinking?" This snaps me back to attention.

I groan and throw my head back onto the couch. "You know I don't drink. I just want to kiss you, okay? With tongue this time!"

I glance sideways at him. I was aiming for levity, but he ignores it and says, "I don't have a girlfriend."

I turn. "Why didn't you tell me y'all broke up?"

He clenches his jaw. "There is no Anna. I lied. I'm sorry. There hasn't

221

been anyone since Palo Duro. I was afraid that if you thought I was single, we wouldn't be friends."

"You lied to me?"

"Sorry." His voice is coiled tight.

I pull my knees up to my chest. "I thought I could trust you."

"Jet, stop. You can. I'm not saying it's good I lied. But I haven't lied to you other than this. Don't make it a bigger deal than it is. I'm not your dad, okay?"

"Actually, this is exactly what my dad did."

"This is different, and you know it. He lied to his wife about an addiction, and I made up a girlfriend. It's not the same. I'm not him. You're not him. Even your dad isn't the same guy anymore."

I say nothing.

"How long, Georgette? How long have you felt this way?"

There he goes *Georgette-ing* me in all his shirtless midnight zeal.

I don't answer.

He moves closer.

He's a hot knife and I'm butter. I squeak out a response. "I don't know." Except I do know. "I guess I've been lying like everyone else. Telling myself it was nothing."

"Why?"

"Fear can make a liar of a saint?" I add quickly, "Not that I'm any saint. But I'm terrified to lose you. You know we've come close too many times."

His jaw tightens. "Yes, I do know."

After a beat, he asks, "What changed?"

"For starters, you went and said all that 'How can you be afraid of something you've never done?' and 'How do you know if you don't try?' stuff. And then the bride said, 'Love is worth the losing of it,' and honestly? Nothing has changed. I'm still about to hyperventilate at the thought of messing up our friendship. People are still awful. But"—I look at him and swallow—"you're not awful." I sigh in surrender. "And I can't stop thinking about you, so I guess I'm trying to be brave or something stupid like that." I burn with embarrassment, too late to turn back now.

"Good to know I'm not awful." A playful smile spreads across his face.

I shove his shoulder. "Glad you're getting a kick out of this." My hand drops down his arm slower than I mean for it to. "Did you start majorly working out or something?" I bury my face in my hands and peek between my fingers. Since my foot is in my mouth and my eyes are partially obscured, I go ahead and check out his abs.

He grins, crooked and inviting. "So to sum up, I'm not awful and you only want me for my body?"

I drop my hands and roll my eyes. "Okay, we grew up together and you"—I hold up a finger—"endured hours on end of playing doctor." Second finger up. "Made rainy-day forts with me." Third finger. "Ate my vegetables when our moms turned their backs." Fourth finger. "Let me beat you in basketball twelve hundred times." Fifth. "Told me about your dad." I give up on the fingers and drop them. "We led the line dance at your mom's wedding, and you were the last person to see my mom alive. You held me when I had nightmares about it and told me you do too. You've been here for me, always. Even after you professed your love and I rejected you. But yes, Kendi, I'm in love with you for something as trivial as your body."

I meet his eyes. He grins that half grin and mimics me, holding one finger up. "First of all, you are legitimately good at basketball." Second finger. "Second of all, is it so trivial?" He lowers those two fingers and grazes my arm like I'm silk. He traces all the way up to my neck, his fingers landing in my hair. I ignite, like he traced me with a match.

He says, "When Jerome called last night, he asked whether I was planning to 'make a move.' But I'm not a 'make a move' kind of guy, you know?"

"Right. Just a 'profess love in a canyon when we have to sit in the car together for five hours' kind of guy."

He laughs.

I reach for his waist, his bare skin, like I need to latch myself on to his happiness and never let go. At my touch, he swallows and the laughter fades. I drag my famished gaze to his mouth, and I unfold one leg.

He pulls me, slowly, to straddle him.

My lips level with his eyes, I tilt my head downward. And of all the things I could do, I smile. He runs his thumb across my smile but doesn't kiss me. Instead, his kiss finds my neck. *Bless.* I close my eyes and melt into his mouth. His teeth skate across the bottom of my ear, his tongue drawing tiny loops I can feel down my thighs.

He whispers, "You said you're in love with me." More loops with his tongue.

"I did say that, yes." My eyes close in pleasure. I add weakly, "But only because your body isn't awful." I feel his smile on my neck.

He takes his time kissing all the real estate of my face except my mouth, and my impatience ticks like a bomb. By the time his lips are finally level with mine, I close the gap greedily. And with tongue.

I reach down and lift my shirt off. He pulls back, just to look. My heart knocks around in my chest so hard that I wonder if he can see it. When he peels his eyes from my chest to my face, he says with a bit of a squeak, "A little different than in first grade when your mom pulled off your shirt in a hurry because you spilled orange juice."

I laugh. "I'm sure I spilled it on purpose. Too much pulp."

He kisses me again, softer, leaving me to wonder when he'll touch me like I crave. Then he pulls back, barely. "Now ask *me* how long."

"What?"

"Ask me how long I've felt this way."

I smile again, aching for him. "How long have you felt this way?"

He kisses the corner of my mouth. "Since we went to dances with other people." He kisses the other corner of my mouth. "The New Year's we practiced kissing." He kisses beneath one eye. "Since those kids called us lovebirds." He kisses beneath the other eye. "Since you'd sleep on our couch." He pulls my bottom lip between his teeth. "Since you brought ice cream to the park in that dress." His hand finally cups my breast. "The night in the tent." He looks up at me and says low, "I can't tell you the number of cold showers."

Barely breathing, I whisper, "Not that far back." I'm clinging to him.

"Yes, that far back," he says firmly. "And always." He twists my hair into his fist. "When your hair grays." He kisses the corners of my eyes. "When your eyes get crow's feet." He brings the back of my hand to his lips. "When your skin is thin enough to see all the veins." He lowers his eyes. "When your breasts wrinkle." He lowers his face, his mouth, until his teeth scrape the fullness of my chest and his tongue flicks fast against me, over and over like the beating of hummingbird wings.

My head falls back, my hips pushing toward him in a plea for more. I run my hand down his ribs, abs, beneath his waistband. He gets still, flutters his eyes closed, grips my back. A low sound of need moves from the back of his throat straight into my fingertips like heat. He pulls me from the couch and shuffles me toward his bedroom from behind, his tongue at the top of my spine, hands exploring, clothes dropping behind us.

His bedroom is dark and clean. I turn toward him, the length of me burning against him in red-hot anticipation. I push my palms into his chest and step into him until he backs up and onto the bed. I kiss my way up him, hair cascading, fear falling off like chains. And then, gaining momentum, I take Kendi flying.

2011

"I SERIOUSLY HAVE TO GO," I SAY HALF-HEARTEDLY WITH Kendi's lips on my ear. "It's Photography Sunday."

We're standing in his kitchen with dirty dishes scattered across the table, and I'm about to make the long drive back home. This has been our routine for almost a year now, splitting weekends between north and south Texas.

He pulls me close. "Actually, you don't."

This isn't like him. He's protective of me when it comes to Dad, but in a way that encourages healthy interactions like Photography Sunday.

A few Sundays after Nana's funeral, Dad asked if I wanted to go out for ice cream again. When he noticed me rushing through my sundae, I told him about a hiking trail I wanted to explore with my camera before sundown. He asked to join, and that's how we stumbled into a tradition of our own: Photography Sundays. Now I pick him up each week and we chase the sun.

It turns out, however, that my forgiveness in that Braum's booth didn't actually make him sober. I'd say six out of seven Sundays, he isn't drunk. The other times, he opens the door and turns me into a ten-year-old. That's about the age I was when I learned to tell if he was drunk. His vacant eyes, dragon breath, and too-loud voice still leave me shriveled in worthlessness.

At the same time, age makes anger give way to something slushier.

226

It's not gone, but it's not as solid. Now Dad's drinking doesn't offend me as much as it breaks my heart.

Whenever he's drunk on a Sunday, I turn my back on him and chase the sun alone. Sometimes I declare to my empty passenger seat that I'm done trying. But always by the next Sunday, I'm ready to risk it again. I won't give up the six times for the one. Mercy isn't a onetime event with an alcoholic.

I lean my head against Kendi's chest. "Tempting, but I really should get going. Dad has gone like eight—maybe nine—weeks in a row now. This is important to him."

"I know. It's important to both of you." He doesn't let go of me.

I laugh, confused. "Okay, so?"

"He's fine with you missing it this once. I asked him."

"You asked him?" I lean back to look at him.

"I have a surprise for you. And he's cool with skipping this one Sunday. So please stay in Houston a few more hours?"

"You talked to my dad?"

"I did."

"Uh, okay." I bite a smile. "What's the surprise?"

"I think you might be a little unclear about the term 'surprise.'" His voice has a wink in it.

I roll my eyes and start clearing dishes, but he says to leave them and get my shoes. I think of weekends when we were little, when he'd wait for me to get my shoes and then fly me away.

The surprise, to my great dismay, isn't so far off: he's taking me flying. Not pretend flying. Real. In a Cessna 172. Maybe *trick* would have been a more accurate word than *surprise*.

My annoyance is crowded out by paralyzing fear. Kendi thinks it's a romantic gesture and is convinced it'll be a life-changing experience for me. I bite my nail. As long as it's not a life-ending experience.

227

Walking out to the little prop plane, I ask, "What about the weather?"

Kendi looks up at a sapphire sky. "What about it?"

"It could get bad."

"There isn't a cloud in the sky. Or the forecast. I checked all of this."

"What about navigation and fuel and stuff?"

He raises an eyebrow and one side of his smile. "Navigation and fuel and stuff? You do know I'm a licensed pilot and have everything prepared for a safe flight."

"Okay, but what about 9/11?"

"What about 9/11?"

"Terrorists? On planes?"

He gives me a look. "No terrorist is hijacking our four-seater Cessna."

I swallow, searching for other ways to hem and haw.

"Jet."

"Hmm?"

"I would never force you. If you're too scared, we don't have to go."

I look from him to the plane to the sky to him. "I hope you know how much I trust you, Kendall Darnell." I take his hand and a deep breath, and I board the plane.

On the runway, with seat belts and headsets on, I cross myself like Nana did at Six Flags when we ascended the Texas Giant. Kendi chuckles and asks through the headset if I'm Catholic now. I say, "I'm just someone who knows how easy it is to die."

In the end, I don't die. But I do hate it. Every second of it, I feel like I'm going to hurl or hyperventilate. I'm so relieved when we land that I could make out with the ground. Risks go this way sometimes—every bit as awful as we feared.

Kendi feels terrible. He takes me out for steak to try to make up for it. Over filet mignon and asparagus, I apologize.

"Why are *you* sorry? I'm the one who's sorry. I thought it would be . . ." He shrugs.

"I wanted to love it and share that with you. I'm so sorry to disappoint you." I look down at my plate, wondering if Leah would be better for him after all. "Your life's passion is airplanes, and I hate flying. What does this mean about us?"

Kendi chuckles. "It doesn't mean a thing." He takes my hand and traces my palm lines. "We share more with each other than with anyone else in the world. I don't need another me. I need *you*."

I blush.

He frowns. "Actually, that's not true."

Nervous curiosity gathers as sweat in my creases. "What?"

"I want to share more with you." He leans in. "A home. A name. A life."

He slides a ring box onto the table, and I gape.

"I was going to do this in the air today, but we saw how that plan went."

He moves to kneeling and opens the box to reveal a pearl ring.

"I love you, Georgette Bright. I always have and always will." His eyes are the held-breath color of hope. "Will you marry me?"

My smile is as wide as a plane's wingspan. "Wait."

A hint of panic spreads across his face. It's my turn to make him sweat.

"We're not already married?" I lean toward him. "We *have* kissed on the lips."

His relief echoes mine as I say yes. Of course yes. A nearby table applauds as he slides the ring onto my finger and rises to kiss me, smiling into my mouth.

We forgo a decadent dessert and stop by the grocery store instead, to pick up some Blue Bell.

Shauna, Michael, and Dad surprise me back at Kendi's apartment, where they cheer and make a fuss and examine my ring. They've been having a grand old time baking a sponge cake while they waited for us, and they seem as proud of their cake as their children's engagement. Dad takes pictures of us and the cake, and he declares it a perfect Photography Sunday.

We tell them about the whole day. They laugh and cry and hug us. After a while, I sneak out to the balcony as the parents discuss how of course they've always known.

I can hardly breathe without her. Ten years and the grief is as fresh as ever, new milestones battering me. I don't know which is scarier: getting married or getting married without Mom. To her best friend's son, who was like a son to her more than her actual son. Speaking of Davis, do I invite him to the wedding? I rest my elbows on the railing, my face in my hands. Children are playing below, their laughter like wind chimes. A mother calls out, "Slow down!"

I need to show her my ring. I need her to help me find a dress, to say she loves the ones I hate and hates the ones I love. I need to argue with her about the menu. I need her to help with my makeup but not my hair. I need to beg for her silence when she tries to tell embarrassing stories about her own honeymoon. I need to tell her how different Kendi is from Dad.

Would she warn me not to do it after all she went through? Would I care what she thinks after all I've been through?

Dad finds me on the balcony and says only, "Mom?"

I nod, and we say nothing else. He puts his arm around me. I don't want him to hug me. But more than that, I don't want him not to.

When we go back inside, Kendi says, "Bright? Darnell? Bright-Darnell? Darnell-Bright?"

Revealing how much I've thought about this, I answer immediately, "Darnell-Bright." Kendi smiles and nods agreement.

Michael tries it out. "Kendall and Georgette Darnell-Bright." Michael Darnell, who took the name of his wife's dead husband. And Bright, the union of Ryan and Lillian. Darnell-Bright: lost loves given new life.

Shauna clasps her hands together. "Y'all know the new thing these days is to create a wedding hashtag. We need one."

Kendi glances at me. "Whoa, Mom, we're not ready for all of that yet."

She ignores him. "Oooh, how about #thefutureisbright?"

"Doesn't it need Darnell?" Michael points out.

"True." Shauna clicks her tongue. "That's harder."

Dad looks lost. "What's a wedding hashtag?"

Shauna explains, "It's where you combine both names into a clever title so all the online wedding stuff can be linked in one place."

Dad grunts, thinks, then bursts out with, "How about #thefutureis darnbright?"

Shauna's expression shines with approval. Kendi and I laugh as the three of them talk over each other. Neither of us cares about a wedding hashtag; the parents can decide. Michael gets a call from a patient, leaving Shauna and Dad to congratulate each other on their hashtag genius as they clean the counter from their sponge cake escapade.

Eventually I pull Shauna aside.

"What's wrong, darlin'?"

I take her hands. "Would you be my matron of honor?"

She gasps. "Georgette Elise!" She squeezes me and blots her eyes. "I will try to be half the matron of honor that your mother was for me."

My nose stings with memory.

As the parents are leaving, Dad says that he understands if I don't want to, but he hopes I'll consider a dance with him at the wedding. I give him a noncommittal nod, far from ready to think about that.

Since driving away from my fiancé is the last thing I want to do, I decide to stay in Houston one more night. It's worth the early morning drive for class.

When we're alone, I tell Kendi about throwing up. Even though it's been a while, proclivity for addiction runs in my blood. A grasp for control in an out-of-control life. It's the fear beneath all fears—that I'll hurt Kendi. That I'll be the Ryan to his Lillian.

I say sincerely, "It's not too late for you to back out."

"Never." And then, "I love you."

We sit in comfortable silence.

He says, "I missed your mom tonight." Pink springs to his eyes, and I press his hand to my lips. He didn't say that for my benefit.

We haven't talked about where we'll live or children or any of the other questions that are much more important than wedding hashtags. But it's early in the engagement and late in the night, so we go to bed. Kendi kisses me with new warmth, and then he drapes his hand across my waist until it's heavy with sleep.

2011

THE FIRST TIME A MIDWIFE HANDS ME A STETHOSCOPE, nobody pays attention to me. They don't know I'm a stethoscope virgin—toy stethoscopes and dogs named Stethoscope excluded.

The midwife focuses on the prenatal appointment card, makes notes about urinalysis results, chats with the thirty-seven-weeks-pregnant mother about signs of labor, and entrusts me to go ahead with the routine heartbeat check. The quiet arrival of a dream.

As I put it in my ears, it becomes pink plastic and the patient becomes Mom, unzipping her fleece. At first, I tried to find Mom's heart in her stomach. (A prophetic mistake.) I begged her, "Tell me how to find it, Mommy." When she moved the pink stethoscope to her chest, I still couldn't hear a heartbeat. It was only a cheap toy, after all. So she took the end of it to her mouth and whispered, "I love you." That, I could hear.

Nonsensical thoughts fly through the minds of those struck with sudden tragedy. When I dropped to her twisted side that horrible night, I desperately, idiotically thought, *I need a stethoscope!* I visualized the pink plastic that had been discarded years earlier. I squeezed her limp wrist. I waited for someone to tell me they'd found her heartbeat, that I'd simply been listening wrong.

When I could no longer deny that her heart was permanently stilled,

233

I remembered she was registered for organ donation. I wanted to claw the people who came for her. I wanted to scream at them, *Don't take it! Don't take it! Don't take her!* Grief can be irrational. Instead, I sat as silent and still as her heart, my unscreamed screams scorching my throat.

When they told us that it was too late, that unfortunately the short margin of opportunity for organ harvesting had passed, that she remained "intact," I was relieved, even as I knew she would have been upset. But she was gone and I was there. Couldn't I have a death that left something intact?

When I paid my last respects, I reached under her dress, laid my shaking hand on her chest, and begged, *Tell me how to find it.*

Her heart is buried in the darkness of the earth, but it is also buried in the darkness of my body. Everyone says "gone but not forgotten," though it's ultimately the other way around: generations later, a mother is forgotten but not gone, a pulse in the bodies birthed from her love.

Shit. I might want to have children. All that resurrection.

I move the stethoscope around on the patient's abdomen. It's a formality at this point. Her baby is actively wiggling, so it's clear that there's a beating heart. But I of all people know that sometimes we need assurance of what's in front of us.

The patient—a first-time mother—watches me as I pull the stethoscope from my ears and let it rest around my neck.

I smile and say to her, "Loud and strong."

Part Three

RYAN

2012

IN MY DEAD MOTHER'S HOUSE, I MEET MY DEAD WIFE'S son. Davis and Jet both smile, four of Lillian's big eyes blinking at me. Her grandchildren are practicing their responsibilities as flower girl and ring bearer. My role is to help plan the rehearsal dinner. Lillian would have loved every bit of this.

Marigold is just like her name, her fairy giggle like a streak of gold across a black canvas. I bet Lil giggled like that as a girl. The imagined laughter rips through my stomach. I'll pick up liquor on the way home.

It's an April wedding. The small chapel has an arched wooden ceiling and red pews.

Per Shauna's instructions, I arrive early for family photos. Davis's parents are here, and I can hardly look away from their family—all they gave Lillian and all she gave them. And still, all the pain in it. Even the best parent can't replace the first parent.

After photos, there's a tizzy of activity in which I have no assigned role, so I scoot out of the way and meander through a labyrinth. Rosemary decorates the perimeter. A blackbird hops the path. I talk to God, asking him to bless Jet and Kendi. I talk to Lil, telling her I miss her more than ever. She's in every camera click and smile of the bride, every pollen sneeze of her grandchildren. The blackbird flies off, its wingbeat steadying me like a liturgy.

The wedding is simple, perfectly Jet and Kendi. I'm reminded of when Lillian was pregnant with Jet and stressed about all the supplies. *Which material of burp cloth should I get? And how many? And why is this so complicated?* My mom advised, "You don't need much. Babies are simple." She looked at us pointedly over her bifocals and said, "Not easy, but simple." Boy was she right.

When I see Jet in her wedding dress, I recognize Lillian's gentle commitment, but I also see the feistiness that is all and only Georgette. Her hair is down, curls reminiscent of her baby curls. Her bouquet is made of lilies, and she has drawn diamonds on the soles of her sneakers. Yes, she's wearing sneakers with her wedding dress, which would have given both her mother and her grandmother conniption fits.

Liam walks down the aisle, handsome and proud.

Then Marigold, rose petals like cardinal feathers.

The crowd rises, the canon begins, and I give Jet away, as though I have any right.

The chapel is dim and the promises heartfelt. Pangs shoot through my abdomen. My discomfort doesn't escape Michael, who puts a firm hand to my shoulder and nods, *Okay?* I nod back, *Okay.*

After the Darnell-Brights recess out of the chapel, we move to the reception. Shauna and Kendi dance to Carole King. Then it's our turn.

While Jet maintains that *Abbey Road* is the best Beatles' work as a whole, she chose a song from *Revolver* for our dance: "Here, There and Everywhere."

The music starts, and I stretch out a jittering hand.

How can her feet dance so gracefully when she only just took her first steps? I missed them, of course, those first steps. But I do remember that the whole process infuriated her, her ruffled bottom plopping onto hard ground over and over.

Jet and I have never danced together before. I twirl her as the lost years stream down my face. I whisper, not for the first time, that I'm sorry.

She shakes her head and whispers back, "Now we're here."

She should hate me. I should be excluded from her wedding and exiled from her life. Instead, grace upon grace, now we're here.

Here, there and everywhere.

2012

THE FIRST SUNDAY AFTER HER PALO DURO HONEYMOON,
Jet texts me: GO FOR GOLDEN HOUR?

I type back, WOULDN'T MISS IT, even though we both know that's
a lie. I would and I have.

I didn't know if we'd keep doing Photography Sundays after she got
married, and I didn't want to pressure her. It's enough that Kendi got a
job in Fort Worth and they're living here.

I put a bottle of bourbon back in my cabinet, and I pack my camera
bag.

Months later, Photography Sundays haven't taken a hit. Though Jet's
car sure has.

"It's just a fender bender, Dad."

"How long do you plan to keep driving this thing without AC?"

It has been many years since I got behind the wheel with alcohol
in my system, but she still refuses to get into any car I'm driving. It's a
source of contention. So we're in her busted-up Corolla as she sighs,
"It's not so bad."

I give her a look as sweat dribbles down my spine. "Come on. You can borrow my car. Or some money."

"I can't drive a stick. And besides, I could replace this one if I wanted. It's not about money."

"What is it, then?"

She checks her side-view and changes lanes. "I don't want to talk about this."

That's when I understand. This is about Nana. Jet rivals me in sentimentality; she just tries harder to hide it.

I try a different tactic. "Can I at least try to fix this passenger window? Without AC in Texas, you've got to be able to open both windows."

"I mean, Kendi or I could do it, but if you—"

"I'm here now. Let me see if the manual has anything helpful." I know embarrassingly little about fixing cars. So I open her glove box.

"Dad! D—" She slinks lower into her seat.

My eyes widen. Directly in front of me is an unopened pregnancy test. "Are you—"

"Maybe," she says, clipped.

"I thought you didn't want—"

"I didn't. I don't. Well, I don't know if I do." She pauses. "I am."

"Huh?"

We pull up to our destination. She parks the tired car and turns a tired face toward me. "Pregnant."

I look back at the unopened test. "But it's not even o—"

"That's like the fourth one. According to the first three, I'm pregnant."

I try to think of what Lillian would say, but then I'm sidetracked by something else peeking out of the glove box.

Jet sees me see it, and she looks thoroughly annoyed.

I pull out the envelope. "Did you not ever open this?"

She rolls her eyes. "It's not really your business whether I opened it. It was your business to give it to me, and you didn't do that until my secret brother found me and I came to you."

"I've apologized for that. It's a bit overdramatic not to open it."

I place the envelope back in the glove box on top of a mess of papers. She just sits there. I can't help but steal a glance at her belly, which of course doesn't look any different than usual.

"Should we . . . take pictures?"

Jet chews her lip. "No."

She unbuckles and stretches across me, pulling the envelope back out with a long sigh.

I eye the glove box suspiciously. "What else is in there, Pandora?"

To my immense relief, Jet laughs. "That's it, I swear. You found all my glove box secrets." She taps the envelope on her leg.

"Why haven't you opened it?"

She shrugs. "Anger? Fear of anger?" Her eyes are searching as she looks up at me. "What if it tells me Mom's not who I thought she was?"

I think back to the night when Lillian told me about her son, the sting of not having known, and the question I asked myself. "Wouldn't you rather know who she really was?"

Jet is chewing her lip raw. "Sometimes you can be such a good dad." She sounds irritated by that admission.

"So, do you want to?"

"Want to?"

"Open it?"

"Now?"

"Why not?"

"Sort of?"

"But?"

"Well, uh . . ." She scrunches her nose. "I want to open it alone."

"Right." I nod. "Say no more."

I gather my gear and head off down the asphalt road, leaving my daughter in her grandmother's clunker with her mother's envelope and a belly full of fear.

The flap of an empty envelope is lifted. A standard white envelope. A woman pauses. She has a headache. She has a history. She slides a photograph sideways into the envelope, followed by a strip of four negatives. Variations on a theme. Her young daughter's voice wafts from the kitchen. "Mommy? Is it time for a snack?"

Eight years later, the woman's widower is drunk and alone, sorting her belongings. Half-used lotions. Dog-eared books. Mugs. Purse clutter. Fringed Justin boots. He is weeping, clutching his hair, his heart, his merciful elixir. Then an unsealed envelope with his daughter's name written in his wife's hand. A photograph. A piece of paper folded into thirds. He unfolds it.

Dear Georgette,
~~*You Today I*~~ *You should know you were my third pregnancy. Before you, your dad and I had a miscarriage. Before the miscarriage (and before your dad), I had a son. I placed him for adoption because I*

It's unfinished. The man refolds the paper and returns it to the envelope. Licks up, licks down, the adhesive taste sticking to his tongue. The flap is lowered and traced with a shaking finger. He sets it aside and moves forward with his task. Receipts. Pajamas. Hairbrush. A half-filled calendar.

Eleven years after that, in an empty parking lot on Photography Sunday, their daughter breaks the envelope's seal. Pulls out the faded photo and flips it over to confirm. *April 1974* in blue cursive, bottom right corner.

Kodak. She holds the negatives up to the sun and squints. Same as the print itself, it's the silhouette of a young woman—her mother—belly round with life awaiting its time. Variations on a theme.

"This isn't even why I picked this spot." Her voice wobbles.

I keep my camera in position. A palomino swishes its tail as sunrays reach through pecan branches. Flies circle the horse's ear. Click. "I know." I lower my camera. "But isn't it great?"

I turn around to see Jet empty-handed. No camera gear, no envelope. Her eyes are puffy. She sits down in the long switchgrass outside the property line fencing and says, "It's beautiful."

I snap a shot of some hay bales and then sit down a few feet from my daughter. "Whatcha thinkin', kid?"

She shrugs, resting her chin on her knees. There's a rustle in the grass near her, and we both jump up. I position her behind me and stretch on tiptoe to get a better look as it slithers past. Jet backs up. "Rattlesnake?"

I exhale relief. "Just a rat snake."

She turns to walk to the car, the sun like a warm hand on our backs. All's quiet except my screaming inability to think of what to say.

Jet eventually breaks the silence. "All I'd have to do is set my child down in the wrong grass and I could lose them."

I nod understanding and blow into the air, trying to scatter her words like dandelion seeds, make them go away. It doesn't work. And I don't tell her that thoughts like this—back when her entire body was the length of my forearm—were soothed only by swallowing sips of fire until a steady buzz silenced my arsenal mind. We walk without speaking for a good while, shoes scraping asphalt.

Jet runs fingers through her hair and watches her feet. "She was so young and had nobody. I used to think she was selfish. That she took the easy way out." She puts a hand to her abdomen and stops walking.

"But there is no easy way out. We just have to calculate between loss and loss."

I want to tell her no, that the gain swallows the loss. But I clear my throat, frown, and say nothing.

She starts walking again. "It's not that she didn't tell me. It's that she hadn't told me *yet*. It's that she died too soon." Her voice cracks. "That's why I've actually been mad."

A bird sings out in the distance like a stray shot of color in a gray-scale world.

We get to the Corolla, and Jet unlocks it. "I don't know what to do. I have Kendi, and I still don't know what to do."

We open our doors and get in the sweltering car where both past and future have been loosed from their glove box cage. Sideways, I peek at my daughter, a woman who was a baby who almost wasn't. Lillian was too scared. Maybe I pressured her, but I don't regret that. Georgette is the greatest non-regret I've ever had. Moving my gaze from her profile to my lap, I venture, "Does Kendi want—"

"I haven't told him."

This unnerves me. We buckle our seat belts. I have no right to say what I'm thinking: *Keep your family close.* Or maybe my regrets give me the right to say it. Instead I ask, "Are you thinking you might—"

"I don't know." Jet starts the car and checks the rearview. "I don't know."

She drives us home, the one working window rolled down as light drains from the sky.

1986 to 1987

I DRAIN THE SHOT GLASS. SATURDAY NIGHT. THE ROOM glitters, people shine, I float, demons flee. Who wouldn't want more of this magic? *Shot.* But more causes the room to spin, people to duplicate, me to spiral, demons to double down. I need the magic back. *Shot.* It's not a problem for me, but Lillian doesn't get that. *Shot.* I see Dad in her eyes when she looks at me. *Shot.* And I don't want to see him anywhere. *Shot.*

By some miracle, Jet's still asleep. Sunday morning. Lil and I make love for the first time in weeks. She worries about the baby waking. I slide a hand beneath her nightgown and tell her the baby's fine and I want to satisfy my wife. She lets me.

Jet's still snoozing when I pull on a shirt and hum my way to the kitchen. Pan, spatula, flour, sugar, fruit, bacon. A perfect morning, and I hardly even have a headache. As I fry the bacon, I think about last night's gallery event and the after-party and this morning's sweet proof that I can have the reprieve of alcohol and still be a family man. In fact, it's possible that alcohol makes me a better man. I'm better than my father, anyway.

and invitations and mementos. I spot sonogram photos of my grand-daughter and, tucked behind those, the strip of negatives from Lillian's first pregnancy. Jet mailed the print to Davis.

I guzzle the milk. I've had no morning drink.

"Well, that's my cue to . . ." Jet clicks her tongue and points finger guns toward their bedroom.

"Yes, of course. Sleep well." Kendi kisses her forehead as she yawns.

If nothing else, I can shove this reality down the throat of my regret: my daughter is living better than her parents.

But then the thought hits me that Lil and I looked a lot like them when we were at their stage. Things turned irreversibly on a dime. God forbid that for these two.

Jet shuffles away to bed as Kendi turns back toward me. "So, do you share Jet's unease about the air?"

"Nah." I shrug. "Just another way to get around."

He takes a big bite of kolache and smiles confidently. "After going up in a prop plane, I think you'll have a higher opinion of flight." He emphasizes "higher" by pointing his kolache at me.

He tidies the counter, hands me a tumbler of coffee, and grins. "Let's fly."

Kendi drives us to a little airport outside Dallas where he has rented a Cessna.

On the plane, he adjusts dials and switches and then calls to get clear-ance for takeoff. I wasn't prepared for how different this would feel from a commercial flight. My own nerves tingling, I can see why Jet hates it.

As soon as we get off the ground, defying the downward tug of gravity, a sense of calm washes over me. And now I can see why Kendi loves it.

The Dallas skyline shrinks below us, Reunion Tower like a thumbs-up. Acres and acres of the Great Trinity Forest scroll by in shades of green, yellow, and rebel pops of red. I've never realized how many trees are in the metroplex. I take photos and itch for a canvas. We're so much lower than a commercial flight—I can see everything.

As we watch the Trinity River snake its way between Dallas and Fort Worth, we talk through headsets about everything from the weather to Rick Perry to World Cup predictions. I snap photographs.

When Kendi asks about the other times I've flown, I admit that it hasn't been much. A few times for work and once to visit my dad before he died. My stomach knots, either from the memory or altitude or alcohol void.

Kendi says, "I doubt anyone could enjoy a flight taking them to say goodbye."

I chuckle, though it isn't funny. "Believe it or not, all he apologized for was 'not being around more.' Nothing else." I stare into the vast blue. "I wouldn't have wanted him around more anyway."

Kendi's brow furrows. I can be such an insensitive oaf. What I just described must be how Jet feels about me. Which must be awful for Kendi, whose dad is gone. I forget about that with Michael. I squeeze my eyes shut as if to erase my insensitivity.

The headset clicks, and Kendi's voice crackles in my ear as though he's reading my mind. "You know, I always imagine my dad as perfect, but it's good to remember that no dad is." He adjusts a control a few degrees and inhales. "Especially since I'm about to be one."

I regard him. Boy become man, pilot, father. When he and Jet were little, I'd show up tipsy and late to spend time with her, but she'd be enraptured by whatever game she was playing with him. Lil would try to shift Jet's attention, and Kendi would respectfully step back, bothered that his friend wasn't more interested in her dad. Lil would send Kendi on home with some message or another for Shauna. *Come over for tamales and the Mavs game.* Or, *Don't forget the parent-teacher meeting.* Kendi and Jet would smile at each other, the gaps in their grins ever-changing like *Tetris* pieces. He'd hug her goodbye. Sometimes, he would even hug me.

Across a sea of static, I tell Kendi, "You'll be a great dad. And—" I pause. "I'm sorry for the ways I've hurt your wife."

We soar through this middle distance, higher than the skyscrapers but lower than the clouds. Kendi swallows. "Just enough distance to make sense of it all." He nods down toward Dallas, but we both know he's talking about something much bigger than a city.

I don't know if there's any distance where family makes sense. All I know is that a man can be sorry from any height or depth, and he had better say it while he can.

Kendi instructs me to put my hands on the yoke. Feel the pull of wind.

Back on the tarmac, there's a group of boys in party hats. They watch Kendi land the plane like cherubs watching God. He gives them high fives before we leave them to their cake and dreams.

On the walk to the car, Kendi gives me a friendly slap on the back and says, "So! Just another way to get around?"

I laugh and squint against the sunlight. "Definitely more than that."

"Well, come up with me any time."

"Thanks, son." I stuff jittering hands into my pockets and nod. "I will."

2013

MY GRANDDAUGHTER IS BORN ON A SUNDAY. I MEET HER when she's eight hours old.

On Monday morning, I realize I was too drunk to remember her face.

My stomach pains are like pacing tigers, and I toss them their meat in the form of Hennessy. Doctors say my symptoms could resolve if I stop drinking, but I'm skeptical. Drinking resolves them much faster. The thing about alcoholism is that there's sickness on both sides. Drink, you're sick. Don't drink, you're sick. A blurred line between medicine and poison.

When Apricity is one day old, a man about my age comes into the gallery during the midafternoon lull. He looks around, sweat stains on his Bass Pro hat. We strike up a conversation about oil versus acrylic. He rambles on, not in any rush. First, he's talking about paints. Then he's volunteering the information that he's a recovering alcoholic.

I ask how long. Three years, one month. I congratulate him and add, "I'm a recovering alcoholic too. Except for the recovering part." I think of the blank spot in my memory where Apricity's newborn face should be from yesterday, and I tell this man who was ten minutes ago a stranger, "Just your run-of-the-mill drunk, ruining his life."

He exhales knowingly. His eyes have too much sympathy for me to meet them. So I ask, "How'd you do it?" I've heard a hundred recovery stories, but I've only forgotten one granddaughter's face. I need this man to have some new solution for me.

"Well, it ain't *done*, for starters." His voice is hoarse, eroded into something that must barely resemble what it once was. "Recovery's an always-doing." He clears his throat and looks around at the art. "Anyhoo, I got sober when my estranged son gave me an ultimatum. If I could stay dry for a month, we'd take a fishing trip together."

He sees my skepticism, holds his hands up, and continues, "I know it, I know it. Let me put it to you this way: alcohol made me feel good. A relationship with my kid made me feel good. And I had to choose. Question was which pain I could tolerate. I'll be the first to say that an easy decision don't make for an easy action, but I'm doin' it. I thank my lucky stars that I was given a chance." He smiles with dark yellow teeth. "Anyhoo. Day after the fishing trip, I went to AA." He nods toward the pen-and-ink he's purchasing—a fisherman I've been trying to sell for months. "And three years later, I came in here and found this gift for my son. Next week's his birthday." He smiles proudly, pulls off his hat, swipes a hand over bald skin, and situates the hat back on his head. "AA meeting's tomorrow at four thirty, brother. Just a few blocks thataway." He points over his shoulder with a stubby thumb. "I can stop here first?" He raises gray eyebrows that still have a few wiry black strands.

"Oh thanks, but I probably can't get away from the gallery then." I ring up the pen-and-ink. "But congratulations again, man." Good for him, but I've already tried AA. It's not the magic new solution I need.

He leaves me his name and number anyhoo. Alan.

A couple of hours later, I lock up, go home, and drink until everything's black.

———

A *beep-beep* slices the dark. My eyelids slowly unstick. No, it's not dark. It's extremely bright. Ouch. I squint at my phone. A text from Jet: COME SEE US SOMETIME SOON. SHE WANTS TO GET TO KNOW YOU. A picture of Apricity fills my phone screen.

My hand jitters as I type: COME GET ME FOR THE MEETING TODAY? THANKS ALAN.

It isn't a new solution, but it is a new day. I want Apricity to have someone different than Jet had. I'll do anything for it. It's not my first rodeo with AA, but it is my first time to feel this motivated since Lillian.

I go to a second meeting. A third and fourth. A ninth, tenth, eleventh.

Twelve years ago, I didn't realize the thirst is like a virus waiting under my skin. I didn't truly know the double mind of recovery until the night Lillian died and I fled. I fought the urge to step off a bridge. Left Jet to fend for herself at only fifteen years old. Got plastered. Didn't step off a bridge, but did fall off the proverbial wagon. *Relapse* is too gentle of a word. Come evenings and weekends, I was catatonic. It was slow suicide. Life can be too long to bear.

In those days, I would crave death and then see a flash of Jet's face. She couldn't be my reason for sobriety—she was my reason to live. That I didn't show it didn't make it any less true. She was baby, child, teen, and then fast and scorching as a lightning strike, I'm holding a granddaughter instead of a daughter. Life can be too short to bear.

I start to pray in AA this time. I can't claim to know what it means, but I can't claim it means nothing. It helps a lot of people turn things around. I see buddies get as dry as deserts, giving all glory to the good Lord. All I know is that I can't judge a man who doesn't talk with God, and I can't judge a man who does.

My liquor cabinet empties of bottles and fills with paints, pictures, books.

A paper flutters from an old book, and I pick it up with an old hand. On it: *ryan brighton (from library)*

2016

Dear Apricity,

Just now I wanted to drink, but then I thought of you and didn't. It has become important to me to write to you about this, and I figure now's as good a moment as any. It's too much for a three-year-old, of course, but when you're older.

I'm not sure how you'll view me as you grow up, but it might impact how you view yourself, and so there are two things I want you to plainly know. First, alcohol is a big part of my life. Second, alcohol is a small part of me. Addiction is only one section in the textbook of a human. Early in mine, I was berated by the question, Why can't I stop? *But over the years, the better question revealed itself:* Why did I start?

From monkey to moose, animals the world over consume fermented fruit and get drunk. The earliest evidence of humans harnessing alcohol to drink is from pottery residue recovered from nearly ten thousand years ago. Imagine. For thousands of years, even the aroma was preserved.

Think of all the generations that came and went, outlived by a fragrance. Think of the apple and barley, wine skins and drinking horns, vineyards and breweries, chemistry and craft, Greeks and Romans, peasants and kings, Egyptians and Mesopotamians, preserving and sustaining, distillation and the global trading of spirits, travel and immigration, banquets and prohibition, rations and speakeasies, merriment and mistakes.

Civilizations across time and space have come to recognize the harms and benefits of alcohol, restricting and prescribing it as they saw fit. Sailors were permitted alcohol off-duty because there are times when one needs a provision that at another time might destroy. And sailors sent to war were all but required to drink—otherwise their consciences interfered with their task.

Addiction and alcohol are not the same, Apricity. Some of us must avoid alcohol to avoid addiction. But for many, this is unnecessary. Like fire, the drink has saved lives and taken them. I actually think I could have been a good sommelier if I hadn't been an addict. But I am an addict.

On a long-ago day that nobody knows, a man or woman or child discovered fermented fruit in the bottom of some forgotten vessel and realized it could make them warm, well, or brave. It could make them laugh, stagger, or sleep. The fruits and their sugars are powerful. But they are also neutral. It is our thirst that drives us. The heart thirsts for comfort like the stomach thirsts for nourishment, and the discomforted move the drink from one vessel to another. That is why I started drinking.

My hope for you isn't to do with whether or not you drink. My hope is that alcohol will be but a peripheral detail in a life drenched with so much comfort that, a thousand years from now, people will still smell the aroma of it.

Yours always,
Pops

2019

FIVE YEARS AND SEVEN MONTHS SOBER. TWO HUNDRED ninety-one weeks.

I shouldn't say my sobriety is because of Apricity, but I also shouldn't lie.

I took her on countless walks in her stroller, where she'd blink awake and let the blue sky into tiny eyes that were still deciding what color to be.

I happened to be at their house when she took her first steps, and she was nothing like her mother. She barreled forward, no frustration at falling every third step, just back up for more, like it was all a game.

At her third birthday party, she pointed proudly to me and told the neighborhood kids, "That my Pops!" A few of the youngest ones started calling me—one word—Mypops. Liam and Marigold were there, both of them the sort of middle schoolers who weren't too cool to play with their little cousin and her friends. Marigold perpetuated the Mypops name because it made her giggle.

Nearly every weekend, I had dinner at Jet's house, where I sometimes got a phantom whiff of rhubarb. I cooked while Apricity entertained us with her antics. She loved fish, hated peas, and always sat on my lap when she finished eating. ("How many more bites 'fore me can sit wif Pops?") She tried on my glasses and asked about the space between my teeth and traced the veins in my hands like I was an artifact. My veins

259

were how she found out blood is blue until skin is cut. After learning this, she asked, "What else do pain make change?"

She painted me, and I painted her. We hung them side by side at the SG. When I sold the gallery to DJ, he kept those two paintings, marked them *Not For Sale*, and hung them beside a little plaque about the founder. I told him I didn't need any plaque, but he said other people needed it and not to be stubborn. So it stayed.

After hearing on the radio that grandparents should be sweet and silly, I stopped by the house on Apricity's first morning of kindergarten and surprised her with a red rose and a red nose. Jet liked how I incorporated rhyming, so I pretended it was intentional. Apricity took the rose and smelled it dramatically. Then I squatted down to her level, my knees cracking. She squeezed the clown nose, giggled, wrapped an arm around my neck, and told me matter-of-factly that I did *not* smell as good as the flower. I watched her go off to big-girl school, growing and shimmering and not looking back.

What that must be like, to not look back.

That was only a few months ago. Now I'm in the hospital, and I will not be going home.

When Jet asks if it's a life-threatening condition, I tell her life is a life-threatening condition. She makes a Lillian face at me.

I had some sobriety, for which I'm thankful. But the damage was done. I healed to die, like everyone who heals. Advanced cirrhosis means I won't live to see Apricity's sixth birthday. She already has a plan for a unicorn princess party, which sounds like a grand idea to me. I don't think people remember much from when they're five, so Apricity's memory of me will be an outline colored in by her mother. She'll have little more than foggy memories of clown noses and thick blue veins.

The wait list for a liver is long. Most livers are shriveled underground or in use among the living. It's strange, body parts as commodities. Medicine is grit and science and business and miracle.

The first time Apricity visits me at Harris, her eyes are big and curved with fear. Hospitals can do that with their lights and tile and needles and beeps. She understands more than I expected, and she cries. So—no surprise—I cry too. Her tears hurt me as much as anything ever has.

The second time she visits, she is prepared for the machine sounds and antiseptic smells and pallor of my face. The yellowed whites of my eyes. Cheerfully, she sings to me: "Twinkle Twinkle," "I'm a Little Teapot," "Itsy-Bitsy Spider." She brings me books to read to her: *Mother Goose*, *Runaway Bunny*, *Are You My Mother?* She gives me trinkets: plastic rings that are too small for my pinky, drawings, a dandelion stem, a heart-shaped rock. I'm sorry I can't take these with me, I tell her. It's okay, she says, they're to enjoy for now. When I read to her, she puts a hand to my cheek and asks if my voice hurts. I've learned the hard way about lying, so I tell her the truth: yes, it does.

When the time comes—and it won't be long—I'll be moved to palliative care, being made comfortable as I "expire" (*die*, I wish they'd just say).

There's a painting under my bed for Apricity, of her with her parents. Jet knows. She is starting to sift through my apartment, marking things as *Keep* or *Go*. I've given instructions about the art. The rest of it doesn't matter. What I leave behind comes down to a daughter, a granddaughter, and a bit of art. An embarrassment of riches.

I ask Jet to bring me the photos she took on the night of my second proposal to Lillian. Some of the shots turned out, while others didn't. I want them all.

At least Jet will get to say goodbye to someone for once. I wonder if she'll have hard words for me in the end. Lord knows I've earned them.

My hands are unrecognizable. I don't like to look at them. I'd rather imagine them young and holding a paintbrush or a camera or the bride of my youth.

I have an IV of fluid and a catheter, water being pumped through me like I'm a straw.

Hospice won't have these interventions. They will simply let me go.

A nurse is here now. Cindy? Cathy? Something like that. She wants me to try some food. Meat loaf.

2019

Dear Apricity,
Remember Penny? I bet you don't, since you were only three years old when she died. Penny was a tabby cat that kept slinking around your house. You wanted to bring her inside and got miffed at your daddy for his allergy. So your mom let you feed her outside. Next came her name and milk on the porch every day. You belonged to each other even if you couldn't live together. But then Penny didn't show up for a few days, and your mom spotted her in the road, all nine lives gone.

When she told you Penny was gone for good, you asked what was good about it. You both cried. The main reason your mom was upset was because she'd had her first loss at work. She had managed to save a baby boy during a difficult delivery, but he had too many complications. He lived only four hours. The next day, she found Penny and cried out, "I can't save anyone!"

Apricity, my standing advice is to always listen to your mother. But on this point, I must say she's wrong. (Jet, if you're screening this letter, then please hear me out.) Those four hours meant something. They meant everything.

You must not measure salvation like an ingredient that's either *there or not. Yes, salvation can be a heroic moment of rescue. But more often, it's smaller. Slower. It's a piece of art that took years to grab the moment in its arms. A mother and son getting ice cream or therapy, week after week. A bowl of milk refilled every day. A skilled doctor pulling more months from a man's life like scarves from a magician's sleeve. A granddaughter giving an old man more years than he would have otherwise had.*

This is why in the same breath I can tell you that you saved me, and I am dying. Both are true, and it was always going to be this way.

When I was about your age, my mom saved a nest of baby sparrows. With a lamp and cardboard box and dropper of formula, she nursed them until a pair of bird rescuers in green-collared shirts came to collect them. This memory, like me, is old. Those sparrows are long gone now. But know this: she saved them. Completely. Like you saved me. Loss doesn't negate salvation, just like death doesn't negate life.

I remember once when I sat at your kitchen bar stool trying to untangle your Elsa necklace. Out of nowhere, you asked your parents where babies come from. I smirked and focused on the necklace while they answered. Sort of. They didn't actually tell you how babies get in, only how they come out, and how your mother gets to help with this. You asked your mom if it hurt when you came out of her bottom. She knuckled your sweet cheek and said, "Yes, you had a big head." The pools of your eyes widened as you responded, "I so sorry, Mommy," with such sincerity that she couldn't hold your gaze. She blinked downward and said, "Oh sweetheart, you did nothing wrong. You were being born, and nobody gets a choice about that."

Through choices made and not made, you entered this world like a starburst, and you let me ride your trail of light through the sky.

264

There is goodness ahead of you. I know this because I know you. You don't hide from pain or from play. Your joy is obstinate, yet you are brave enough to break. You have open eyes and an open heart—a rare combination in a world where one of those usually closes the other. You are your mother's daughter, who is her mother's daughter. You are, and you will always be, radiant.

Yours always,
Pops

2019

JET COMES ALONE TO VISIT ME IN HOSPICE. SHE'S WEARING scrubs because she delivered a baby five hours ago. She has helped deliver at least a hundred already. When she learned how to insert an IV, she practiced on me. She got squeamish isolating my vein and said, "I don't want to hurt you." Now if that isn't a miracle.

She brings news that Apricity is going to be a big sister. They plan to tell her soon with Blue Bell. Telling me this now, she sniffles, sitting gingerly on the edge of my bed. A nurse peeks in and backs away, closing the door.

"I hate that you won't be here."

It requires all my strength to lift my arm, but I do it. I tilt her chin until she gives me her bloodshot eyes. I use yelling effort, but all that comes out is a whisper. "Georgette Elise." I lower my shaking fingers to her heart and say slowly, "I will be here." I move my hand to the life in her belly and say, "There." She closes her eyes and tilts her face upward, a lone tear trailing down as she whispers with me, "And everywhere."

Hard words, but not in the way I expected. So much can be lost and still so much remains.

She curls up beside me and I hold my daughter, remembering her newborn form and the time I nuzzled her smooth baby cheek. She opened her mouth and gummed the tip of my nose, creaturely, searching for milk. I once told her that made me her first kiss, and she scrunched her face.

I drift to sleep beside her soft whimpers.

Shh, shh. Your mom will be here soon to feed you. We're here at the beginning. I'll paint a bottle of milk for you. I will not throw it. But I left my white crayon under the table. If we can't take a drive, how about a little walk?

I wake. Startle. She has been fed. Grown up. Hated me. Loved me again. I am old. Dying. And she is still here. This is a forgiveness I never gave my own father.

But—Georgette!

I close my eyes. Georgette.

Out my window is a Methodist church where the choir comes and goes.

I'm afraid of the unknown. It's all that remains, this forced unburdening. This chrysalis room.

My breath snags. Air hurts. I'm a dwindling mass of bone and water and memory.

I grunt at the nurse when she tries to close the window. I need the church. The dawning sky.

If you're in either of those, God, have pity.

Have pity.

Soon, Jet will go home, weary feet dragging her through the door. She will set down her keys. It will be late. Kendi will come around the corner from the kitchen, where he will have been finishing the dishes. He will have given Apricity macaroni and cheese and let her stay up late watching soccer with him until she fell asleep, ready to be carried to bed. He'll look at Jet to ask, *Did he?* And she'll look back at him to say, *Yes.* He'll quicken his pace to her and guide her to the couch. This will be the second time he helps her grieve a parent.

They won't speak. He'll hold her. Get her water and tissues. She'll say she has to pee, and it will be ten more minutes before she gets up and does it. When she comes out of the bathroom, she'll turn left instead of right, walking toward Apricity asleep in her bed. She'll pull her daughter's airplane blanket down enough to press lips to her cheek. Apricity's face will be rosy, young, soft, and this will be a shock to Jet's lips, which will have last kissed her father's corpse.

Kendi will hold her through to sunrise. Apricity will wake the next morning with the same shining sun, ticking clock, chirping bird, and leaking faucet that was there the day before. But something will be missing. Kendi will tell her that I died. Jet will sit looking downward, tears dripping onto uneaten eggs. Apricity won't know what to do. She'll want to talk about it more than her mother does, and Jet will give her that. She will give Jet that.

There will be a funeral. I've asked only that some paintings are displayed, and a selection of photographs. I want to be seen with Lillian and Mom because perhaps, by some mystery, I will be.

Jet will be sad and tired for a while. But then she'll have a new baby, another birthday, another Christmas with Shauna's handmade red-and-white stockings. She'll have hugs to give Kendi before takeoffs, brisket to enjoy, new shoes to buy growing children. She'll have golden-hour photos to take and babies to deliver into this world that needs them. She'll have dentist appointments, school dances, graduations, her grandmother's rhubarb pie recipe to share, and library books to return to the place where her parents met.

There will be atrocities, too. Pinched fingers, hurt feelings, schoolyard bullies, snakes in the grass, lies, betrayal, sickness, war, addiction, and the death of the young.

But if I know anything, I know Jet will keep her family close. Together, they will visit the hill where her parents lie in rest. And the oak that was once a sapling will spread wide its canopy.

EPILOGUE

2019

"TIME FOR BED, KIDDO." KENDI RESTS A HAND ON HIS daughter's shoulder.

Apricity's tongue peeks out of her mouth as she colors.

"What're you coloring?"

"A picture for Pops."

Kendi's face pinches as he squats and says softly, "Remember, Pops isn't here anymore."

"I know." She points to her drawing. "He's here."

Kendi looks down at a stick man and a big yellow sun.

Apricity gazes out the window at the night sky. "You said the sun shines on the other side of the world when it's night on our side. So somewhere else there's sunshine even though I can't see it from here."

Her father nods slowly. "That's right."

"I think too somewhere else there is Pops, even though I can't see him from here."

Kendi leans closer to her drawing and says, with a catch in his voice, "So this is—"

"Pops!" Apricity flashes a knowing smile. "In the bright place."

ACKNOWLEDGMENTS

THANK YOU TO EACH PERSON WHO IS WORKING FOR sobriety.

Thank you to Jane Dystel for your belief in this book.

Thank you to Carina Guiterman—and the entire Simon & Schuster team—for seeing where I was taking the Bright family, and helping me get there.

Thank you to Laurie Grassi, Jenny Alton, Sarah Smith, Anna Carol DuBose, Jeanne Damoff, Emily Larzabal, Ben Larzabal, Sheiliann Chilli Peña, David Lewis, Melissa Smith, Becki Howard, Esther Luna, and Grace Romjue for your insightful feedback.

Deep gratitude to Amelia Fischer and Grace Cowan Padua.

These pages are indebted to three people whose lives ended too soon: Ninette, Ryan, and Cecilia.

Thank you to Naomi, Eliot, and Haven, my brightest lights.

Thank you to Lucas, my first reader and favorite risk.

Thank you to the One who created this world with its sun and shadows, and who offers redemption to those of us who seek.

And thank you to everyone who reads this story; it belongs to you now.

ABOUT THE AUTHOR

SARAH DAMOFF lives in Texas with her husband and children. Her work has appeared in *Porter House Review*, *Ruminate Magazine*, and *Open Global Rights*, among other publications. *The Bright Years* is her first novel.